WELCOME TO THE
CAMEO
HOTEL

USA Today Bestselling Author

K . I . LYNN

Cover image licensed by shutterstock.com/ © prometeus
Cover design by RBA Designs

Editor
Nancy Smay @ Evident Ink
Marti Lynch

Formatting
Elaine York, Allusion Graphics, LLC (http://www.allusiongraphics.com)

Publication Date: May 14, 2018
Genre: FICTION/Romance/Contemporary
ISBN-13: 978-1948284028
ISBN-10: 1948284022
Copyright © 2018 K.I. Lynn
All rights reserved

WELCOME TO THE
CAMEO HOTEL

Lobby

I was tired. Dead tired.

As I stumbled into my apartment, my foot caught on the step and I tripped, nearly face planting into the wall.

"Shit!" I hopped in place. The shock was a hit of adrenaline that raced through me.

Thankfully I was able to catch myself before I bruised something.

After two grueling mid-term presentations, all I wanted to do was fall into bed and wake up the next morning. Unfortunately, my work wouldn't allow that. At least I had the peace of mind that my projects were complete, and I was pretty sure I did a good job.

"Crap!" I hissed as I glanced at the clock. I stripped off my clothes as I headed toward the bathroom to shower. It was a good thing I'd picked up food on my drive home, but it'd cost me about fifteen minutes I desperately needed.

Once out of the shower, I toweled off my hair before twisting it up into a tight bun. With it wet, my hair looked almost black instead of its normal bronzy brown. My reflection showed just how tired I was, with dark circles under my hazel eyes. My eyes were a mix of honey gold and green, and the darkness only made them pop more, especially when they were lined with the black of the mascara and eyeliner.

When all was done, I had just over a half an hour to get to work. A little too tight for comfort, but doable.

Sometimes I thought my decision to work full time and get my MBA at the same time was not the sanest decision. I went right from my undergrad to grad school without slowing down, but the rent still needed to be paid. Luckily my apartment was close to Boston College.

That decision was responsible for the fact I'd had almost no sleep in two days. The commute alone was a daunting task in front of me. I could take the subway, but that took longer and I didn't like taking it home at midnight when my shift was over.

Why did I say I could work a shift right after midterms? Because, I reminded myself, I was a masochist in dire need of some money, and could sleep tomorrow. Rent in Boston was astronomical, and a single day out of my paycheck equated to one of my bills not getting paid. There were always my vacation days, but I held them back for when it came time for finals. I'd already requested most of a week off in May.

As I headed toward the door I grabbed a couple of energy drinks, ripping one open and chugging it on my way down the stairs. Any kind of boost was welcome. I'd probably get a huge latte once I got to work.

The traffic gods seemed to have been smiling down on me, and I was able to get to work with no problems. After finding a parking spot, I tossed an extra energy drink into my purse, grabbed my heels, and headed in.

The Cameo Hotel was a large, five-star hotel situated on the water in the north end of Boston. The least expensive room was hundreds of dollars a night. It wasn't out of the ordinary for us to see celebrities and corporate CEOs.

It was eerily quiet in the employee lounge, nobody in sight, which was not the best sign. Any prayers I had of an easy night were blown to pieces as soon as I walked from the office and out to the reception area of the lobby.

It became glaringly obvious that I should have called off.

Customers lined the desk, and all managers and supervisors were out. I couldn't even hear myself think over the decibel level at which the complaints were being screamed.

The awaiting shit storm was not what I needed. The temptation to turn around and run was severe. I was tired and didn't think I was strong enough to get through the night after the day I'd had. As I stood there like a deer in headlights, a set of eyes locked on me.

Fuck.

I watched the blue eyes of my manager, James, grow wide with relief, and I realized I'd lost my chance to sneak out the way I'd come. I'd been spotted.

I shuffled my feet, about to run as he headed straight toward me.

"Thank God you're here," he said with a heavy sigh. By his clothing and features, you wouldn't think anything was wrong. Every part of him was put together, from his perfectly styled blond hair to the starch of his suit. Even his smile was intact, looking no worse for the wear.

It was all a lie. I knew James well, and behind that calm exterior he was freaking out. His superpower was never letting it show as he calmly defused any situation the hotel hurled at him.

"What is going on, and how do I get out of it?" I whispered.

He let out a dark chuckle. "Sorry, Emma. The only way out for *you* is through."

I narrowed my eyes on him. "I'm not sure I like you right now."

"Don't be that way; you know you love me."

Damn him for being right. For three years I'd worked my way up at the Cameo, all the way to taking James's supervisor spot when he was promoted to manager. With his quick wit and charm, we had even ended up dating for a short period, but the timing had been off.

"Keep telling yourself that," I said, teasing him.

His lips drew up into a smile as he ran his fingers down my arm. "Every day."

I bit my bottom lip as I looked up at him. "All right, quit stalling."

The smile on his face fell, and he cringed at the level of one voice that boomed out above the others. "Housekeeping missed an entire floor."

"What?" Maybe at some low-end hotel it wouldn't have been so bad, but the Cameo catered to a higher level of clientele, and they had *high* expectations.

He nodded. "Nothing was done. Not the rooms that were occupied, or the ones that checked out."

"Shit," I hissed under my breath. "What's being done now?"

"They're working on the floor now, and minor complaints are getting comped meals and discounts. We're moving and upgrading the incoming guests as well as comping others, case dependent."

I nod. "Make them happy. Whose floor was it?"

"Valeria is looking into the matter. Right now, we're just taking care of the fallout one case at a time."

He inched toward the door, and I sidestepped to block him. "Where are you going?"

"I'm sorry, Emma," James said as he took my hand and pressed the keys into my palm before he pushed through the office door.

I swung my arm out and stopped it from closing behind him. "Coward!" I hissed.

He turned back to me and smiled. "Let's get a drink tomorrow. You're going to need it."

I shook my head and rolled my eyes. "You're paying."

If I didn't like him so much, I might have punched him for the mess he was leaving me, though I wasn't really alone. Miguel, the hotel assistant manager, was standing with Jaqueline, one of the clerks. Hopefully he wouldn't abandon me as well, but he often stayed after five.

With a hard sigh, I straightened my jacket and walked over to Shannon, who was helping a very red-faced man. She seemed flustered, her hands were shaking, and she seemed to have difficulty stringing her words together. Then again, he refused to let her speak.

4

I set my hand on her shoulder. When she turned to look at me, relief flooded her face.

"Go take a break," I whispered to her.

She mouthed a "thank you" before scurrying off.

"Hello, sir. I apologize for your experience with us today."

"You should! That room should be condemned! Beer bottles, condoms, broken mirrors, and trash everywhere. I needed a damn tetanus shot to set foot in there. How was that acceptable?"

"It in no way is. We experienced a technical difficulty today."

"That's not my problem!"

"No, sir, absolutely not." I scanned the computer to find an open room. "I would like to comp your room tonight and move you to one of our junior suites at no extra charge for the rest of your stay. Is that agreeable?"

He pulled back, no longer leaning over the counter like he wanted to throttle me. In a way, he looked defeated. Almost as if he wanted to fight me, but my response wasn't what he expected.

He nodded. "That works."

One of the most valuable tricks I'd learned in my years working at the hotel—never let people see when they're getting to you.

I gave him my best smile, making sure it reached my eyes, while my ears were bleeding from the shrieks of a Barbie-esque socialite at the other end of the counter. Her complaint was minor compared to the man in front of me. Not that what happened was excusable, but not having two towels exchanged and her garbage can emptied was hardly something to shriek about. Complain? For our guests, yes. Shriek? No.

"Here you are, sir," I said as I handed him his new keys. "You will be up on the sixteenth floor. Once there, take a left and your room will be on your right." I gave him a smile and watched as he huffed away.

Angry customer after angry customer were defused over the next hour. Screams of displeasure and threats still echoed in my ears by the time we were done, but the night was still young.

Once we were clear for a few minutes, Miguel headed back to the office, and I followed behind him after letting Caleb go home.

"What happened?" I asked as I sat in the chair across from Miguel.

He shook his head before running his hands down his face. "I talked to Valeria, and somehow the crew assigned to the floor accidentally released the whole floor before working it."

My expression dropped. "How does that even happen? I hope she fired them after what they just put us through and the money the hotel just lost."

He nodded. "They were placed on final notice."

I groaned. "Meaning they still have another chance to do this all over again."

"You did good," he said, ignoring my comment. I knew he agreed with me. If any of the reception staff did something like that, they would be gone.

"Thank you. Are you heading out now?" I asked as I glanced to the clock. It was after five.

"Yes," he said as he stood back up. "Hopefully everything is taken care of, and nothing else will pop up and you'll have an easy night."

"An easy night? We haven't hit peak weeknight check-in yet, and I already need a huge Margarita."

He gave me a rueful smile. "You get off at midnight."

"That is way too many hours away, especially after the day I've already had."

He gave me a thin-lipped smile. "Sorry."

I shook my head. "No you're not."

He chuckled. "No, because I think I'll go have one. I'll think of you. Does that help?"

"Nope."

"Goodnight, Emma."

"See you later." I stood and headed back out to the front desk and to Shannon and Jaqueline.

"Thank you so much, Emma," Shannon said as she walked over to me.

"He was over the top."

She laced her fingers together in front of her. "He was, and he just kept yelling. I couldn't think."

6

"You did fine," I said, trying to calm her. "Why don't you fill me in on what I missed?"

After talking with the two of them, I found that most of the other rooms had the basic dirty beds, dirty towels, and trash; the usual. After the first wave, we upgraded seventeen rooms and comped four of those. Not to mention all the perks we gave away, like free meals at the hotel restaurant.

The upgrades depleted most of our available rooms, as the hotel was at eighty-percent capacity.

All in all, it was one of those nights I *hated* being a supervisor. Sure, we'd dealt with the bulk of the guests, but it was only a short reprieve. Another small wave of people called or came down to talk about how their room hadn't been serviced. We held lots of business travelers during the week. Luckily they were all current guests, so it was mostly minor things, and a few free breakfasts seemed to appease them.

The hotel was almost full *before* everything happened, and with the room exchanges, there wasn't allowance for much more room switching or new guests.

The call of the Margarita was strong—or a shot of tequila—anything to take the edge off. I was waiting for the axe to drop on my shift, because with the slow rate at which housekeeping was getting through the floor, it was bound to happen.

On a quick break, I was able to look at my phone and read a few texts I'd received from James. One was a photo of Margarita mix next to a full bottle of tequila.

James: Tomorrow night?

I smiled before quickly typing back: **Tease**

James: Yes, but what about tomorrow night?

It was so hard to shoot him down, but we were stuck until I graduated and got out of the hotel. **Sorry, but my manager put me on the schedule.**

James: Damn that asshole. I'll have to talk with him

A chuckle left me as I read his text, and I responded. **You give that blond bastard in the mirror a right talking to.**

James: Will do. Raincheck?

Emma: Hmm, you and me and a bottle of alcohol at your place? That spells trouble

Very enticing trouble, but trouble nonetheless. In the few dates we had two years ago, the chemistry had been there. We'd shared a few make-out sessions, but nothing more.

James: Trouble can be lots of fun

Emma: True, but trouble can also cost me my job

James: I'll make sure your manager doesn't know ;)

Emma: Yeah, I'm sure you will

For years we'd skirted the line between friendship and a romantic relationship, only to constantly be reminded that he was my boss, and therefore off limits. Then there was my schedule. I just didn't have time for a relationship. Still, the flirting never stopped.

James: I can keep a secret

But not for long

I don't want you to be a secret

My heart fluttered in my chest, and I bit my lip as I smiled down at the phone. I couldn't wait until I was out of the Cameo for good. Not just for the more normal schedule, but because I could finally date James without it being a conflict and against company policy. Ever since the New Year, our flirting had picked up in anticipation that we could actually act on all the flirting in a few months' time.

I closed up my locker and headed back out to the lobby to find out how things were going. It was almost seven, and check-ins had slowed down. I was about to head over to the lobby Starbucks when I looked toward the front door and was struck by the man walking in.

It was straight out of a movie—the scene where time slows down as the gorgeous stranger walks in, the wind blowing around him and a ballad playing in the background. He struts in, oozing sex and making all the women's panties wet.

Yeah, it was one of those moments.

At least until he tripped on the floor mat and nearly tumbled to the ground. He straightened up as quickly as possible, glaring down at the flooring as he continued on, but it was too late. The three of us at the desk had seen it all and were now in love, even with the less-than-graceful entrance.

A little clumsiness was endearing, because with the aura he was giving off, I was pretty sure he could prove to me just how manly he was in many ways.

Jaqueline and Shannon snickered at his klutzy move, which he noticed right away.

He approached the desk, his eyes going between the three of us before staying on me. The eyes always scanned to me. After all, I had the more formal uniform and the title of supervisor printed on my name tag.

That, and the girls were still giggling.

Once again, I pulled out my best, friendliest smile. Though the friendliness well was running dry, I wasn't sure I could look at him *without* smiling: sharp features, chestnut hair, broad shoulders, and full, kissable lips.

He wasn't a vacationer—not with the way he was dressed: navy suit with pinstripe vest, Rolex watch, garment bag on his shoulder, and the iPhone that was glued to his hand with the car rental keys. Everything about him screamed, *I'm here on business.*

"Are tripping hazards a common thing in this hotel?" he asked.

It caught me off guard, and I just stared at him. "Sir?"

He motioned to the rug. "Your rug tripped me," he said. No smile returned as he stared at me. He was curt and looked like a boardroom giant. "Someone failed to make sure it was laid properly."

He was right—the rug was all wavy with the end curled up.

"I am so sorry, sir. I will get someone right away to get rid of that." I shot a look over to Shannon, who immediately picked up a phone to dial maintenance to replace it. The curled end would continue to trip people if we didn't get it out of the way.

He huffed, clearly annoyed. "I need to check in."

"Name on the reservation?" I asked, not wasting any time. I was immediately in work mode.

"Grayson," he replied, pulling out his identification and a credit card. I glanced at his ID and took in his full name and age— Gavin Grayson, thirty-five.

Damn, he didn't look thirty-five. There wasn't a line on his face.

I scanned the computer and found he was booked for two weeks. "Thank you, Mr. Grayson. I've found your reservation. It looks like you have one of our beautiful executive suites. You are all set up, so let me get your keys and a signature from you," I said with a smile, taking small notice that he was staring at me.

I pulled the receipt from the printer and coded the keys. "Please sign here. You'll be in room 1208. Elevators are across the hall. Once on the twelfth floor, you will take a right and your room will be on your right. Is there anything else I can help you with, Mr. Grayson?"

He glanced over at Jaqueline and Shannon, who were still smiling at his trip. I watched his jaw clench, and he stared at me for a moment before shaking his head. "No," he replied curtly, any fleeting cordiality gone.

I stayed extra friendly; his mood swing wasn't going to get me down, especially since it was nothing compared to what I'd faced earlier in the day. "Thank you for staying with the Cameo Hotel. If you need anything, please don't hesitate to call."

"Thank you," he said with a nod and headed toward the elevators, his large, expensive rolling suitcase in tow.

He was way out of my league, but it didn't hurt to look. We received a lot of good-looking guests, along with celebrities, but he was in the top ten in the looks department. At least to me.

"Wow," Jaqueline said from beside me. "Girl, I don't know how you do it sometimes."

"Do what?" I asked.

"Be so professional all the time."

I smiled and gave a little laugh. "Years of practice."

We checked in another guest, and then Mr. Grayson appeared again. His face was twisted in fury, making the hackles on the back of my neck stand up.

"Are you fucking kidding me with that room?" he yelled once he was within a few feet.

"Sir?"

"It's a fucking disaster! You people couldn't even bother cleaning it between guests?"

The blood in my veins froze. Fuck. I was so enamored with him that I didn't even notice his reservation had been defaulted to the cursed floor.

"I am so very sorry, sir."

"I highly doubt that. Are you so incompetent you can't even read the screen to show if a room has been cleaned?" he seethed.

"I apologize, we had an issue earlier—"

"I don't care what you had . . . What's your name . . .?" he trailed off and looked down at my name tag. "Emma. Emma, is there anywhere clean in this entire building?"

"I assure you that all of our rooms are very clean."

"Not from what I just saw."

"That was a very unfortunate incident," I said as I scurried to upgrade him. With such limited availability, there wasn't much I could do. "I sincerely apologize. I should have noticed the room number."

His glare narrowed even more. "Yes, you should have."

He was breaking my cool and my smile, but I forced it to remain intact as I quickly booked him into a slightly better room— it was one of the few left. Inside, I wanted to slap him for being such an ass, then shove the maid responsible at him and let him light into her.

"I've upgraded you to one of our executive suites with a water view," I said as I coded new keys.

"Are you going to personally be responsible for the cleanliness of *this* room?"

I slipped the keys across the desk. "I can assure you, Mr. Grayson, it is a beautifully kept room."

"We will see about that," he sneered before storming off again.

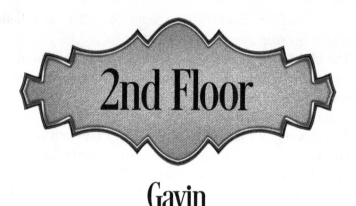

2nd Floor

Gavin

Boston was never where I ever saw myself living. I spent my formative years in Ohio, wanting to get out of suburbia. All my life I was taught that you go to the job, and you didn't expect the job to come to you.

That was how I ended up in Chicago, then New York, and finally, to the Cates Corporation headquarters in Boston. For twelve years I'd worked myself to the bone climbing the corporate ladder.

In thirty-five years I followed careful and strategically laid plans. Until Boston. Until *her*.

For over a week I'd adjusted to a new office, new assistant, and new city. In that time, my nights were spent at the Cameo Hotel. I should have spent my evenings looking for a new home. I even had a realtor, but one thing besides acclimation stopped me—Emma.

From the first moment I saw her, there was an attraction I couldn't comprehend. Feelings I didn't want consumed me for a woman I didn't even know.

Nearly every night when I walked in, there she was. Unassuming. Beautiful. Fucking alluring.

She was a conflict of interest and a distraction I didn't need.

As I walked across the marble floor of the Cameo Hotel, my body searched for her while my eyes tried to ignore the call. I flicked my gaze up and sure enough, she was watching me cross the lobby, lips slightly parted.

Fuck, her lips. Indeed, fuck her lips.

My cock twitched, begging for the image my thoughts had conjured.

I blew out a breath when I stepped onto the elevator and away from those eyes.

When I'd moved to Boston from New York, it was for a clean start as much as it was the first step of my promotion. I knew no one outside of the people I worked with, and that suited me just fine.

But fuck if I didn't want to know her.

She made me want to fight with her, just to watch the anger flare in her eyes while the smile never left her face. Professional to a fault. A fault I wanted to crack, to break open, to see inside.

It was a feeling I hated. Work was my life. It demanded all of my time and energy, leaving nothing for personal relationships.

As soon as I was through the door of my room, I shed my suit piece by piece, a very noticeable tent in my trousers.

"You don't fucking dictate my actions," I grumbled down to the bulge pulsing beneath the fabric.

It was a lie. The desire I had for her was what led me to call her for the most innocuous things. Simply to see her, to have her close.

To breathe her in was an aphrodisiac.

I despised that she made me feel that way, because it left me wary of her. My ex-wife had used her sexuality to get to me, used my desire to get a ring, and used my money to finance her lovers. The bite of that betrayal had never left, and had never healed.

It angered me to want Emma. Angered me that every night I pumped my cock to thoughts of her.

In a petty move, I took that emotion out on her. It was an attempt to push her away, which was thwarted by my inability to keep her there.

While my first room had been a disaster, the room she moved me to was actually very nice. There were a few small wear-and-tear things that came with age and use, but they had done a good job of maintaining the space.

I'd have to let Richard Hayes, the president of Cameo International, know how nice his hotel was. Even if I complained every day.

After a week, the housekeeping staff had upped their game, making it harder every day to find fault with something, some reason to bring her up.

"You don't need to see her," I said to myself, but as I stared at the coffee pot on the wet bar, at the assortment of drinks and sweeteners, at the single packet of sugar, a new plan formed.

Before I could stop myself I was at the phone, dialing down to reception.

"Good evening, Mr. Grayson." Her voice hit my ears, and a shudder rolled through me. The formality that she addressed me with always set off my fantasies.

"There is only one sugar packet, Emma. I need two more."

There was a small pause, and it made me smile, knowing she was probably cursing me out.

"Right away, Mr. Grayson."

The anger in her voice only fueled my own. I wanted to take her down a peg, take her down to her knees.

I was so hard that the slightest touch had my head falling back. How would she react if I opened the door stroking my dick?

That idea was a little sobering, calming me down enough to position my length so it wasn't obvious.

Control and planning were my strong suits, but she continued to wreck them, while I continued to let her. It was a dangerous game, but with every bite I took, every hit of her, she beat me down.

While I won every battle, she was slowly winning the war, and I couldn't stand for that.

The soft rap of her knuckles on the door pulled me from my thoughts of her to the actual physical version.

My nostrils flared as I opened the door and glared down at her. Her breath hitched, making my hand twitch at my side. The lust running through my veins struggled to take over. All I wanted was to drag her in, bend her over the couch, and fuck all of my frustration out on her.

"Your sugar." She held out her hand, palm up. Five little brown packets sat against the creamy white of her skin.

I snatched them up, forcing myself to ignore the fire from the brief contact with her skin. "I said two, Emma. Can't you count?"

"Anticipation, sir."

"What?" I asked. My attempt not to groan out at her words were masked by the growl of my singular question.

"If you need two more, it means you'll need three for a second cup."

Was she truly anticipating my needs, or making it so I didn't call her for sugar the following day?

"Nice to see you know basic addition. Did you need a calculator?"

A smile drew up on her face, forced but with a glimmer of hatred. "Is there anything else I can help you with tonight, Mr. Grayson?"

Yes, get on your fucking knees and choke on my dick until I come down your throat.

Eloquence went out the window in her presence. All I wanted to do was devour every inch of her.

"You're dismissed."

That fire flared again in her eyes, accentuated by a brief widening. "Have a good night."

I said nothing more, gave her no return gesture, simply slammed the door in her face. Anything else would have led to a case of sexual harassment, and I would not allow myself to fall that far.

"Really, Gavin?" I said as I propped myself against the door.

Guilt and anger flooded in. I was an asshole by nature, but I still didn't take pleasure in being one to her, even in my state. Still, Emma took everything I threw at her in stride. She never backed down or cowered at my intimidation.

A strong woman was exactly what I wanted, but not what I needed with everything that was going on. There was no time for niceties, for my affections to grow. The only thing I had time for was sex, but Emma evoked more than the desire for her pussy.

A quick fuck wasn't what I wanted, but what I did want from her was still a mystery. I couldn't seem to leave her alone, which made one thing for certain—she'd be back. I'd find another reason to have her in my space the next day, and the day after, and every day following until I'd had enough.

The sugar packets fell from my hand into the trash.

I drank my coffee black.

3rd Floor

Mr. Grayson quickly became infamous around the hotel. The first night made him so angry that every single day there was a new issue with his room. He nitpicked everything, and it was always when I was on duty. The concierge desk emptied at five, leaving the reception desk to answer his calls, meaning I was always the one who had to deal with him.

Lucky me.

Normally, I was pretty invisible to guests, but Mr. Grayson was dialed in to me. My experiences with him were the first time I'd wanted to punch someone. In all my twenty-five years, I had never met anyone as infuriating as Gavin Grayson.

"The tourism guide has been defaced. Bring up a new one with no scribbles," he said on day two.

I blinked and looked down at the phone before replying. "I'll be right up, sir."

On day four, he called to tell me, "I have no washcloths."

My smile was plastered on, but I knew it was no longer in my voice. "I'll have housekeeping bring you some right away."

It only took a few days until I was no longer delegating the responsibility of delivering whatever was missing or needed replacing, but rather I was the one knocking on his door with whatever he requested.

"There is only one sugar packet, Emma. I need two more," he complained on day seven.

I ground my teeth. "Right away, Mr. Grayson." More sugar wasn't going to make him the least bit sweeter.

Every time I saw him, I was gobsmacked by his good looks, even when he was glaring at me. I hated the way it made my heart speed up. Even more, I hated the butterflies that fluttered in anticipation each time I was about to see him.

If I disliked him so much, why was I reacting that way?

"I can talk to him," James said as we sat in the lobby Starbucks.

"Really, it's fine," I stressed. The last thing I wanted was for James to confront him. The man was demanding, and I could deal with him on my own.

"No, it's not fine. His behavior is unacceptable," James said, his forehead furrowed, and his jaw ticked. It wasn't often he let his anger show. "For fuck's sake, you're not his personal assistant, at his beck and call."

"I can handle him." I leaned forward to try and catch his eye. It worked, and he seemed to calm down a little bit. "He's just nitpicky and rude. Besides, he'll be gone soon."

"I still don't like it," he grumbled.

"That's fine, but it won't even be an issue soon. We'll look back on it one day and laugh."

He grimaced. "I'm not laughing now." He blew out a breath and reached out, placing his hand on mine. "I know I have no claim over you, but that doesn't mean I'm not protective of you."

The warmth from his hand was comforting and sent tingles through me. They reached my chest, but something was off. The blossoming in my chest didn't seem as full and expansive as it normally was when James touched me.

"I know," I said, giving him a smile. "Come on. Your break is over, and I need to get home."

We got up and headed back to the reception desk. As we walked across the expansive lobby, a familiar figure came into view. Mr. Grayson was entering from the parking garage. My heart started doing double time as I watched him head straight toward the elevators. He shot a quick glance at us, but I couldn't stop watching as he got onto an awaiting elevator. Our eyes locked, and a wave of heat flowed through me.

"What kind of mood do you think he's in?" James asked, pulling me away from Mr. Grayson's intensity.

"Not a good one. Good luck tonight."

He let out a groan. "I can't stand him."

"Just breathe, and remember, it's only a few more days. Then you'll never see him again."

He nodded. "You're right."

"I wonder who he works for," I said. It was obvious he was high up on the totem pole, wherever it was.

"You didn't hear?"

"Hear what?"

"He's the VP of the Cates Corporation. Next in line to be CEO. I heard he was the head of the New York offices, but since he's moving up, it was time to come back to headquarters."

Cates was a huge business consulting and technology company. The hotel had hosted a few of their functions over the years. Mr. Grayson seemed young to be taking over such a position, but with his attitude, I wasn't surprised.

We stepped into the office, and I headed toward the hall the led to the break room when James reached out and pulled me so my back was against his chest. The sudden movement caught me off guard, and I froze.

"What's wrong?" he asked.

"You surprised me." James hadn't touched me like that since our last date three years ago.

"Sorry, I just . . . Can't we just start now, in secret? Be a couple?" His breath was hot against my neck, sending tingles through me. Once again, I noticed a reduced response to him. It was still there, the urge to pull him close and kiss him as the heat flared inside me, but it wasn't the normal blaze.

"No," I said with a sigh.

He groaned against my skin. "Why do you have to be so levelheaded when I'm dying over here?"

He wasn't the only one. "Because I have to finish this program, and if we start dating now, my grades will tank. I've worked too hard to let anything stop me."

He nodded and released me while stepping back. "You're right. I would definitely distract you and try to monopolize your free time. I'm sorry."

I turned to him, and my chest began to ache. It was so hard turning him down. "This isn't easy for me, either."

"I know. I'm just selfish."

"Why selfish?"

He gave me a shy smile. "After three years, you're still the only woman I think about. We didn't get a fair chance back then, and I've been waiting so long to try again."

"Just hold on a few more months."

He nodded. "I can do that."

My lips turned up into a smile, and his did the same. "Have a good night."

"You, too," he said with a wave.

After getting my things from my locker, I headed toward the parking garage. It was hard having those conversations with James, because each one broke me down more and more. I wasn't going to think about the strange lack of response I felt, chalking it up to PMS.

At the same time, just one look from Mr. Grayson held more fire than James's touch.

There was nothing wrong with that. Mr. Grayson was just a hot guy. Why wouldn't my pulse speed up when he was around? It was normal. Healthy, even. And not a hiccup in my path. No, Mr. Grayson was just a guest, nothing more.

When I got to my car, I pulled out my phone and noticed the date. Crap. I hadn't talked to my parents since February, and March was closing up.

Not wanting to forget, I pulled up my contacts and hit send. It rang a few times before the click of someone answering.

"Hello?"

"Hi Dad," I said into the receiver.

"Emmybear! How are you doing?" His voice was instantly happier than it had been when he answered.

Calling my parents had become a couple-times-a-month thing, and like always, hearing my dad's voice was soothing.

"Busy as usual."

"How are your classes going?" he asked.

"Almost over." That alone was a huge bright spot. Years of hard work and sacrifice were coming to a close.

"And then that's it? MBA?"

"MBA."

"I'm so proud of you, baby. I'm so sorry I wasn't able to help you."

"Daddy, don't worry. I worked hard, just like you taught me, and I did it and only missed a meal or two," I said, trying to cheer him up. It was the truth. It was hard, but I always had a place to lay my head and a meal to fill my belly. I sacrificed in other ways— friends and other relationships. Most of my college friends moved away after graduation, and those who were still in Boston were just as busy as I was.

"Still, when we moved out here I had every intention of helping you out financially. I've barely seen you because you've been forced to work so much."

They moved hundreds of miles away for my dad to get a higher-paying job, only for the company to fold a year later. The recession had improved, but he still had trouble finding a job there or back home. I hadn't even seen my parents in over two years, having been forced to work most holidays.

"Hopefully that will change and I can come visit you soon."

"I would love that." I really would. I missed my parents so much.

I missed his hugs. Then again, I missed any hugs. The lack of physical contact of any kind was depressing. I craved that connection desperately. When James had wrapped his arms around me, it was the first type of hug I'd gotten in a year or more.

"How's everything else there? Any job prospects after graduation? Men in your life?"

"No prospects yet, but the school is helping me. As for men . . ." James weighed heavy in my chest. I just wasn't sure if it was feelings built up over years of thinking about it or something real. "There is someone, but we'll see what happens with that."

"Well, hopefully I'll get to hear more on that next time," he said with a chuckle.

"Is Mom there?" I asked.

"She's at work. Can she call you when she gets home? Or are you going to be working?"

"I'll be in class, but I'll catch up with her on the weekend."

"Sounds good. Love you, Emmybear."

"Love you, too, Daddy." I hit the end button and let out a sigh at the same time. Another night ahead of me. I couldn't wait to be done with school, because I was tired down to my bones.

The saying about burning the candle at both ends? Well, all the wax was gone, and my flames were about to meet.

Every night there seemed to be some complaint from Mr. Grayson, but on the ninth night all was quiet. The clock neared eleven, which signaled one hour left until the end of my shift when I would be handing the reins off to Rob, the overnight manager. There was only a small amount of time before I would have my first night free of Mr. Grayson's complaints.

"Nothing?" Shannon asked as she crossed the lobby with one last cup of coffee from the lobby Starbucks. They were closed, but Shannon was friends with one of the girls that worked there and was able to get her hands on another cup while they cleaned up.

"Not yet." I was about to say something else when the phone beside me rang. I glanced down, a familiar number flashing on the screen, then glared up at Shannon. "You did this."

She held up her hands, eyes wide. "I'm sorry!"

I blew out a breath, then picked up the receiver. "Good evening, Mr. Grayson."

"There is a *fucking party* going on in the room next to me. Shut them *the fuck up!*"

I had to pull the phone away from my ear as he yelled, clearly more agitated than normal.

"Right away, Mr. Grayson." I hung up the phone and looked at Shannon. "Does he do this when I'm not here, or am I just lucky?"

She nodded. "I heard he cracked James's perfect smile yesterday."

"Insufferable," I mumbled as I stepped around the desk. "I'll be right back."

"Good luck!" she called as the elevator doors closed.

Due to the ire I'd heard in his voice, I figured the party must be really loud. The hotel was built with great sound barriers between rooms to make sure guests slept their best.

The music was loud enough that I heard it almost to the elevators. I was surprised Mr. Grayson was the only one who complained. The realization dawned on me that he didn't tell me which room it was, but by the volume of the music, it wasn't hard to figure out.

I rapped swiftly with my knuckles on the door and waited. There was a cascade of laughter on the other side, but no response. The second time I knocked much harder, making sure they took notice. When the laughter died down, I knew I'd been heard.

The door swung open, and I was greeted by a guy that looked to be around my age, maybe a little older. There was a beer bottle in his hand and a big smile on his face.

"Hey, sweet thing," he said, somehow sounding smooth though I could tell he was drunk.

"Good evening. We've received a few noise complaints and need you to turn the music down."

"It's a party, baby. There's got to be music," he said before holding his arms out and gyrating his hips at me.

"Party or not, you're being too loud and we have guests that are trying to sleep."

"Just listen to her and shut up," a gruff male voice called from down the hall. The sound lit up every nerve ending as it traveled down my spine.

Fifteen feet away in front of his door was Mr. Grayson, standing in nothing but a set of plaid sleep shorts. My mouth dropped open as an unfamiliar, warm feeling spread through me at the view of his bare chest and just how fit he was. His hair was not in its usual impeccable style, but sticking up in every direction. The frown he wore was something I was very familiar with, but it gave him a gruff sexiness.

"Shut the fucking music off. Some people are trying to sleep," Mr. Grayson growled, clearly aggravated.

"Whatever, man," the drunk guy said.

I looked back to the occupant, noticing that his four friends were snickering. "Turn it down, and keep it down, or I will be forced to remove you."

"Bitch, we paid. You can't do shit!" one of the occupants yelled out.

The guy at the door wore a smug smile. "Maybe you can come in and help us quiet down."

In my periphery, Mr. Grayson took a step forward. "Don't talk to her that way."

"Dude, go back to bed. We just want to have some fun," the creep said as he wrapped his arm around my waist.

It stunned me, and took me a second before I realized what was happening, and then I was pushing against his chest. He was laughing, but I didn't have time to react further before Mr. Grayson ripped the creep's hand from me and pinned it behind the guy's back as he pressed him against the wall. His bottle of beer fell to the floor, spilling some of the leftover contents onto the carpet.

"Don't touch her," Mr. Grayson spat. "She isn't some street whore."

My heart slammed in my chest as I watched him manhandle the guy. I had to admit, it was a turn-on. Especially knowing it was in my defense.

The creep struggled to get out of his grip, but Mr. Grayson only held him tighter. "Get off me, man!"

"All she is asking is for you to quiet down so that I am not up her ass about the noise. It is *not* an invitation for you to hit on her or touch her in any way. Do you understand?"

All of his friends stayed in their place in the room, watching the events unfold.

"Let me go," was the guy's only response.

Mr. Grayson moved his arm, tightening his grip as he pulled more, making the creep wince in pain.

"I said, do you understand?"

"Yeah . . . y-yes!"

Mr. Grayson released his hand as he shoved him back into the room. They closed the door, and the music immediately died down. He came over, stopping in front of me.

"Are you okay?" he asked as he looked me over before his eyes locked onto mine.

It was the first time I'd been close enough to notice his eyes. While there wasn't much noticeable difference from a few feet away, with barely a foot separating us, the color difference between his eyes was obvious. He had heterochromia—his right eye was a crystal-clear sea blue, while his left eye was green.

"What?" he asked, noticing my pause.

"Your eyes . . ." My gaze flashed between the two, bouncing between them to compare. "Your eyes are beautiful. I hadn't noticed before."

The tightness in his features relaxed. It was only a brief moment before they hardened again and he stepped back. "Yes, this entire hotel staff seems not to notice a lot of things." With that, he headed toward his door.

"Thank you very much for your help, but I could have managed without it," I said to his back.

He glanced over his shoulder at me. "Perhaps, but sometimes it takes a strong hand to handle those who are out of control."

"Do you use force often?"

That stopped him, and he turned back to me. "Physically? No. There are other ways to get people to do what I want."

"Like yelling at them."

He didn't respond as he stepped back into his room. "Goodnight, Emma." Then the door slammed.

"Goodnight, Mr. Moody," I said before heading down the hall toward the elevator. I needed to find Miguel and file a report about the room next to him.

Still, even though he was cold as per the usual, there was something about the way he came to my defense that had warmed me up to the man. At least a little, anyway. Especially my body.

4th Floor

The alarm went off, startling me awake. I was disoriented. What day was it? What time? The clock read nine, but was that morning or night?

I went through a list.

Groceries? Done. Homework? Done. Work?

I let out a sigh and pulled the blanket over my head. Oh, that was why the alarm was going off.

One day. That was all I wanted. Just one day that was free of both school and work. One day to stay curled on the couch with takeout and binge Netflix.

At least Mr. Grayson's reservation was almost over and there would only be a few more days of dealing with him.

With a groan, I peeled myself out of bed. I *hated* third shift. Nothing like going to work in the middle of the night and coming home when the sun was creeping into the sky. Each step to the shower was torture. I had taken about a three-hour nap, but it just seemed to have made me more tired.

Instead of being awake, I was a zombie. A quick shower didn't help, and my body was still sluggish as I walked to the kitchen in search of something that would help. Inside the fridge, I found a Rockstar Energy Drink and began eagerly sucking it down.

With a few ounces in me, I returned to getting ready. It took a few minutes, but I began to feel more and more human with each sip. Once dressed, I returned to the kitchen to grab another for work.

"Shit," I hissed as I looked to find there were no more. I'd just gone to the grocery that afternoon, so how could I have forgotten?

Starbucks was closed and didn't open until almost six. I wasn't sure I could hold out that long without my head falling onto the desk. Nothing I could do about it, so I was stuck with the half a can I still had left. Hopefully it would do. There was a coffee maker in the break room, but I hated coffee that wasn't watered down with steamed milk and some vanilla.

The can was completely empty by the time I pulled into the parking garage. At least I finally felt awake and energized. Being almost eleven, everything was quiet as I headed toward the office. If it'd been a Friday or Saturday, things would be different, but it was Wednesday. There were bound to be a few stragglers at the bar, but the lobby was going to be empty.

When I entered the office, James was headed toward the door I'd just come through, and his eyes popped open in surprise.

"Good evening," I said with my arms open wide like I was presenting myself.

James chuckled and shook his head. "That's an invitation."

"An invitation for what?"

He stepped forward and leaned down to my ear, his hand resting on my hip. "For me to wrap my arms around you."

"All touchy touchy." I giggled.

He furrowed his brow at me. "Are you all right?"

I nodded. "I had a Rockstar, and I'm tired. Think I'm a bit slap happy."

He chuckled at me and shook his head. "That'll do it."

"So, what's on the agenda for tonight?"

"Reports."

"Yay," I said with little enthusiasm and a roll of my eyes. "That won't put me back to sleep or anything."

He shrugged. "I have a task for you."

"Oh, yeah?"

"And it's more than looking beautiful."

I couldn't help the blush that spread on my cheeks. "James . . ."

"Okay, in seriousness . . ." he reached over to grab a small stack of papers ". . . when Valeria gets in, I need you have her double-check this inventory and product list ASAP. Miguel is going to send out the order as soon as he gets in at seven."

"Got it."

Caleb arrived a few minutes before James headed out the door. Once he was gone, it was just the two of us. The nights were normally pretty quiet. We used the time for tidying up the front desk, dealing with the occasional request or drunk, and watching the late night partiers crawl in.

The hotel bar closed at one, and after that, silence. It was a drag, and I found myself napping on my break only to be startled awake by my alarm.

"Slap me," Caleb said around four.

"Can't, I'm your boss."

He let out a groan and then whipped his hand across his face, tousling his perfectly styled dark brown hair. The smack resonated around the silent lobby.

"Ow," he said.

His cheek started to turn red, and I couldn't help but laugh. "Did it at least help?"

The corners of his lips turned down and his bottom lip jutted out. "No."

I slipped off my heels, my feet killing me, and let out a sigh.

"Whoa, when did you get short?" he asked, his brown eyes wide.

Normally, Caleb and I were eye to eye, but with my shoes off, I was my regular five feet, five inches.

"Ha, ha," I said with a roll of my eyes.

"I hate third shift," he said after a few minutes of silence.

"Ditto."

The hours that followed continued to drag on, but around five thirty, activity started to pick up in the lobby.

Just before six, I headed toward Valeria's office. I was just passing the fitness center when something caught my eye, causing me to stop. A very familiar man was working out and looking very different than when I normally encountered him.

It was Mr. Grayson. The muscles in his arms and chest flexed as he pulled on the handles of the cable crossover frame, the weights rising and falling with his movement. It was hypnotizing. I couldn't stop watching him, and my heartbeat increased while the blood pumped in my veins in time with his movement.

At least watching him I understood how he'd handled the creep from two nights prior. He was very fit, but I saw how strong he was as well. Not bulky like some of the meatheads I'd seen, but lean with broad shoulders.

I was lost in a trance when he looked up and our eyes met through the glass. The force of his stare startled me, and I made an embarrassing little jump before continuing on my way down the hall.

What was wrong with me? The man was infuriating and maddening and drove me crazy, but one look at him and for a few seconds I forgot all that.

Looks shouldn't trump attitude, but somehow, his did. Which left me a weird mess of confused and turned on. Again, him coming to my aid all shirtless and manly and peeling that creep off me . . .

My hormones were a mess. Maybe my period was near or I was ovulating. Something had to explain my irrational responses to him, because I'd never had such a strong reaction to any man before, even James.

I shouldn't get caught up in strange hormonal reactions to asshole guests that were going to be gone soon.

But that was when the doubt started to creep in. What if my desire to be with James was only a product of what-ifs? I liked him, there was no doubt there, but was there more than like?

Valeria sighed as I entered her office. "What now? Haven't I bent over backwards enough for that man?"

I held up my hands and pursed my lips. "He's very particular."

"He's a diva, Emma."

"I'm not arguing. I'm the one that deals with most of his complaints."

"What is it now?" she grumbled.

I knew that Mr. Grayson had made a reputation for himself, but his high standards seemed to hit Valeria hardest.

"It's not him."

"No? Then why are you down here?"

I held up the papers. "Inventory and reorder of Cameo logo material. I need you to double-check the numbers."

She blew out a breath and took the sheets from me. "Why can't we all do this on our own?"

I shrugged. "Company policy."

She nodded. "I know. It's just a colossal pain."

She checked her computer against the list and made a few corrections and notations.

Valeria's black hair fell out of her loose ponytail, her glasses slipping off the end of her nose. Normally, she was very put together, but I'd heard that her youngest was sick, which probably accounted for the less-than-pristine look. At only around five feet tall, new employees assumed she was harmless. Small but stern, she fired faster than any manager, which was why I was surprised by the pass she'd given to whomever released the floor of doom a few weeks back.

She'd been with the hotel for a decade, starting when she had taken classes for a hospitality degree. Her end goal was to take Phillip, the hotel manager's, job. I was certain she'd be better at it than he was.

"Is Miguel sending it in?" she asked after a few minutes.

"As soon as he gets in."

"Good. That means we should have everything by the end of the week." She handed the order form back to me. "Thanks, Emma."

"No problem. Word of warning, don't go near the fitness center for a little while."

That piqued her interest. "Oh?"

"Mr. Demanding is in there."

31

"Well, now I have to go just to see." She slipped off her glasses and stood as she attempted to wrangle her hair into something presentable. She pretended to need to walk back to the front with me. "*Ay, papi,*" she whispered as we slowly passed by the large glass windows. "*That's* him?"

I nodded, engrossed in watching the new angle he was working. "So nice to look at, but that mouth."

"Isn't that what duct tape is for?" she said as we continued down the hall.

"Oh, my God, now I'm having thoughts of him scowling while . . . you are so bad!" I laughed. I glanced over, an electric shock running through me as I found him staring at me. My lips parted as I drew in a sharp breath, my cheeks warming.

"Ooh, Mr. Santos is getting some tonight."

I understood where she was coming from. Watching Mr. Grayson was an aphrodisiac, and it was turning me on. The way he looked at me didn't help.

After making up a fake excuse, Valeria headed back to her office, fanning herself with each step.

Less than two hours later, I kicked my apartment door closed, pulled my clothes off, and fell into bed to get some sleep before my afternoon class.

The next day I went in for my normal second shift, happy to have gotten a full night's sleep, even if it was three in the morning by the time I got to sleep. Sleeping after third shift always made it difficult to get back to normal. At least I'd gotten a good chunk done on my final project.

There were only three days left on Mr. Grayson's reservation, and I was going to be so happy when things returned to normal.

Normally the phone ringing wasn't anything out of the ordinary, but when Shannon backed up and shook her head, I knew who it was.

"I can't talk to people like him," Shannon said, her back against the wall as she stared down at the phone in horror. Angry customers left her flustered, and after the first night, she was scared of even the possibility of a confrontation with him.

"It's okay, I've got him." I took a steadying breath, plastered on a smile, and answered the phone. "Good evening, Mr. Grayson," I said into the receiver.

"I want a cheeseburger." No pleasantries, straight to the point.

Oh, good. Somebody else's problem. "Let me connect you with room service."

"No. I want you to handle it."

The vein in my forehead began to throb. "Sir?"

"They fucked it up last night," he grumbled. "I want it right, and I want you to make sure it's right and delivered as soon as it's done."

His demands were going above and beyond my duties, but I'd do anything to keep him happy and not yelling.

I held my hand over the receiver and closed my eyes as I took a deep breath. "Of course. What would you like?"

After taking down his order, I left Shannon to man the front while I headed over to the kitchen.

"Hey, Emma," Omar, the head chef, called as I entered.

"Hi, Omar," I said with a smile.

He was expertly cutting up some vegetables at a speed I would never attempt unless I *wanted* a trip to the emergency room. "What brings you down here?"

"I have a special request from a guest, and I need it made *precisely* as he wants it."

With a quick swipe, the vegetable joined a large stainless steel bowl with some waiting ingredients. "Is this the guest I've been hearing about?"

"His infamous status has reached even back here?"

He grinned as he wiped his hands off. "This isn't his first room service order."

"Ah, yes, he did mention something about an order." I used to think I was the only one that took the brunt of his demands, but it became obvious I wasn't the only one—just the only one face to face.

"What can I get for you?" he asked.

"I need a cheeseburger and fries," I said before diving into the list of specifications. "Cooked medium, not under, not over. One slice of sharp cheddar cheese, three strips of bacon, mayo, ketchup, pickles, white onions not red, and tomato on a toasted cornmeal bun."

"Because that's not specific enough," he said with a shake of his head as he headed to the walk-in to pull out ingredients.

"Tell me about it. There's more." I glanced down at my paper. "Fries need to be hot and crisp when I take it up. No funny business, please. For my sanity, make it exactly as he requests."

"Got it. I'll let you know when it goes up."

"Oh, no, no, no," I said, halting him as I shook my head. "I have to wait and take it up myself."

"Seriously?"

"Yes, because if it's not right, I'll be coming right back down." I plastered a fake smile on my face while Omar shook his head.

Omar didn't pass the order off, and instead, made the entire thing himself.

"Hopefully that satisfies the king," he said as he laid the plate down on the cart.

"Thank you, Omar."

"Don't take no shit from him."

The corner of my lip slid up. "From him? Never."

"Good girl. Now go on before his fries cool down."

With one last wave, I headed to the service elevator and up to his floor. The ride was short without evening activity creating stops. As I pushed the tray down the hall, I prayed that it was exactly as he wanted it. The last thing I needed was more of his mouth.

After a swift knock the door swung open and, as always, I was stunned by how overwhelming he was. Still in his slacks, vest, and dress shirt with the sleeves rolled up, the tie and jacket were gone. The sight, along with his presence, sent the butterflies in my stomach into overdrive. It was all overpowering when I was near him.

Why did the first man to make me feel this way have to have the worst personality?

"Emma." He stepped aside and held the door open for me, which seemed a little odd.

I picked up the tray with some difficulty as I attempted to not spill the drinks, and headed in. "Where would you like it?"

"The desk is fine."

I set the tray down and straightened up, eager to leave. "Is there anything else I can help you with tonight?"

"Wait," he said, stopping me from pushing past him and getting the hell away.

I clasped my hands in front of me and stood watching as he lifted the covers, a low hum of appreciation rumbling as he looked it over. First, he tried out a fry, seemingly pleased with its state, then he picked up the burger.

The second he bit in, he began to moan. The sound was bordering on erotic and sent a tingle down my spine and heat pooling between my legs.

What the hell?

"Perfect," he said, his voice low and, for the first time, appreciative. "Now this is a good burger." Another bite, and another moan left me weak. "Good job, Emma. I knew you would get it right."

A compliment? After so long, I hadn't been sure he was capable of such a thing.

I had to focus on that because I wasn't sure why I was having such an extreme reaction to him. That moan . . . that moan would do me in if he continued.

"Thank you, sir. Will that be all?" I needed to get away from him and the magnetism that surrounded him.

He shook his head as he took yet another bite. "Who made this? Because I need him to make me one every night."

"Every night?"

His eyes went wide for a fraction of a second before he cleared his throat. "I may have a bacon cheeseburger obsession."

"If this is your reaction to a cheeseburger, please let me know what else gives you pleasure and I will do everything I can to get it for you."

He stared at me, his eyes somehow darker, heavier as he sucked some of the juice from the pad of his thumb. I froze, almost as if I was trapped within the intoxicating vibes he was giving off.

"There are many things that give me pleasure, Emma." The gravel tone of his words had my brain short circuiting, especially since our eyes were locked.

I couldn't look away, couldn't think of any response, but instead was stuck in place, hypnotized, feeling my face heat up. "What would those be, sir?" I asked, my voice barely a breathy whisper.

Another low moan, but this time not from the cheeseburger. "Get out of here."

I blinked at him, confused as he sat at the desk, his attention focused on the tray. My dismissal was obvious, but I was still stunned at the sudden shift in his mood. It took a second for that to wear off, and my feet began to move, carrying me away from him.

When I got back to the lobby, I ran to the restroom to try and cool down. In the mirror, my whole face was pink. He hadn't touched me, but I was burning for him to. That look, the way he'd licked the juice off his thumb, was the sexiest thing I'd ever seen.

The horror lay in realizing I'd never felt that to such a degree with James or anyone else.

I almost asked myself what I was going to do, but stopped. Mr. Grayson would soon be gone, and things would go back to normal. I would forget all about this feeling and chalk it up to his good looks and the fact he was probably teasing me just because he could.

"I heard you made him happy last night," James said from behind me, his mouth close to my ear.

I turned and glanced around, making sure nobody was around. Not that we were doing anything wrong. Everyone was used to seeing us close, but even so, we were only inches apart.

It was odd—James was close, but my normal reactions to him were missing. Or maybe they were just dulled. There was little warmth or longing, the butterflies barely flapping their wings. I had thought the other night was a fluke. That I just wasn't feeling well or something, but again, the lack of reaction was strange, especially considering how I felt ten feet from Mr. Grayson.

The finish line was in sight, and once I found another job, we wouldn't be trapped. He knew it and I knew it, but for some reason the idea of being with him didn't fill me with the same excitement it used to.

No, I knew now, though it was very hard to admit: the even more unavailable Gavin Grayson had somehow taken over James's place.

Still, I smiled up at him. "About time I did something right."

He let out a chuckle. "That asshole just doesn't know what he's talking about. Being a pain just to be one. I'm sorry you seem to take the brunt of it."

"He seems to have taken a liking to beating me down. I wonder if he's betting with himself when he'll break me."

"Never. Emma Addison is unbreakable."

"Thanks for the vote of confidence."

"No problem." He leaned in closer, his breath hot against my neck. "Go out to dinner with me tomorrow."

"James . . ."

"As friends."

I shook my head. "You know that's a lie."

He let out a sigh and stepped back. "Yeah. I guess a guy can dream. I just . . . I feel like you're somehow slipping away from me and I don't know what to do."

I wasn't sure how to react or what to say. I'd felt the same way for about two weeks, slowly, ever since Gavin Grayson walked into the hotel.

"There's a lot of pressure right now," I finally said, not even sure I believed it.

He nodded. "That could be. I know you've got a lot of stress with school and then your bitch of a landlord raised your rent."

"Yeah, I didn't need that headache of trying to scrounge up an extra two hundred a month, especially since nothing else changed." The whole rent thing was frustrating and infuriating. "It's not like she upgraded anything."

He shook his head. "Rent is ridiculous."

"One entire paycheck now goes just to rent," I grumbled. "If I didn't have this job, I don't know what I'd do."

"Move in with me."

I rolled my eyes. "You just can't help yourself, can you?"

His lip twitched up into a smirk. "With you? No. Plus, if you didn't have this job, nobody would care if you lived with me."

I didn't know how to respond to that, so I continued on my way out. "Good night."

"Same to you."

I shook my head and stepped out into the lobby to where Caleb and Jaqueline were, and away from the awkward way I felt after what James had said.

"How's today?" I asked.

Jaqueline smiled and shrugged her shoulders. "Pretty easy. There was a big luncheon in the Midas ballroom. Some fiiiine men came through. Mmm!"

It was pretty slow, but there were people coming in every few minutes to check in, and occasionally there would be a short line of a few guests.

An hour later, I let Jaqueline take her break.

"So, what's with you and James?" Caleb asked once Jaqueline was gone.

I blinked at him. "What?"

"He's super friendly with you. Touchy-feely, nice. Real looker with those blue eyes."

"Fine. He likes me." That wasn't hard. But if he asked me more . . . my heart seemed to be turning on me, and it scared me.

"Are you two together?" he asked.

My mouth dropped open. "Caleb!"

He threw his hands up. "I'm just asking."

"No," I stressed. "That's against company policy."

"But you want to."

My lips formed a thin line. "Maybe one day. For now, it's flirting."

I hoped that put Caleb off the subject, especially since I was having doubts. Why were things changing?

5th Floor

Valeria's mention of duct tape kept me up at night with fantasies about Mr. Grayson. Tied to a chair, scowling at me, nostrils flared as I rode him. It was exactly the image I was trying not to think about, but after the cheeseburger incident, I couldn't stop.

I couldn't stop thinking about him.

The night had barely begun when the phone rang. That stupid flutter in my stomach kicked in at the number.

"Good evening, Mr. Grayson," I said.

"There is water all over the bathroom floor," he said in a low, clearly aggravated tone.

Water? Floor?

"Did you hear me, Emma?"

I blinked, trying to get my brain to function. "I . . . Is there a leak?"

"I don't know, but why don't you get up here with someone from maintenance." The ire in his tone was very noticeable, probably due to my delayed response.

"Yes, right, sorry, sir." Since when did I become a bumbling idiot in front of him? It was probably the surprise of something actually wrong versus some perceived slight. I picked up the phone

40

and called for maintenance to meet me up in his room, and then waited for Caleb to return from his Starbucks run.

From thirty feet away, Caleb could tell I'd received a call. "What is it today?" he asked as he held out a fresh latte.

"Thanks," I said as I took it from him. "A possible actual issue."

"Yeah? Good luck."

I took a quick sip of my latte before setting it down. "I'll be back."

By the time I made it up to the fourteenth floor, Joe, the maintenance supervisor, was heading down the hall from the service elevator.

"Hey, Emma," he said with a smile.

"Hi."

"What do we have?"

I blew out a breath before reaching out and knocking on his door. "We'll see."

The door swung open, and I almost stumbled from the impact of seeing him. Every time it got harder, not easier. Power and strength exuded from him with almost palpable force.

Unfortunately, so did his sexuality.

"About time," he grumbled.

He held the door as Joe and I walked through, Joe heading straight for the bathroom. I followed behind, my eyes going wide at the water covering the bathroom floor.

"Whoa." I stepped back to let Joe find the source and returned to facing Mr. Grayson.

"Exactly," he ground out. It was a different level of annoyance than I was used to. He was genuinely irked.

"I apologize for this inconvenience."

"Can't this hotel do anything right?" he asked as he removed his cuff links, and we heard the sounds of the maintenance man, clinking away in the bathroom.

"Once again, I apologize—" I began, but was cut off.

"Enough with your damn apologies. Over two fucking weeks of them, and they don't fix a fucking thing," he sneered. "If my company was run the way this hotel is, I wouldn't have a job. Fucking incompetent idiots."

41

"Please, sir, your language is inappropriate. I am trying to rectify the situation." I'd had about enough of his mouth. The language he used was inappropriate in my mind, given that I'd been bending over backwards to make him happy and that the issue was truly a fluke. The problem was that nothing seemed to make him happy—with the exception of berating me.

"There shouldn't be a situation," he nearly shouted, glaring at me as he yanked the tie from around his neck.

I stood my ground, facing him, my spine straightening. "I agree, but unfortunately there is. For the inconvenience, we would like to upgrade your room."

"No."

"I'm sorry . . . no?" The vein on my forehead started to throb, and my ever-present smile faltered. He was going to drive me to homicide at this rate. Maybe that duct tape idea wasn't so bad.

"Are you deaf as well, Emma?" He walked toward me and stopped just short of my body, invading my personal space, and leaned in close, his hand resting on the wall beside my head. I could smell him at that distance, and the bastard smelled divine. "You've moved me already, and besides the leak in the bathroom, I quite enjoy *this* room." His gaze moved up and down my body and his tongue peeked out to lick his lips. "You will just have to find another way to *compensate* me."

Blood rushed to my cheeks as my hands fidgeted with the hem of my jacket. We were inches apart, and all I wanted to do was lean forward and press my lips to his. The heat rolling off him lit up every nerve in my body.

I had to be misinterpreting him. I had to be. The strange quickening of my pulse when I saw him, the butterflies. It was just another overreaction from my body, finding what it wanted to hear and see and turning it into something seductive.

"At your service, Mr. Grayson," I squeaked out, flustered.

I was close enough that I could have sworn I heard him groan, which almost made me groan in return from the rush of heat that moved through me.

He pushed off the wall and resumed unbuttoning his shirt. "Get out of here."

It was the second night he'd dismissed me the same way. An electric pulse seemed to circulate between us, then suddenly, he became cold and calculated.

"Hot, demanding bastard," I grumbled as I walked down the hall, cursing his name as I fanned my face.

My steps slowed as I got to the elevator and my heartbeat regulated. I hated what he was doing to me, the doubts he was instilling. Each encounter with him was destroying everything I thought I knew and wanted.

Dealing with Mr. Grayson had pushed me to the point of losing sleep, which was something I definitely needed. Between his anger and his sexual presence, I was at my wit's end.

His stay was extended another week and I desperately wanted him to just leave, to let me get back to normal. I was tired of dealing with him, tired of being berated, and tired of lust-filled dreams about him.

"Hey, are you all right?" James asked.

"Hmm? Oh, I'm fine."

"Are you sure? You just seem . . . out there."

I tried to give him a smile, but a strange heaviness in my chest stopped it. "Yeah, I'm just tired."

There seemed to be an invisible wall between us, but that didn't stop James. Maybe he didn't feel it the way I did. It was almost like my personal space barrier had popped back to life with him.

He rubbed his hand up and down my arm as he leaned down to catch my eyes. "You've got tomorrow off. Get some rest."

I heaved a sigh. "I've got class at nine."

"Well, that sucks. Okay, then go home and crash, then relax tomorrow night. You work day on Saturday, so rest up. It'll be busy with the race."

"Crap, I forgot about that."

"It's during the day," he pointed out. "Take the subway, and you'll be fine. I know you don't like doing it at night, but the sun will still be up when you leave."

I nodded. "That's true." Taking the subway that day wouldn't be bad at all.

"How's Grayson treating you?" he asked after a minute of silence.

"Grayson? Same as always, but it's fine."

"I don't like that he's always calling on you," James said, his normal smile gone, replaced with something I couldn't place, but if the tightness of his jaw was any indication, it was nothing good.

"He does it when I'm not here as well," I reminded him.

"Yeah, but not every night."

"What?" I blinked up at him. Every night I was on, there was a call from him.

"There are complaints, but nothing like when you're working."

I shrugged and tried to play it off, but it left me curious. Did he just like picking on me? "Maybe I'm just his favorite punching bag."

His lips formed a thin line. "Maybe, but I don't think that's it."

My brow furrowed and I waited for him to elaborate, but he didn't.

"Well, I'm out of here. Have fun tonight," he said with a wave as he headed toward the door.

"Hey, James?" I said, stopping him. He turned and smiled at me, and for the first time ever, my body gave no response. "Have a good night."

"You, too."

I stared after him as a lone tear slipped down my cheek. There was such a weight in my heart, a weight that hadn't been there a few weeks prior. He'd done nothing wrong, yet I no longer felt connected to him. What was happening to me?

My lunch break was spent in the lobby Starbucks, downing a quick latte and a sandwich as I read up on my business economics and statistics. I was actually absorbing it and getting my mind thinking about my next project when I was rudely interrupted.

"I didn't realize they taught such high-level academia to hotel supervisors," a familiar, snide voice said, pulling me from my zone and speeding up my pulse. "I didn't think one had to have more than a high-school education, based on my experience these past weeks, and someone with a high-school education would not be able to understand that subject."

I sighed, getting my bearings in place before I lit into him. "If you must know, Mr. Grayson, I am finishing up my MBA in just a few short weeks. No, this is not standard reading for a lowly hotel clerk. I work here so I can eat and have a place to live. A full course load combined with forty hours plus of work every week. Not to mention all the homework, and I still somehow manage to cook, clean, and maintain over a three-point-five grade average."

I sat back, folded my arms, and pursed my lips at him. He looked . . . surprised.

"Well done, Emma. I knew you were somewhat more intelligent than the others, but that is beyond my expectations," he said with his trademark frown.

That only irritated me more. Was he making fun of me? The blood vessel in my temple began to pulse as I glared at him.

"Excuse me?" He was lucky I didn't bite him at that point.

Pulling out the chair on the other side of the table, he inserted himself into my personal space. I hated the way my skin heated when his knee brushed mine. It was so contradictory to how my mind felt about him.

"What I'm trying to say, Emma, is what you have accomplished is quite impressive."

"You've already managed to insult me, Mr. Grayson, by implying that you thought I was intelligent, but only slightly."

He blinked at me. "I've upset you. Interesting."

"Of course you've upset me. I've worked very hard to get through this program and still have a place to lay my head. I don't have copious amounts of money to throw at an upscale hotel to live there for weeks on end. One night in your room is almost a month's rent to me."

"I didn't say you don't work hard, Emma. I know you do, I make sure of it. I just . . ." he trailed off, his hand flying in agitation.

And hitting my latte.

The cup bounced on the table, popping the lid off and creating a latte explosion.

All over my book.

All over my clothes.

"Shit!" I jumped up from my chair and picked my book up from the lake of latte that was swallowing it up.

"Fuck," he cursed before he turned to grab some napkins.

I yanked them from his hand and began patting down the pages. "Great. Just fucking great," I muttered. The book cost me over one hundred dollars used.

"Don't worry, Emma, I'll get it. Go get yourself cleaned up," Andrea, the barista, called from behind the counter.

"Thanks!" I replied before giving her a strained smile as I ran out.

"Emma," I heard him call out as I stormed across the lobby, my book still dripping latte. "Will you let me apologize to you?"

"No." My heels clacked loud on the tile floor as I raced away from him.

"Why not?"

I whirled on him. "Do you really want to know that, Mr. Grayson? Hmm? Because I can assure you I have more than enough ammo to throw at you."

I spun back around and headed through a door that led to one of the employee corridors, walking at as swift a pace as I could manage. The stress washed over me, swallowing me up. Still, I could hear his footsteps behind me.

"Emma, will you just stop. Please."

"Go away!" I cried out. Tears stung at my eyes—the last thing I wanted him to see. Couldn't he just leave me alone? Why did he have to keep picking on me?

He grabbed my arm, and sparks ignited my skin as he pulled me back. My foot slipped at the sudden shift of my weight, and I crashed into his chest. The book dropped to the ground, and his arms wrapped around me as the momentum caused us to spin into the wall. The breath flew from my lungs as my back slammed into the concrete blocks with him crashing into me.

Once we'd stopped, he pulled away from me and the tears started to spill from my eyes, flowing down my cheeks. My chest constricted to keep from sobbing, but it was no use. Panic filled his features: his eyes widened and his mouth opened.

"Why won't you just leave me alone?" I asked. He'd been torturing me in more ways than one since he walked in. Changing everything I thought I wanted.

"Please, don't cry," he begged. His hands cupped my face, his thumbs brushing away my tears.

"What did I do to you?" I asked, really needing to know the answer. "Why do you keep doing this to me?"

"I like you," he answered, just as plain as anything, and I could see the truth in his eyes. My sobbing reduced to just tears streaming down my face, and I stared up at him like he was mental. "I've gone about it in a very juvenile way, I admit."

"How so?"

The corner of his mouth ticked up. "Don't little boys pick on the girl they like?"

I gawked up at him. "You're an adult, you know. If you like someone, you don't beat them down and make them feel inferior. It's called wooing. I have a dictionary, you can look it up."

He smirked down at me, wiping the remainder of my tears away, and I couldn't help but lean into his touch. It was so much more than I could ever have anticipated. Such a small gesture, and yet my every cell lit up and begged for more. More of his hands on me, his lips. More of all of him. Maybe it had been so long since I'd had anyone touch me like that, or it was the attraction I had for him, I wasn't sure.

"I need to go change," I said, forcing myself to pull away from his warmth.

He nodded and stepped back, releasing me. "Let me pay for the replacement of your book."

I glanced up at the powerhouse that had rocked the hotel for weeks, into his beautifully different eyes. There was no malice, no anger, none of the emotions I was used to with him.

"Okay," I said, not knowing how else to respond.

"Have a good night, Emma," he said in a low voice.

My heart thumped hard in my chest. "You, too, Mr. Grayson."

6th Floor

After our encounter in the hall, things changed. He still complained about everything, and even wrote a nasty letter to Alana, the maid Valeria had assigned to him. Apparently, he didn't like the way in which she folded the towels.

His stay was extended indefinitely, making the staff less than excited. I, on the other hand, was finally starting to understand him after his confession.

"Really?" I asked with a quirked brow as he pointed to his latest irritation. My usual demeanor with him had become a little more relaxed.

"There are spots. On the inside."

He wasn't wrong about that, and based on the layer of dust around the windows, some were quite old. The windows were spotted on the outside due to the rain, but window washers came frequently to clean them. I wasn't sure how often housekeeping cleaned the interior windows or if it was even part of their job.

"I'll have someone come clean it tomorrow," I told him.

His brow quirked up. "Tomorrow?"

"Are you that demanding?"

His lips twitched up. "Tomorrow is fine."

The way he smiled at me had my heart racing.

"Oh, by the way." I reached into my pocket and fished out the folded-up piece of paper, then handed it to him.

"What's this?" he asked as I handed him the receipt for my book replacement. I'd warred with myself about having him pay, but the book was ruined and my budget couldn't take the hit for more than a few days.

"The book."

"Right." He pulled the wallet from his back pocket and fished out a few bills and held them out to me.

Two one-hundred-dollar bills were pinched between his fingers and thumb.

"It's only one-fifty," I pointed out.

"Keep the rest," he said. "Besides, I don't have any smaller bills on me."

I wasn't so sure about that, and stood my ground. "I can't do that."

"Why not?"

I blew out a breath. "Because I had a hard enough time deciding if I'd ask for the replacement money."

"Why is that? It was my action that caused the damage to your book."

"Because you're a guest, and it was an accident," I said as I took the bills from him. I kept one, then handed the other back. "Here."

He gave the bill a dirty look, then shook his head. "Take it."

"Mr. Grayson, I can't. That's like a tip or a bribe, and I can't take it." Why was he giving me such a hard time?

"If you don't shut up, I'll kiss you to make you stop talking."

My mouth went slack as I stared at him. "You wouldn't."

He stepped forward, his hand reaching out and settling on my hip before snaking around my back. With a sharp tug, he pulled me against his chest.

"Oh, Emma, you have no idea what I would do to you." The way he said my name was different than before. Tender, almost.

My hands rested on his chest, the bills long forgotten as I shuddered at the feel of his body against mine. Every inch of our bodies that touched was alive, pulsing with a need I'd never known. I kept my gaze locked onto the collar of his shirt, knowing I couldn't control myself if I looked up.

"Why are you breathing so hard?" he asked.

Was I? I leaned forward, my forehead resting on his collarbone, my fingers digging into his chest. The way he made me feel with a single look was nothing compared to the system hijack of his touch. Every part of me responded to him in the most violent, lust-filled reaction I'd ever had. The intensity was dizzying.

"You should go." His voice was thick and rough and licked at the flames inside me. His hand dropped from me, and I reluctantly pulled back.

The dismissal was so similar to previous ones, but unlike the past, when I looked at him, he was staring back. His features were still as neutral as ever, but his eyes . . . his eyes sent a shiver through me.

"Good night, Mr. Grayson," I whispered as I turned to leave.

"Emma," he called out.

I blinked back at him. "Yes?" He gestured to the ground and the bills that had fallen. "Oh."

Just as I began to lean over, he stepped forward and snatched the bills from the ground and held them out for me. "I really can't take you bending over in front of me right now."

The fire that pulsed through my body at the thought of him being so tightly wound for me was empowering. I hoped maybe he was having a similar reaction to me like the one I was having to him.

Twenty-four hours of yearning simmered inside me as I stood behind the front desk. That was how long it had been since I'd seen my torturer, Mr. Grayson.

Just after six, the phone rang and the fire inside me flared. I knew immediately who it was.

"It's Mr. Grayson," Caleb said as I looked down at the phone. Without flinching, he picked up the receiver. "Front desk, good evening, Mr. Grayson." There was a pause, but I didn't hear any yelling. "We will remedy that right away, sir." When he hung up, he turned to me. "They didn't get the windows cleaned or something. He wants someone up there."

"Meaning me, right?"

He nodded. "You're the boss."

I sighed. "Joy. When I get back, you can go on break," I said as I stepped around the counter and headed toward the elevator bay.

There was a request in—I'd made sure of it—which made me wonder if there really were any spots or if it was just an excuse to see me. I really liked the latter.

It had taken me almost a half hour to calm down after I left his room the day before. I still couldn't believe what was happening between us. I just wished we could behave like normal people and not in secret.

The walk to his room was second nature—a quick elevator ride, take a right and go down four doors. A swift rap of my knuckles against the door, and then I waited for the overwhelming force that was Gavin Grayson.

"Hello," he said as he opened the door. No scowl to greet me, no anger. There was a small upturn of his lips, a little more prominent on one side than the other.

A shudder rolled through me, my heart doing double time again.

"What's wrong tonight?" I asked as I stepped into his room.

"You're not in it," he said.

My stomach flipped, and I felt heat flood my cheeks. How was it that in a few short weeks he had taken over my heart? I wanted, yearned for his praise. To get caught up in his eyes, loving the way they would soften and grow heavy as he looked at me.

I drew in a stuttered breath as he stepped forward and towered over me. In heels I was a decent five-feet-eight, but Gavin had to be a few inches over six feet tall—a commanding presence as he loomed over me.

"Emma?" He was so close I could feel his breath on my skin.

"Hmm?"

"I want you."

The muscles in my thighs clenched and I stretched up toward him, almost begging him closer. "Yes."

"To stop looking at me like that."

The haze he covered me with suddenly cleared as I looked up at him. My stomach dropped as I tried to comprehend what happened. "What?"

He stepped away, his back turned to me. All of his muscles were tense, his fists clenching at his side.

"If that's what you want, what do you need?" I asked.

His head fell back. "I thought I'd made that obvious."

"I'm not sure," I replied, more than a little surprised at how breathy my voice was. "I've gotten a lot of mixed messages."

He moved back toward me. "You have me conflicted."

"How so?"

"Because the last time I wanted a woman anywhere near this much, things didn't end so well," he began. "Because you're young. Because you work for the hotel and not for me." He reached out, his fingers caressing my clavicle before slipping up my neck. "Because nothing has ever seemed as taboo as your lips."

My knees felt weak as he moved closer, my nipples tightening. There was no resistance as I waited with bated breath.

His lips were soft against mine, supple. A taste, a sample. It was perfect, and an electric pulse moved between us. Every ounce of want and desire sat in the small gap between our lips.

A squeak left me when he suddenly pressed forward, kissing deeper and more intensely than before. His free arm wound around my waist, pulling me closer to him while his mouth opened. I followed suit, wrapping my arms around his shoulders, pulling him closer. It was forceful and filled with more passion than I'd ever encountered, so much that it ignited an inferno inside me.

All I wanted was for him to keep touching me, to never stop.

"You should go," he said with gravel in his voice.

I didn't want to let go. No, I wanted to continue. To finally scratch the itch that had pestered me since the day I first met him.

"No." My voice was breathy and so unlike any sound I'd ever uttered. I pulled his face back down as I arched up into him. With millimeters between our lips he let out a groan before pushing on my waist.

"Now," he growled as he stepped away.

He was breathing hard, nostrils flared and his eyes so hooded that my thighs instantly clamped together.

"Go."

I drew my lower lip between my teeth before reluctantly turning and leaving.

With each step away, my head cleared and my smile grew. My fingers ran against my still tingling lips. It was by far the best kiss I'd ever had.

One kiss, and I knew my life was changed. I wasn't naïve enough to think we could really have any sort of relationship, but it ruined any lingering thoughts of a relationship with James.

7th Floor

When I arrived to work the next day, James was working on something at his desk.

"How was class?" he asked.

"Fine," I said with a sigh. "Only a few weeks left."

"You're going to leave us, aren't you?" James asked.

My mouth popped open, but then closed. It was an odd question, because we'd talked about it before. "You know I am."

"I'm going to hate seeing you go."

"I'll visit."

He rolled his eyes. "No, you won't."

"No, I won't."

"Good thing I've got your number," he said with a smile and a wink.

Whatever I had with Mr. Grayson was so new and strange and overwhelming that I'd forgotten about the feelings I'd once had for James. They'd disappeared, completely overtaken. I didn't know how to break it to him.

We both walked out to the counter to give Caleb a break and catch up on business when Mr. Grayson walked in through the door leading to the parking garage. He glanced over, and for a brief moment our eyes locked before he returned to looking forward. Even that small look held so much promise and sent the butterflies in my stomach into overdrive.

"That's weird."

I turned to James. "What is?"

"He's early."

"You know what time he arrives?"

He nodded. "Oh, yes. With a guest like him, I've got his schedule down. I know you'll be here to take the brunt of him."

"Gee, thanks."

He turned to lean on the counter to face me. "You have a relationship with him."

That kicked my heart into overdrive. "Excuse me?"

"You've built up a rapport with him," he clarified. Internally I sighed in relief. "He only wants to talk to you."

"Do you ever think he continues to be an ass because he started and doesn't know how to stop?" I asked.

James laughed. "I'm not sure. All I know is that he likes picking on you. Maybe he likes you."

I rolled my eyes and tried not to blush as I played it off. "He's a grown man."

"I'm a grown man."

I quirked a brow at him. "And?"

"And I like you." Our eyes were locked and I could see how much he meant it, how deep his feelings were.

I looked away, out into the lobby. "And you're my boss, remember?"

He shrugged and moved closer. "One small detail. For now."

A few months ago, I'd welcomed his advances, a chance to try again, but the only man I could even think about now was the enigmatic Mr. Grayson. James was a great guy, but Mr. Grayson made me feel so much more.

We returned to the daily update before James headed out for the night, leaving me with Caleb and Jaqueline to handle the check-in rush.

It didn't take long before the aforementioned Mr. Grayson was calling me up to his room.

He was taking off his watch, his jacket long gone but his vest still on. Rarely did I see a three-piece suit, but he wore one every day, and I happily enjoyed looking at him. His suits were my favorite. Sexy, powerful—just like him.

Watching him was my version of a strip tease. I began to wonder what he would look like in jeans, since he was sin in a suit. His chest was beautiful, and I could just imagine a pair of jeans hanging low on his hips.

I was lost in my appraisal, glued to his body and the way it moved.

"Emma, are you listening to me?" he asked, one of his brows quirked. He was fighting a smirk, and I knew I had been caught staring at him. Either way, it was bad.

Flustered, I spoke without thinking. It was the answer for most everything, after all. "Yes, Mr. Grayson, you were complaining yet again about the staff and how we are all incompetent morons."

He stared at me, wide eyed for a moment before his head tilted back and he let out a loud laugh, making me jump in shock.

He was laughing so hard he had to lean over, his hands braced against the edge of the dresser. His shoulders shook.

"That's new," I said as I watched the very unusual behavior.

"Well, that was quite far from the conversation that you missed out on. Though true on all levels with the exception of the inclusion of yourself," he said.

He stalked toward me, a grin still lighting up his face, and I was mesmerized by it. He leaned down to my ear, and his hand settled on my hip, breath tickling the hairs on my neck. My need for him combusted the second he touched me.

"What I was saying was how delicious you would look splayed out naked on the bed. Your thighs open, exposing your sweet pussy, and how I would love to taste you on my tongue." Heat flooded my face, and I swallowed hard. "You would like that, wouldn't you, Emma?"

My hip unconsciously pushed up into his hand, and I felt myself getting wet. Yes, I would like that very much. Weak knees, trembling body, I desperately wanted that.

He pulled away, smirking at me as he backed up, returning to unbuttoning his dress shirt.

He turned from me before speaking again. "Actually, I was asking what your drink of choice was at Starbucks."

My legs lost all strength, weakening and almost collapsing out from under me, forcing me to lean back into the wall before sliding down. The room became unfocused as my heart beat at a rapid pace and my blood heated to the point of boiling. In three sentences he had managed to reduce me to a puddle on his hotel room floor. Then again, he'd been chipping away at me for two weeks.

I heard his heavy steps as he dashed over to me.

"Are you all right?"

I tilted my head up, and even I knew my lids were heavy and full of lust. My tongue peeked out to wet my lips as a small moan slipped out.

I watched the way his eyes darkened as he gazed down at me, lighting me up even more. He reached up and tugged at his hair.

"Fuck," he growled, his hands braced on the wall before me, his torso and hips rocking as he reined something in.

"Please," I whispered, my hand slapping over my mouth almost immediately.

"You don't know how much I want you," he ground out, his hands clenched into fists against the wall.

After staring up at him for a moment, I decided to take the initiative, to be bold. Otherwise, how else were we going to get over the constant game that left us both a mess of need?

I leaned forward and nuzzled the bulge, the evidence of his arousal, through his suit pants. "No, but your friend here wants to tell me." He let out a groan as I ran my nose and lips from the base to the tip of the large, hard cock that lay beneath the fabric.

I held his gaze as I closed my mouth around the head, causing him to draw in a sharp breath.

My hands moved to rest on his thighs before walking up to his belt buckle.

"Emma . . ."

"Yes, sir?" I replied in a husky tone, my fingers pulling the leather through the hook on his belt.

I watched his chest heave, and in his expression I could see the carnal desire of what he wanted.

"Suck it," he commanded.

"As you wish, Mr. Grayson," I replied, licking my lips.

I worked his pants open and hooked my fingers under the waistband of his boxer briefs, pulling them over the bulge beneath. It had been too long since I'd had sex and I was dripping in anticipation for the beast that stood before me.

As soon as the head was visible, my lips and tongue were on him. It'd been years since I'd given head, and I was a bit apprehensive, but the obscenities coming from him as I sucked his length into my mouth encouraged me. I hummed around him, earning an involuntary thrust of his hips.

I swirled my tongue around each inch I worked into my mouth, tasting every bit of him I could.

"Fuck . . . that's it, baby . . . you're so fucking good," he mumbled.

His hips began to flex, thrusting his cock further into my mouth until I was gagging each time. He was braced against the wall while my hands were braced against his thighs as he fucked my mouth. It was only a few strokes of him pushing in as far as he could before he tugged at my arm.

"Up."

The second I was on my feet, he was pulling my suit jacket from my shoulders, then hastily working open the buttons of my blouse. Dipping down, his mouth latched onto my lace-covered nipple before he grabbed it with his teeth. A cry left me, my nipples hardening and sending sparks directly to my clit.

The sensation caused an involuntary arch of my back and my fingers to pull at his hair.

He must have liked that, because he immediately detached. His mouth was electric as he licked, sucked, and nipped his way up my neck and pushed me back. As soon as my back pressed into the wall, his lips found mine. Soft, hard, needy, delicious, pussy exploding.

I lost all train of thought when his lips met mine. All that was left was need. I needed him closer. I needed him deeper.

I needed him inside me. Fuck, did I need him inside me.

"Jesus fucking Christ, are you wearing thigh-highs and a garter belt?" he asked, panting into my neck. I hadn't even realized he'd been pulling my skirt up. His hands stopped on the back of my thighs at the flesh just above the silk stockings.

"Yes," I was barely able to reply before he was kissing me again.

He reached down to grab behind my knee and pulled my leg up to his hip. I wrapped my arms around his neck before he dipped down to repeat the move on the other side.

A moan left me as my legs wrapped around his waist and I felt the heat of his cock at my clit. A little piece of cotton and lace was all that separated us.

"I need you," he whispered against my lips.

"Then take me," I replied, taking his bottom lip between my teeth.

"I hope these aren't your favorites." There was a pull between my legs, then the sound of fabric ripping as he destroyed my panties.

My nails dug into his shoulders and my head titled back into the wall, mouth slack, eyes wide, as he lined up and pushed forward. My breath hitched before a mewling sound left me. Every nerve tingled at the sensation of being so completely filled.

I couldn't think of anything except the feeling of his toned body pushing me into the wall, his hips crashing into mine.

The sexual tension that had been building between us these past weeks fueled us. His hands dug into my ass, pulling me down harder onto his cock, pushing him deeper.

"Mr. Grayson!" I cried out.

He chuckled into my ear. "Gavin."

His lips found mine again and my tongue found his as his hips sped up their motion. Faster. Deeper. Driving me to the point of insanity.

Everything tightened and then suddenly snapped.

I screamed out his name as I clenched around him, his thrusts never letting up, unrelenting and manic in their drive.

"Shit, baby, uhg . . . coming."

Reality dawned after a brief second. "Wait! I'm not on the pill!" I cried out in panic.

"Shit!" he cursed.

He frantically reached down between us and pulled his cock out. His moans echoed around the room as his hips bucked, his cum spraying all over the wall just beneath my ass, a few droplets hitting my skin.

"Fuck," he growled.

I nearly came again at the expression on his face, twisted in what looked like pain, but there was nothing but pure pleasure in his eyes.

He leaned forward, his forehead resting on mine for a moment before he pushed off of the wall and dropped to the floor. I flopped forward onto his chest when his back hit the ground. We were both breathing heavily and I was afraid there would be an awkward silence, but Gavin had me giggling with his first sentence.

"This hotel is growing on me," he said between pants, his fingers lightly threading through my hair.

I shook my head, smiling. "Such an ass."

He chuckled. "Yes, but I'm growing on you."

"If you're lucky," I scoffed.

"I believe you make your own luck, and therefore I am a very lucky man."

"I'm lucky you were able to pull out," I said. The last thing I needed was some accidental pregnancy.

"It was difficult, believe me," he said with a groan. "Not coming inside you is a tragedy. I'll pick up some condoms for next time."

"Next time?" I asked.

"A big box of condoms."

I shook my head, then glanced over to the clock. Panic shot through me as I realized I'd been away from the lobby for almost an hour. I pulled myself from the warmth of his arms, grabbed my blouse, and ran into the bathroom to straighten myself out.

"Shit, shit, shit," I chanted over and over as I frantically put myself back together. I heard Gavin get up in the other room and jumped when he appeared in the doorway.

"I shouldn't have done that," I said absently.

"Emma?"

"I can't afford to lose my job over sex. Even if it was great sex." I looked into the mirror and pulled at my hair to get it back up into a ponytail.

"Great?" His lips twitched into a smirk.

I rolled my eyes at him. "You know you were great."

"So were you." He reached up to caress my cheek.

"What was wrong today?" I asked.

A confused expression washed over his face before it dawned on him what I was asking. "I'm out of coffee."

"Coffee? Seriously?" I quirked a brow at him as I buttoned my shirt.

He shrugged his shoulders and handed me my jacket. "The maids are doing too good of a job now. I'm grasping at straws to get you up here. Coffee is all I had to go with."

"That's because you threatened to have them all fired," I said with a sigh. "Your eccentricity knows no bounds."

He leaned down and pressed his lips to mine one last time. "Good night, Emma."

It was enough to level out my panic a little. "Good night, Gavin."

With an alibi for my absence—coffee of all things—I headed back down to the lobby. Shannon stared at me as I walked across the marble flooring, searching for battle scars. I looked for patrons and found the lobby to be empty before I went into my cover rant about the asshole and his damned coffee.

8th Floor

The next day I awoke to a soft ache between my thighs and a smile. Being with Gavin was better than any of the fantasies I'd come up with. Those fantasies could never have anticipated his strength and intensity.

There was also the unsettled feeling in my stomach. I had tried to play off my absence, but I felt like everyone could see that I'd just had the most powerful orgasm of my life. It wasn't that I regretted being with him by any means, but I needed my job.

No sleeping with guests was just about the number one rule of the hotel, and I'd broken it.

Somehow, I couldn't even be sorry about it. Gavin's touch was hotter than any other.

"Gavin," I said out loud, then giggled. I liked calling him by his first name and not the stuffy Mr. Grayson. It was almost like they were two different people.

As I clipped my garter belt to my stockings, I remembered his reaction to them. They were a bit of a luxury, even though I bought cheap, but I much preferred a garter belt over pantyhose. There was no mess dealing with them while going to the bathroom, and they gave me an air of confidence, though the breeze against my clit the night before had been interesting and left me wondering what Gavin had done with my thong after I left. Maybe next time he wouldn't destroy my underwear.

If there was a next time. What if that was all it was? Once, and then I was out of his system, while I was forever changed?

I tried to push those thoughts out of my mind as I headed out of my apartment and to work.

As soon as I clocked in, there was a note waiting for me to see Valeria.

"Hi," James said as I entered the office.

I almost tripped when I saw him. Guilt crashed down on me. Years of pining for him, and it was all gone.

"Hi."

"Are you okay?"

I nodded, a little too vigorously. "Yeah, I just got this note to see Valeria and wanted to check in before I headed down."

"Okay, I'll see you when you get back."

I headed down to Valeria's office and as soon as I walked in, I knew what it was about. Or rather, who.

"What is his problem?" she asked.

"Valeria, don't take his complaints seriously."

"Don't? Emma, he's making my staff look like incompetent morons. Each call and reason is logged and sent to me *and* corporate.

I hated that she was right about that. It was not fair for her to be dinged each time Gavin threw a fit just so that he could see me, especially for the smallest of things. "They can see the list is trivial."

"Missing towels? No soap? Coffee not refilled?" Her hands flew up. "It adds up, and it makes Phillip wonder where else they are messing up, and assuming guests just aren't mentioning it."

Phillip was the overall hotel manager and not someone anyone liked interacting with due to his short fuse. He was a pompous, self-righteous asshole that made Gavin look like a saint.

"I'm not entirely sure those things are true," I said.

"What?"

"I think he just likes to complain."

"So he's one of those assholes who likes to ruin the lives of others for the fun of it?" she asked.

My lips formed a thin line. "Possibly, I'm not sure."

"You seem to know him best."

I laughed at her statement. "Picking on me doesn't qualify me as knowing him." Even though I did have an intimate knowledge of him no one else did.

"No, but maybe if you say he is bullying you they'll kick him out?"

I shook my head. "You know they'd just tell me to suck it up because he spends so much money here."

"There are things worth more than money."

"Like sanity," I replied.

"Exactly."

In truth, some of the things Gavin complained about would have been noticed by any of the hotel reviewers who came in. However, I also knew he was abusing his complaints just to get me up to his room.

I wasn't even sure if I minded that anymore.

If he wanted me, he had me.

The day had been long and hard. I got home after midnight, and I'd been up by six to get to my eight o'clock class. It was four in the afternoon, and I was having trouble keeping my eyes open while I climbed the stairs to my apartment. I just hoped to make it to the bed for a long nap before my third shift.

I was putting my key in the lock when I looked down. There, on the floor next to my front door, was a huge bouquet of flowers. Not just flowers, but about four dozen large red roses. Sticking out of the top was an envelope with my name written on it.

I managed to get the door open and walked inside, flowers in tow. After setting them on the counter, I opened the envelope. It was hand written, and not typed up by the florist.

Emma,

I didn't have a dictionary to look up "wooing," but I do have an iPhone and Wikipedia is a great resource. In the article it mentioned traditional exchanges; letters (see this), gifts (to come), flowers (see attached), and songs (I am not musical in any way, shape, or form so do not expect this, and no, I will not hold a boom box in the air outside of your window). I have watched many movies and often wondered what all the nonsense was about. Thank you for opening my eyes to this. Oh, I've also heard from my assistant that chocolates are an acceptable gift. Are you a fan of chocolates?

Yours,
Gavin

I smiled down at the note, giddy. If he kept this up, I was going to fall head over heels for him in no time . . . if I hadn't already. My fingers traced his elegant script, over the word "yours." I wasn't going to get my hopes up, but it was nice to dream.

"I wonder how he got my address," I said to the flowers as I leaned in. The smell was strong and succulent.

Then again, I was talking about Gavin Grayson. He had his ways.

After a couple-hour nap, I was back up and getting ready. My heart skipped when I saw the roses again. I gave them one last sniff before heading out.

The sad part was, Gavin was probably already asleep and I didn't know when I was going to be able to thank him. Though the flowers were an indication, at least to me, that maybe he wanted more from me.

"What's with the smile?" James asked as I walked into the office.

My smile slowly fell as a heaviness rested on my chest. Gavin had taken over every aspect of my life in such a short time. I was ashamed to admit I'd completely written off James.

"Just smiley tonight. We'll see how long it lasts until the sleepiness takes over."

"Nothing wrong with that. I like seeing you smile." He reached toward me, and I unconsciously backed up. His brow furrowed at my movement. "Emma?"

I hooked my thumb over my shoulder as I walked to the lobby door. "I just need to get out there."

He nodded and cleared his throat, but I could see the disappointment. "Right."

"Good night."

"Night."

The awkwardness was heavy, but it was probably for the best. A way to distance myself.

The plan we'd had just wasn't going to happen.

"Hi, Caleb. It's you and me again."

He yawned and nodded. "The only reasons I pick up one of these a week is your smiling face and the extra money."

"Let's be real about this—it's the money."

He laughed, hard and loud. "Yes, the money, but you're my favorite to share the evening with."

"Don't let Dante hear that."

"Oh, that's true. Eh, it's not like he's home right now either."

Caleb's partner was the head waiter at an exclusive restaurant downtown, which was why he loved his normal second shift so much. That way, their schedules were fairly close.

Hours later, our smiles were gone and Caleb was slapping his face once more.

"What time does Starbucks open again?" I asked as I stared longingly across the open lobby to the gated, dark store.

"Not soon enough."

With a sigh, I pushed off the counter. "I'm going to go work on the reporting."

"I'll try not to fall asleep, but no guarantees."

"There's always coffee in the break room," I pointed out.

He turned to me, his eyes in slits. "That is *not* the nectar of the gods. Don't speak those blasphemous words to me!"

We both broke out into laughter. Neither of us was a regular coffee drinker, and the coffee pot in back had become a reoccurring joke in the slap happy early hours of the morning. It really was tempting, a fresh pot, but a little cream and sugar didn't make it a latte.

About an hour later, I was almost done with the reports when Caleb opened the door.

"Emma?"

"Yes?" I replied, not even looking up.

"I've got a problem. Mr. Grayson requested a wakeup call, but I think his phone is off the hook. I've been trying for the last half hour."

He did, did he? Sneaky bastard.

"You want me to go wake him, don't you?" I asked in a whine.

"Please?" he begged, giving me his best puppy-dog impression.

I rolled my eyes at him and sighed, making sure the information was saved before I stood. "Okay, but you owe me!"

"Anything," he promised as I exited into the lobby and headed to the elevator bay.

It was a trick, I just knew it. He was getting clever.

When I made it to his room, I barely had to knock when the bastard flung the door open, wearing nothing but a towel around his waist and a smirk on his gorgeous face. Beads of water still trailed along his skin, dripping from his shower.

"I can't stay," I said immediately as I crossed the threshold and closed the door. I didn't hear him step up behind me, but I could feel him. The sparks that flew between us, even from a few feet away, were a palpable energy. So were the tingling sensations that coursed through my body and the wetness that settled in my panties.

"Yes, you can. Just for a few minutes. I need you, baby," he whispered in my ear. His hand had worked its way under my skirt, up to my panties, where he was massaging my clit, his fingers teasing my entrance.

"Miguel is due in shortly, I have to report . . . oh, God!" my protests were drowned out by the cry that left my lips when he slid two fingers in.

"Take your skirt off," he commanded, the husk in his voice sending shivers down my body that concentrated between my thighs.

His hand gripped my arm above my elbow as he led me over to the bed. I slipped my skirt off, followed by my jacket and blouse until all I was left in was my stockings with garter, panties, bra, and my heels.

"Fucking beautiful. I think you may be the sexiest thing I've ever seen," he said before laying me back on the bed and slipping my panties off. At least they'd been spared this time. He leaned down until I could feel his breath against my folds. I felt his tongue on me and nearly jumped from the bed as he began eagerly licking and sucking.

"Gavin!" I cried out. My eyes were wide, mouth parted from the overwhelming electric charge that swept across each nerve ending.

A groan vibrated against my clit before he straightened back up and licked his lips. He was just teasing me. Reaching over to the nightstand, he picked up a condom and rolled it down his length. My hips rocked toward him, calling to him. There was something fascinating about watching him, his fingers gliding up and down his hard shaft.

He climbed back onto the bed and pushed my knees down, spreading me open. His hips rocked, and he slid his hard length against my wet entrance and clit before lining up and pressing in all the way. My eyes fluttered shut, rolling back; my head fell down onto the bed as he entered. I would never get used to how good he felt.

"Damn, baby, you are so fucking tight," he moaned, and leaned down over me.

His hands ran up the length of my arms, pulling them above my head, pinning them there. He smirked down at me momentarily before adjusting his position slightly.

"Hold on," he whispered.

His hips moved back before returning, slamming against mine. My back arched off of the bed, and a strangled cry escaping my lips as his relentless pounding took hold of my body. I couldn't move, I couldn't breathe. I could only feel.

His lips found mine, a moan slipping from his mouth to mine. I tried to take charge of the kiss, to have control of something, but he wasn't having any of that. He wanted complete control, and he was going to have it.

My body was shaking, my legs quivering. He sped up, thrusting harder and faster. I couldn't take any more.

"Gavin!" I cried out, clenching around him, my back arching against the bed.

Seconds later he followed, my name slipping past his lips.

He collapsed on top of me. "Mmm, just what I needed for a morning wake-up call."

"Are you awake now, Mr. Grayson?"

"Definitely. You?"

"Surprisingly, yes. You're as good as a cup of coffee."

He laughed and kissed me full and hard.

"Thank you for the flowers," I said.

His lips pulled up into a smile. "You're more than welcome."

We rose a moment later, and I dressed quickly before running out.

"Wait! Have a good day, Emma," he said, kissing my forehead before kissing my lips. I was stunned by the gesture, but greedily accepted it.

"You, too."

As I exited his room, I glanced down at my watch to see only fifteen minutes had passed, though it felt like so much longer.

"Was he there?" Caleb asked when I returned to the lobby.

"Yes. He's awake now."

"Did he complain about the phone?"

The phone? I scrambled for a moment to understand, then it clicked. "It wasn't settled right on the receiver."

Miguel arrived a few minutes later, and I went over the evening reports and filled him in on the news before returning to my apartment and crashing for six hours until my afternoon class.

After a week, it was official—I was addicted to sex with Gavin Grayson.

The college boyfriends I'd had couldn't compete with his skills as a lover or with the raw passion I felt with him. They had been all about themselves, but Gavin wanted me to come before him. The more times, the better.

I was breathing hard, lying flat on my back on Gavin's bed after a thorough fucking.

"You're going to get me fired," I said from beneath him, his cum cooling off on my skin. He lost control and was inside me before he put a condom on, but by the look in his eyes as he watched his pearly drops land on my skin, he didn't care.

"What a way to go down."

I quirked a brow at him. "You think your cock is worth my job?"

He fell beside me on the bed, his breath labored. "Maybe not my cock, but I am."

"Jury is still out," I teased, but wasn't entirely sure he was wrong. As much as I liked him, we hardly knew each other and I wasn't sure where we were going, if anywhere.

"No hung juries, Miss Addison, just hung me."

A laugh sprung from me as I shook my head. "That was bad."

He shrugged. "I tried."

"It wasn't wrong, either."

"One thing is for certain." His fingers danced around my skin, spreading his cum all around, making sure it dried and stayed on my skin.

"What's that?" I asked.

"You're not leaving this room until I have your number."

"Asking for my digits?"

"I've been trying to ask for weeks now, but you keep distracting me."

I turned to look at him in disbelief. "I'm distracting you? You do know you are the definition of a distraction, right?"

"What do I distract you from?" he asked.

"Work, mostly," I replied. "School. Sleep. Life."

"Life? Really?"

"Yeah. You are very demanding that I pay attention to you even when I'm miles away."

He trailed his fingers up my stomach, between my breasts, all the way to my lips. The heavy look in his eyes as I licked his fingers, moaning at the taste of him, was intoxicating.

"You do the same," he admitted. "You've invaded my work life. It makes it very hard to concentrate when all I can think about is being between your legs, hearing you moan."

My heart sank a little bit. "So, the physical stuff?"

"Try and tell me it's different for you."

I did think about the physical stuff. A lot. But his room wasn't the only place where I dealt with him.

"It is. You know you have a reputation, one you've worked hard to cultivate. I have to deal with that version of your persona more than this one."

"I should rectify that."

"More sex?"

His thumb caressed my cheek as his eyes locked on mine. "More me."

My lips drew up into a smile. "I'd like that."

9th Floor

The last few weeks had been interesting. Gavin and I had entered into a sordid relationship of sorts. Always in his hotel room, always when I was on duty. He would pitch an ungodly fit about anything and everything to get me up there. The managers were happy that I seemed to have a calming touch, even though it never lasted long. That, and they had no idea what kind of touch I used.

Gavin Grayson was a force to be reckoned with.

Not just as an asshole. He was also quite a lover and, as I was beginning to see, so much more.

Behind his cool, abrasive exterior laid an extraordinary and affectionate man . . . one with an incredible intellect.

However, he did have a very demanding side—Mr. Grayson.

GG: I want to see you

I looked down at the screen and blinked, smiling. He was contacting me outside of my working hours. When he had asked for my number, I didn't think he would really contact me. I was in complete shock. He actually did it. I mean, wasn't I just a fling for him? Was this more than just great sex to him?

Emma: I don't work tonight.

If I had thought my reply was the end of the conversation, I was greatly mistaken. Gavin Grayson was used to getting what he wanted, and that night he wanted me.

GG: Come over

I sighed. Did he really want me to lose my job? It was bad enough I'd been having sex with him in his hotel room during work hours. I was already sick about what would happen when or if it was found out just what went on in his room.

Emma: You know I can't

GG: Fine. Let's go to dinner then

A date? Was he serious? My pulsed raced. I wanted a date with him, badly, but I couldn't go out even if I wanted to. So instead, I offered another alternative, one I could live with.

Emma: I have homework. 415 Cherry St Apt 2C

I shot him my address, unsure if he'd kept it after he'd sent me the flowers. The ball was in his court. I didn't have time to entertain him, or fall to his whim. If he wanted me, he had to come and get me.

I didn't hold much stock in him actually coming, but I desperately wished he would. Just to show me I was more than just convenience. That I meant more than what we had at the hotel.

A few hours later I was on my couch in lounge pants and a tank top, my hair thrown back into a loose bun, papers surrounding me. I was so thoroughly engrossed in my project I almost didn't hear the knock on my door. Granted, the TV was on and drowned out the sound.

I was a little peeved when I stood up from my lake of papers and made my way to the door. To say I was surprised to see Gavin standing there was a great understatement. It was after nine in the evening. He hadn't replied, so I never expected him to actually show.

I stood, staring at him. "Wha . . . Gavin?"

"You're being rude, Emma," he said.

That seemed to wake me from my surprise, and I stepped aside to let him in.

He smirked down at me as he entered. "You look cute."

I looked down at my PJs and really wished I'd been wearing something . . . else. "I . . . I'm just working on homework. I didn't think you'd actually show up."

"I said, you look cute. I like the look. Much better than your uptight supervisor suit. It looks more . . . you. Not to say I don't like the suit, because you are usually hiding those fucking stockings underneath."

"Says the man in the uptight-asshole power-trip suit," I shot back, ignoring his comment about how hard my stockings made him. I smirked over my shoulder at him as I locked the door.

He frowned and proceeded to rid himself of his suit jacket, tie, vest, and dress shirt. He stripped off his belt as well and removed his leather shoes, leaving him in his undershirt and slacks.

He held his arms out and spun for me. "Better?"

"Marginally," I muttered and then mourned the loss of his suit. The man looked damn fine in one and knew how to work it.

"What are you working on that's keeping me from taking you out?" he asked as he looked around. "Wow, your apartment is small."

"I know," I replied. "Not all of us are incredibly wealthy. This is how the other half lives. 758 square feet, baby."

"Your apartment is smaller than my room at the hotel," he noted.

"Yeah, well, like I said . . ." I trailed off, annoyed, and turned to walk away.

"Hey, hey," he said, grabbing my arm and pulling me to him. "I'm sorry." His arms wrapped around me and nuzzled into my neck as he held me tight. "What are you working on?"

"It's a presentation for my management course," I replied with a sigh.

"What do you plan to do once you have your MBA? I assume you aren't staying at the hotel," he asked with honest curiosity.

I shook my head. "No. I am out of the hotel as soon as possible. I'm looking for jobs right now. Mostly treasury departments, staff accountant positions. Maybe once I have more experience, a controller."

"Hmm. Do you need any help?" he asked. His offer was genuine, but I was used to faring on my own.

"No, I don't need help. I can do this myself," I replied, walking away from him and back to my sea of papers.

"Let me rephrase that; would it help if I was your audience?"

I stared up at him, still curious why he was there since I was sure he could tell I wasn't going to jump into bed with him.

"Okay," I conceded. "That would be helpful."

A huge, uncharacteristic smile broke out on his face before he sat down on the couch across from me.

For the next two hours we worked on my presentation. He helped me fine tune a few things and finalize my edits, making it a masterpiece of a presentation that was sure to impress my professors.

Afterwards, we curled under a fuzzy throw blanket and watched a movie. Gavin had me pulled tight into his chest, and about an hour later I heard the soft sound of snoring from behind me. I turned and looked up, and his eyes were closed, his mouth slightly parted.

I hated to wake him, but he needed to get some sleep.

"Gavin," I whispered, the back of my fingers caressing his cheek. "Gavin, you need to go to bed."

He groaned, but reluctantly opened his eyes. I stood and took his hand, guiding him to the bedroom. Eyes half closed, he peeled off his undershirt and slacks, leaving him in his boxer briefs.

If he hadn't been mostly asleep and adorably cute—words I would not normally associate with him—I would have had thoughts of taking advantage of him. He fell into my full-sized bed, much smaller than his king at the hotel, and pulled the cover over him. I stared down at him for a moment, but a moment was all I was allowed before Gavin's hand reached up and grabbed my own, pulling me into the bed. A giggled erupted from me before I settled under the covers, his arm around my waist as he snuggled into me, spooning.

In minutes I was dreaming, secure in my Gavin cocoon.

It was early the next morning that I was woken by a very hard cock sliding against my panties. A moan left me and I opened my eyes. Gavin was above me, his gaze hooded. I sucked in a breath; he looked so sexy like that, his need showing.

Every cell awoke and my hips rose to meet his, rubbing my clit against his hot shaft. I watched his eyes flutter closed before he grabbed his cock and slid between my folds.

My back arched off the bed, and I cried out in pleasure as he pushed all the way in. We rocked together, slow and sensual. Soft caresses and tender touches; very different than our previous encounters. Something had changed.

"You really should get on the pill," he groaned.

"Are you saying you're keeping me?"

He nodded. "Yes. You're mine and I want to fuck you like you are mine, which includes coming inside you." He took my bottom lip between his teeth and pulled. "I want to fill you without getting you pregnant."

"As soon as school's out," I said.

He pressed all the way in. "Good."

Two nights later, Gavin showed up at my door, food in hand. My heart sped up as I stared at him, a huge smile on my face. The two nights I wasn't working, he had searched me out. He wanted to see me as much as I wanted to see him.

"So, what were you like as a kid?" I asked as we sat curled up on my couch after dinner. It was odd to see him on a Friday night, but it was also somewhat unusual for me to be off on a Friday. "Were you always an ass, or is that a recent personality trait?"

He laughed at my question before glaring slightly. "I . . ." He began before letting out a sigh and eyeing me. "I was a book nerd." He stopped to gauge my reaction before continuing. "A gangly teen who was in all the advanced placement classes who had no friends."

"I'll tell you a secret . . . Nerds are hot," I admitted with a wink.

"Well, it wasn't until college that I seemed to grow into my body and fill out. It was there that I started to grow into my current personality. I'd be in classes with assholes and jocks who I'd be paired with on a project, and they assumed I'd do the work for them. Instead, I would do my part of it and then write who was supposed to do the next section."

"I can just imagine the beating you got for that."

That made him laugh. "Yeah, the high school me, maybe. But by then I was tired of being picked on, tired of being used for my intellect. I'd had enough, and I wasn't taking their shit any longer. Anyway, one time a guy in my project group approached me with three of his friends. I may have ended up with a broken hand, cuts and bruises, and bleeding everywhere, but I left with self-confidence and four jocks crying on the ground."

I stared at him in shock. From the incident with the party boys in the room next to him I knew Gavin could hold his own, but winning a fight against four guys was a huge accomplishment.

"What?" he asked.

"Umm, wow."

He gave a shrug. "Once out of college, those jocks were working for me, and I may have been a bit vindictive."

"No," I said in mock credulity as I sat up. "You weren't mean to those poor jocks, were you?"

"I'm not very nice with people who don't work for me. How do you think I am with people who do?"

"Remind me never to work for you."

That made him laugh, and he pulled me up to straddle his lap. "But I have all these fantasies of you on my desk I *really* want to try out."

"After-hours fun." Reaching up, I set my arms on his shoulders, my fingers playing with the hair at the nape of his neck.

A contented moan vibrated from his chest, and his hands rubbed across the outside of my thighs. "Then the risk of getting caught is significantly decreased."

"Exactly."

"Well, what about you, Emma?"

I shrugged my shoulders. "Not much to tell. I'm originally from North Carolina and moved to Boston about twelve years ago. The youngest of two kids. My older brother, AJ, is an engineer in Cincinnati. A few years ago my dad was recruited by a company in Texas, and my parents moved down there, but it folded a year later."

"That's terrible."

I nodded. "Yeah. I haven't seen them in three years because of it."

"Why don't you go visit?"

"Because my vacation days are spent on things like finals, and I work most holidays. Plus, I can't afford to and they can't afford it either."

His brow scrunched up. "Is he still without work?"

"He is," I said with a nod. "My mom works, but it's barely enough to pay the bills. So, I work and I go to school so I can make a better life for myself and my family."

"That's very noble."

I shook my head. "I'm not noble. If anything, I'm plain."

"You are anything but plain, Emma. You are the bright spot in my day."

I caught my lip between my teeth as I smiled at him. Sometimes he said the sweetest things. "See, there's the guy I like."

Gavin's lips turned into a crooked grin before he pressed them lightly to mine. "Only for you."

"I feel like we're doing things backwards," I said as I pulled back a little.

"What?"

I waved my hand between us. "This. Us."

"Because we've had a lot of sex and not much else?"

I nodded. "Yes."

"That is exactly why I came over."

My brow quirked up as I looked at him. "Not for sex?"

His fingers flexed against my hips. "Well, there is that. After all, having you within ten feet of me turns me on. But I want more than that with you."

In a fit of excitement, I slapped my hand down on his chest. "I have an idea. Let's play twenty questions."

"I don't think I've ever played that," he said.

"It's easy. We can alternate. I'll ask you a question, then you ask me, and we can both answer."

He gave a nod. "All right."

I tapped my finger against my lips and hummed. "What do you like to do in your free time?"

"Before you?" He settled back into the couch as he thought about it. "Work occupies a lot of my time, but I used to love going out to Caesar Creek and fishing."

"Where is that?"

"Ohio. Northeast of Cincinnati. It was a long time ago, back when I was in high school. When I had time to sit in a boat and think about nothing."

"When did you live there?"

"It's where I grew up. I left for college and only go back to visit my family."

"Siblings?" I asked.

"I have a younger sister, Samantha, who is a nurse, and my parents."

We both had family in the Cincinnati area. That was convenient. Maybe we could go together and I could see AJ. "Okay, what do you currently like to do?"

"I like going to live baseball games. I *suppose* I could become a Red Sox fan since I'm here," he said with a sour expression. "After that, having a drink with colleagues."

"Not friends?"

"You're the only friend I have in Boston," he said with a rueful smile. "What about your free time?"

"I honestly don't know what that is." I heaved a sigh and moved my hands across his chest, loving the feel of the slow, steady rise and fall beneath. "I've been working and going to school full time for the last six years. When there are breaks between semesters, I try to relax and binge Netflix. If the weather is nice, I like to drive to the beach and sit and look out at the water."

"Just look?" he asked. "You don't get in?"

"That water is fucking cold," I said with a laugh. "I imagine one day how I might go to a warm-weather beach and how nice that would be."

"Maybe we can take a vacation down to the Virgin Islands in the fall."

I blinked at him. "Seriously?" The idea excited me, because it wasn't just about a trip with him, it was talk about a future for us.

His eyes were locked on mine when he nodded. "Yes."

I leaned forward and threw my arms around him. "I would *love* that," I said as I pressed my lips against his. It was something I'd avoided for a half hour because I knew where it would lead, especially with me on his lap. When I pulled back, his eyes were heavy, and I forced myself not to kiss him again and take things elsewhere. I cleared my throat and sat back. "Your turn."

"Where do you see yourself in ten years?"

I quirked a brow at him. "Is this a job interview?"

He chuckled and shook his head. "It's just a question."

"Ten years . . . hmm . . . Married with a couple of kids and working as a controller."

"Kids, huh?"

"What about you, mister?"

"Running Cates, having a family of my own, and ruling the world."

Family of my own, repeated in my head. Maybe we could have a family together.

"Ruling the world? Getting aggressive in that drive to the top, huh?"

Another chuckle. The sound always put a smile on my face. I loved it when he was relaxed like that. Those moments together were my favorite, because it was then I knew we were more than just sex.

"I don't think I ever set out to get to the top, but as I worked, I realized that was where I wanted to be. I love being in control."

"You are quite commanding."

"Commanding, hmm?"

I nodded. "Quite. Demanding, too."

In a shift, suddenly I was on my back with him nestled between my legs. "Aggressive, overbearing. I've heard them all before. But do you want to know what I really am?"

"What is that?"

He hovered over me, his lips inches from mine. "*Passionate.*"

10th Floor

I didn't see Gavin the next day at work, nor did I hear from him. After three days, an ever-expanding pit began to form in my gut. Worry that I'd been thrown aside, that he was finished with me, because he hadn't contacted me. Not even a two-second text reply.

All thoughts of that were pushed from my mind when I returned home after classes that day.

There was a box sitting outside my door. It was weird, because I hadn't ordered anything, but sure enough, my name was on the label. The name of the company wasn't familiar, but I pulled it inside with me.

When I opened it, there was an envelope on top of yet another box.

"Okay . . ."

There was no name on the outside of the envelope, but when I pulled out the small card, my heart skipped a beat. I recognized the handwriting instantly, because I'd spent so much time studying the previous letter.

Emma,

Gifts. Though I'm not sure if this is for you or more for me.

Yours,
Gavin

A huge smile spread over my face as I stared down at the note. It was short, but again, the "Yours" captivated me. It took me some creative jostling to get the box out of the box, but finally I was able to pry it out.

It was shiny black, with gray trim, all tied up with a matching fabric ribbon. I couldn't remember the last time I had received a gift from a guy; then again, I hadn't had a boyfriend since sophomore year.

Not that Gavin was necessarily my boyfriend, but he sure was acting like it.

"Oh." Inside the box were layers of glossy grey paper and underneath was a silk bag. There wasn't just one bag, but multiple. "What . . ."

My brow furrowed as I opened the top bag and fished out the contents. It was fabric, black lace, and after turning it a few times, something fell and I realized it was three pieces—thong, bra, and garter belt.

Then I understood his note. While I would get use out of them, he would get pleasure from seeing them on me.

He didn't go cheap either. The quality was exquisite, the fabric soft.

When I reached the bottom of the box I looked over everything. I had four new sets of matching panties, bra, and garter belts, as well as eight new sets of silk stockings and two corsets. What really struck me was that they were all my size.

"Oh, he's good."

The man was making it hard not to fall for him. After the horrible beginning, his ferociousness had converted to passion. Intoxicating and consuming.

I pulled my phone from my pocket and immediately sent him a text.

Emma: Come over soon

GG: Be there in an hour

An hour. It was enough time. I headed toward the bathroom, stripping off my clothes as I went.

He was going to be in for quite the show.

After two months at the hotel, I had learned many of Gavin's habits. He kept to a schedule, and with the hours he worked, I understood why.

On Mondays, he worked late, usually getting room service for dinner. Dry cleaning and machine-washable items went out on Tuesdays. He worked late on Wednesdays because I didn't, and he'd begun to come over to my apartment after he was done. On Thursdays, he usually went to dinner with clients or the CEO of his company. It was Fridays when he found some way to drag me up to his room. Saturdays were the wild card; it all depended on whether or not he had to go into the office. I was off on Sunday nights, and he had begun spending the night with me.

He had made sure his package arrived on Wednesday for our date. Though it wasn't a date, per se. He came over and we spent time together.

The stockings went on like butter, so smooth. Somehow, I felt even more powerful in the new set than I did in my old ones. I left the corset for another day.

I was working on my makeup when I heard the knock on my door. "Shit." I took one last look, giving my hair a quick fluff, then slipped on my heels.

Through the peephole I double-checked it was Gavin, then blew out a breath before opening the door. I threw my hip out and rested one hand on it while the other was on the door.

"Good evening, Mr. Grayson."

His eyes popped wide while his jaw ticked. "Fuck," he ground out as he stepped forward and pulled me to him. He kicked the door closed and locked it before letting his hands explore. "Mmm," he groaned against my skin. "Now those are silk stockings."

I giggled. "Do you like your present?"

He nodded. "I'd love to show you just how much."

"Oh, Mr. Grayson." I pulled away. "This is just a modeling. I'm not that kind of girl."

He chuckled, low and deep as he yanked me back to him. "Why don't we see about that?"

An hour later, we were sitting on the floor at my coffee table with an array of Chinese boxes and two sets of chopsticks—dinner for the night after an early evening of fucking.

"I'm sorry I didn't contact you," he said.

My stomach dropped a little. "I was beginning to think . . . I don't know."

"That I didn't want you?" he asked, then shook his head. "Please, don't ever think that. We had a meltdown and I ended up at the office for too many hours."

That may have explained it, but he could have at least replied to my texts. "Can you do me a favor next time?"

"What's that?"

"Can you give me the courtesy of a text to let me know?"

His eyes softened, and he reached out to squeeze my hand. "Yes."

I twirled the chopsticks around the noodles. "I've been wondering . . . why are you living in a hotel?"

It took a second for him to finish his bite before responding. "I'm still at the hotel because I haven't found a home, not that I've even had time to search yet."

I reached into his box with my chopsticks and stole a bite of his sesame chicken. "You could be looking tonight instead of fucking me," I noted.

He smirked and licked his lips. "Yes, but fucking you is infinitely more enjoyable than searching for a new abode, Emma. In fact, spending time with you is more enjoyable then most activities that come to mind."

"More enjoyable than . . ." I trailed off thinking of some of his favorite things that I'd picked up on. "Watching baseball?"

"I get a much better view watching you."

"Spending ridiculous amounts of money on women's lingerie?"

He chuckled. "That's a trick question, Emma. Because I love to see you wearing that."

"Thank you again for the gifts," I said, my cheeks heating.

His tongue swept across his lips as he reached into the box in my hand and pulled out some lo mein noodles. "Thank you for wearing them."

"Okay, more than bacon cheeseburgers?"

"Eating you is much better."

I shook my head and sighed. "You are incorrigible, Mr. Grayson."

"And you need to eat up, Ms. Addison. Fuel your body. You're going to need it to get through the night."

I swallowed hard and felt my body flush. It was going to be a good night.

I couldn't wait for the day when we could go out, maybe on a real date and start a real relationship . . . if he wanted one. I honestly wasn't sure what he wanted. He said I was his, but I still felt like his girl on the side.

In order for anything to change, for us to really be together, Gavin had to move out of the hotel.

The sun was out when I left my morning classes, making me smile. It was finally May, and the temperature was warming up. Only two more weeks until I graduated, until I was done.

I had been putting out my resume since January with little response. As soon as my classes were over, I would be spending my days off searching and submitting.

Until then, the Cameo Hotel would continue to be my source of income. I anxiously awaited a set Monday-through-Friday schedule and standard hours with no customers.

I didn't think I'd ever be able to handle another Gavin Grayson again without going off.

"Good afternoon, Miguel," I said in greeting as I entered the employee lounge, ready to clock in for my shift.

His face lit up when he saw me. "Emma! Oh, thank God you're here!"

"What's going on?" I asked dubiously. He was being overly friendly, which usually meant he needed or wanted something.

"Laundry lost one of Mr. Grayson's suits, and we can't find it anywhere!"

My eyes grew wide, the blood draining from my face, and I shook my head. "No, please don't make me tell him." Even with our relationship, it was a task I really didn't want.

"He already knows it's missing," he said. "He just doesn't know it's disappeared. Gone. We can't find it anywhere."

I sighed and scrunched my eyes closed. "Great. What are we going to do to make it up to him? You've seen his suits; they aren't cheap."

"Give him whatever he wants. He's spent more than my salary already during his stay, just . . . whatever he wants. A week's stay, monetary compensation . . . combination of both. Whatever, to make him happy," Miguel instructed.

Too bad I knew exactly what Mr. Grayson wanted and knew I'd be the one paying for this screwup. Though I had to admit, I was a little bit excited to experience his anger in a sexual way.

"I will hopefully return. But if I'm not back in an hour, send up a body bag."

With great trepidation I made my way along the familiar path to his room. I slowly lifted my hand to knock, unsure what kind of reaction I was going to receive. Most of his complaints had been fluff to get me up there, but this was a serious issue.

I knocked on the door, and a moment later a very agitated Mr. Grayson answered.

"Good evening, Mr. Grayson. I was wondering if I might have a word with you about your suit?" I asked. He stepped aside and let me in.

"I take it because *you* are here, that my suit has not been found?" he asked, and I could hear the ire in his tone. "Otherwise they wouldn't have tasked you to speak with me."

"No, and I have a whole speech prepared. Would you like to hear it?"

His brow twitched, his jaw set. "All right, what does Emma the hotel supervisor have to say?"

"I apologize, Mr. Grayson," I said to start, in my professional tone. "The laundry staff has been unable to locate it. It is our hope that it will turn up shortly. The hotel would like to compensate you to make up for the loss of your property. We are fully aware that it is of great expense and we by no means think that what happened is excusable, but we are trying to make amends for the error."

"Oh, there will be some serious compensation needed, Emma," he growled. "That suit cost more than you make in a month, and your canned apology doesn't make anything better. The hotel can compensate me for the suit, but the rest will come from you." He pulled me to him, his hands kneading my ass, his lips an inch from my own. "I think your ass will be able to make it up to me."

I blinked up at him. "What?" That wasn't the direction of sexual payment I was expecting. It was also something I'd never done before.

He leaned in further and nipped at my jaw. "I'm going to fuck this fine ass of yours, Emma," he reiterated, his hands working their way under my skirt. "I want you naked, on my bed. Now."

While I was nervous, my whole body was on fire. His voice alone could drench my panties. I did as he commanded and began stripping my suit off. I was bent over, trying to get my skirt off, when Gavin stopped me, his hands on my hips, his cock rocking into my center.

"Fuck! I swear you wear this shit just for me, just to tease me. Is that it, Emma?"

"Yes, Mr. Grayson," I answered.

He pulled me up and spun me to face him.

"Gavin, Emma." He leaned down and pressed his lips against mine. In seconds the kiss heated and our hands were roaming all over each other, wherever we could touch.

"Gavin," I whimpered. Yes, he was my Gavin, though a little more abrasive than normal, and I loved it.

His lips opened to mine, and his hands dug into my skin, pulling me as close as he could.

"Gavin," I panted.

"Lay face down," he instructed, pushing himself away. He turned toward the nightstand, and I watched him pull out a condom and some lube.

I was only lying there for a second when I felt the bed shift and Gavin's knees straddle my thighs.

His hands massaged my cheeks, pushing them together and pulling them apart. Cold droplets hit my skin, making my jump, but they quickly warmed as he moved it across my skin, his thumb pressing against my tight hole.

It felt wrong.

"Relax, Emma," he said, pushing his thumb through the tight muscles.

"I've never . . ." I trailed off, my voice wavering.

"Don't worry, baby, I won't hurt you. This is for both of us," he reassured me. He leaned down and kissed my shoulder, working his way up to my lips.

He used soft, slow strokes as he worked his thumb in, stretching me open. His cock was hard and hot against my thigh. I moaned at the heat it radiated, my hips rising to get closer.

Suddenly I felt two of his fingers slide into my soaking pussy. I cried out, my hands clenching into the sheets from the sudden move. He started pumping his fingers in and out until I was panting.

With a groan, he removed his fingers. I whimpered at the loss, but rejoiced when I felt his cock working its way in.

He was filling me slowly at first before he worked all the way in. More droplets hit my warm skin, his thumb replaced by the two fingers he had used to work my pussy. With each thrust, he pushed his fingers in.

The slow rhythm normally wouldn't get me too worked up, but the position had his cock rubbing the perfect spot, warming me, pulling moans and soft cries from my lips.

"Gavin . . ."

The pace increased, and so did the mind-numbing pleasure that washed through me.

"Come for me, Emma," he groaned. "I need you to come, baby."

"Fuck," I hissed. He changed his position slightly, and my eyes flew open. A few more strokes, and I shattered around him, screaming into the blanket as I clenched.

"Fuck, so good." He continued a slow and steady pace as I rode out my orgasm. "I think you're ready now."

My mind was still clearing when he pulled out and I felt the head of his cock poised at my asshole. There was a snap from the container of lube, more drops on my skin, then the wet sound of him stroking himself. Gently, he began to slowly push in, testing me, before pushing in further. It was . . . uncomfortable, but not painful like I expected.

"Oh, shit, baby. Yes!" he cried out as he began to move in deeper. "What a fucking sight."

He worked his way up in speed, slow at first, then building.

His hands reached between our bodies and began massaging my breasts, pulling and twisting my nipples. He knew my nipples were a weak spot and had me whimpering and moaning in no time.

"That's it, baby. Feels good . . ."

His moans, deep and resonating, moved through me, turned me on.

His grip tightened. "Fuck! Coming!" He let out a strangled cry, his head burrowed into my shoulder. His hips were flush against my cheeks, each jerk of his cock, sending sensations of pleasure through me. After a moment his body relaxed, his chest resting against my back.

He stayed there for a moment before pulling out and rolling off and onto his back. He worked to catch his breath for a moment before leaning over and kissing one of my ass cheeks.

"Now that was fucking perfect compensation!" he said. "About time this hotel came up with something good." He rolled onto his side and pulled me to him, kissing me.

"I'm glad that we could come to an agreement," I replied before I let my ire show. It was only fair. "Though, next time you want to try something kinky, can we do it when I am not on duty, and also, when it is not because of some screwup the hotel did?"

He grimaced. "I was an ass again, wasn't I? I should have asked you first. I'm sorry. I was so worked up and let it get the best of me."

"Just keep that in mind next time, Mr. Grayson," I said, giving him my best glare.

His eyes grew wide. "Yes, ma'am."

I stared at him, trying to figure out if I'd heard him correctly. "Oh my God."

"What?"

"You have manners?"

His lip twitched up. "My mother may have instilled them in me in my youth."

"You should utilize them more often. Chicks dig manners," I assured him.

"I'll keep that in mind as well. Perhaps you should write a handbook. All of this wooing and manners stuff gets confusing."

I scoffed. "You can run a multi-billion-dollar business empire, but can't handle courting a woman?"

"Obviously not. I've screwed up a lot with a particular woman that I am quite fond of. Besides, it's been a while since I've done any of this," he said, and I sensed a story there, but he didn't expand.

"Well, I think you can make it up to me. Just refer to your Wikipedia article on wooing," I said with a smile.

He got up from the bed and headed toward the bathroom. "Flowers? Letters?" He turned to look at me. "Gifts?"

"How about a date out?" I asked, quirking my eyebrow at him. His eyes widened.

"Or not . . ." I trailed off, suddenly feeling very insecure about whatever was going on between us. I looked away, unable to take his rejection after everything.

The bed dipped, and suddenly I was on my back again, caged beneath him. His eyes were soft, his touch reverent as he cupped my face, forcing me to focus on him.

"I think that's a perfect idea."

"Yeah?"

"I see I've been selfish with our time together. Believe me, when we are both gone from this hotel, I will take you out on a date anytime you want."

Relief and joy flooded my chest. All I wanted was more time with him out in the open, and I was finally going to get it. Not only that, but there was the promise of more, of a future outside the hotel.

11th Floor

First shift always seemed to fly by. There were people checking out until noon, and then lunch, then people began trickling in for check-in. It allowed me to work and the hours to fly, but I only saw Gavin in passing. Even second shift was fast paced. But third? Third was the worst.

For some reason, I'd been put on an extra third shift for weeks. It sucked, but it allowed me to watch Gavin head back from the fitness center.

"Have a good day, Mr. Grayson," I called out to Gavin's passing form. I try not to blatantly stare at the sweat rolling down his skin or the way his muscles flexed.

"Good night, Emma."

He was so different looking in his workout clothes. Very opposite the fitted suits, though I wasn't sure which version I liked more.

Naked. Yes, that was my favorite.

I'd just had another sip of my latte when James appeared beside me.

"Hi," he said as he looked at me. His normal, happy smile was missing.

"Hi. How are you?" The tension between us was so awkward and very different than we'd always been.

He nodded. "Fine."

Fine. Not good, which for him, meant bad.

"Everything okay?"

"I think so, just have some things on my mind."

I gave him a small smile. "Me, too."

The awkwardness lingered as we went over the night's reports. Not much happened, and in no time I was in the break room pulling my purse from my locker and kicking my heels off.

I still had Gavin on the brain, and when I pulled out my phone, I found out he had me on the brain too.

GG: I'll have a good day when I empty my balls inside you

My eyes were wide as I stared down at the message.

Emma: You're mean to tease me like that when I can't come see you

While I slipped my shoes into my bag, my phone went off, signaling another text.

GG: You could always come to my office. We could play dirty boss/naughty secretary ;)

Oh, I would so be down for that.

Emma: You wish. I need sleep.

I closed the door to my locker and spun the internal lock. In those few seconds, my phone went off again.

GG: You're right, I do wish. Sweet dreams

Emma: Sweet dreams of you, right?

GG: Preferably

Emma: Have a good day

I blew out a breath as I headed out to the parking lot. It took everything in me not to go up to his room. My brain ran through all the options, different ways I could make it upstairs unseen. That was the problem, though. Nowhere was unseen. There were cameras everywhere. The service elevator would be worse than the guest elevators.

I made it to my car and started it, but didn't put it in reverse. It was so tempting. He was so tempting.

With a groan, I texted him again.

Emma: I haven't left yet and it's all your fault

GG: Where are you? His text came in seconds later.

Emma: The parking garage

GG: Move over to the guest side. Black Audi SUV, 3rd floor

I stared down at my screen and nervously tapped the side of my case. Should I? What if someone saw? Then again, what were they going to see? Gavin was sometimes unpredictable, but he was also not likely to risk me losing my job. Well, any more than we already had.

After a long minute of debate, I threw my car into reverse and backed out. Each floor I moved up made my heart beat faster in my chest. I was excited to see him, be with him, even if it was for a brief second. It pulled at me more, the want inside me, the desire to have him as mine.

I crept through the third floor of the garage. It was full of expensive vehicles, but thankfully I knew the Audi symbol and what to look for. There were two Audis, but only one black one that happened to have the spot next to it open. A few maneuvers and adjustments, and I was able to back into the spot so that our driver's side doors were next to each other.

A few minutes later I spotted Gavin walking down the aisle and rolled down my window.

"This is your car?" he asked.

"Well, if you're saying it like that because you're comparing my nine-year-old Corolla to your shiny new Audi, then yes, this is my car and it does well by me."

His eyes were wide as he looked it over. "Okay."

"It's what I could afford. There has to have been a time in your life you couldn't afford much."

"There was. It's just been a while and I forgot what that was like."

He leaned down and into the car, and I couldn't stop the flutter in my chest. The gorgeous man in front of me was leaning in for a kiss. I was lost to sensation—softness when our lips touched, mint when his lips parted, and the silky roughness of his tongue against mine. Fire zipped through me, and I felt my nipples tighten in response. He started to pull away, but I reached out, cupping his face to stop him. I didn't want it to end, didn't want to face the realities of the day.

Nothing calmed me like Gavin. What I wouldn't give for a day wrapped up in him.

A growl vibrated from his mouth into mine before I felt the sharp sting of teeth on my bottom lip. My eyes popped open to find him staring at me as he pulled back, taking my bottom lip with him.

"You're causing trouble, Miss Addison."

"I would never."

He smirked down at me. "Yes, you would. Now, get to bed."

"So demanding."

"With the state you've left me in? Very. And I'll be sure to show you just how demanding I can be tonight."

A moan slipped from my lips, and I noticed a jump of the cloth at his crotch. It was then I saw just how hard he was.

"But I don't work tonight."

He stopped and spun back to me, his eyes wide. "What?"

"I worked the overnight. I'm not back until tomorrow night."

"You have Saturday off?"

I nodded.

"Then get some sleep. I'll pick you up for dinner at six."

"Wait, dinner? Where did that come from?" I asked, though I didn't really care, because my heart was soaring at the idea of a date.

"From your demanding boyfriend. I want you beneath me, then in my arms tonight. If it has to be in your apartment, so be it."

Boyfriend?

My mouth popped open as I looked up at him.

He let out a groan and reached down to adjust himself. "Don't look at me like that."

"Like what?" I asked.

"Like you want me inside you right now."

I felt the heat rise in my cheeks. "I didn't know I had that look."

"Well, you do. So save it for tonight, because I *will* be inside you later."

Boyfriend. The word repeated in my mind as I pulled away and headed toward home. Maybe I wasn't the only one who felt like this was so much more than sex.

Maybe there was some sort of future for us.

After a solid seven hours of sleep, the light peeking through my window woke me up. A groan left me as I turned to look at the clock. My eyes popped wide, and I shot up. It was almost four.

"Fuck, fuck!" I jumped out of bed and ran to the bathroom. Clothes off, water warmed, and I was in the shower.

I slept longer than intended and was only left with just over two hours to get ready for the first date I'd had in years. Not only that, it was with Gavin, which sent me off into a whole other panic.

What did I have to wear?

The answer came pretty fast as I shampooed my hair—nothing. Everything I owned was either for work or school. While my work clothes were nice, they were *not* date material. There was no time to go buy anything, so I was going to have to come up with something.

Maybe one of my skirts with a cute top?

The water was off, a towel on my hair and one wrapped around my body, and ten minutes were gone when it hit me to check if he'd texted me. Maybe the time changed and I could run out real quick.

"Shit," I hissed as I looked down at my phone. There were five missed texts from Gavin.

GG: Sweet dreams

That one came in just after I fell asleep.

An hour later I got: **Dinner is set for 7pm**

Followed by: **It's upscale, do you have something?**

GG: Never mind

GG: Check your front door

Check my front door?

I ran out of my room and down the short hall to the door. Sure enough, on the other side was another one of the black boxes with gray trim. I managed to keep my towel up as I maneuvered to pick the box up.

I chewed on my bottom lip, a smile on my face as I stared down at it.

Then I ripped into it like it was Christmas morning. There was another note on top.

> *Emma,*
>
> *I hope you slept well. This is just in case.*
>
> *Yours,*
> *Gavin*

The smile refused to leave my face. However, I was also left wondering how a busy man like him had time to shop. Maybe his assistant found it. Kind of weird, especially if that had been the case with the lingerie, but I was just going to assume it was all him.

"Oh, wow." Inside was a black dress. Simple, but the epitome of the little black dress. It was sleeveless with a sweetheart neckline and looked to be around knee length.

I spent over an hour and a half doing my hair and makeup, leaving little time to get dressed. It had been so long since I'd been on a date, I forgot all that went into getting ready for one. And I'd never been to what was bound to be an expensive restaurant.

The dress fit perfectly. Again, I was amazed by the man.

It was a simple black dress, but made with fine fabrics that hugged my body just right. I also made sure I was wearing one of the silk stocking sets he gave me.

Just as I finished putting on my earrings, there was a knock at my door. One last look in the mirror, and I headed to the door. I took a steadying breath, then opened it.

Gavin stood with a single rose. His mouth dropped open as he looked at me, and I loved the spike of confidence it gave me.

"You look . . ." he trailed off as he took a deep breath. "I'm not sure I have the vocabulary to describe your beauty."

"Can you finish zipping me up?" I asked as I held my hair up and turned around. With one hand on my waist, his other took hold of the zipper and began slowly dragging it down. "You're going the wrong way."

"Am I?" His voice was low and deep.

"I was promised a date."

"That you were," he said as he drew it all the way up.

I stepped forward to grab my clutch, where I'd thrown the few essentials I thought I might need, and turned back to him. Arm in arm, we walked to the car where he held the door open for me.

"Quite the gentleman tonight," I noted as I carefully slid in.

"I have to make a good impression," he said as he climbed in the driver's side. "After all, this should have been the first thing I did with you."

"True, but who says things have to happen in a specific order?"

"I like order."

"I know you do."

His hand reached out to rest on my thigh as he drove. It was nice to sit in a comfortable silence, not having to speak. We had dinner for that.

"I'm sorry this is so delayed. I wanted to take you out months ago," Gavin said as we pulled up to a restaurant I would never be able to afford.

"Really? You seemed a little shocked when I asked for a date."

He shook his head. "That was more at the realization that I was so addicted to you, I forgot all about the wooing. When I admitted I liked you, it wasn't just to get you in my bed. That was just a perk."

"I think you're just a little too slick sometimes, Mr. Grayson."

His lip twitched up. "Perhaps."

The Bay was the top of the top when it came to steak houses, and I knew from rumors at the hotel just how hard it was to get in. They were almost always booked a month out, from what I'd heard.

The posh decorations and modern arrangement mirrored the huge price tag that went along with a meal. The chef was said to be phenomenal, and the nights he headed the kitchen were when you wanted to go.

"How did you get a reservation?"

He smirked at me. "Haven't you learned yet that I know people?"

The entrance was crowded with those hoping to get a table, making it somewhat difficult to make it to the hostess stand.

"Reservation for Grayson," Gavin said, drawing the girl's attention away from another hostess.

"Grayson, yes, sir. We have your table ready," she replied with a smile.

Another girl led us to a table near the back. Being ever the gentleman when he wasn't at the hotel, Gavin waited until I sat before pushing my chair in. My face flushed a bit at the chivalric gesture, as I wasn't used to it.

The waiter appeared at our table almost as soon as Gavin was seated. "Hello, my name is Daniel, and I will be your waiter for this evening." He filled our water glasses, then handed the pitcher off to what I assumed was his assistant or something. "Can I get you a drink from the bar, or are we interested in some wine?"

"A bottle of Domaine de la Vougeraie Clos de Vougeot Grand."

I didn't miss the slight surprise that crossed the waiter's face. "Very good selection, sir. I'll be back in a few minutes with that."

Once he was gone, I leaned forward. "What did you order?"

He chuckled. "It's a red Burgundy. Very good with steak."

"I just heard a bunch of gibberish."

My eyes bulged when I looked down at the menu. Appetizers cost more than I usually spent on a full meal.

"Do you like crab cakes?" he asked just as I was moving on to gawk at the entrée prices.

"You have me salivating."

He grinned at me. "That answers appetizer. Unless you see something else?"

I shook my head. "That's perfect."

Daniel returned with the wine, pouring it and then setting the bottle on a coaster.

Gavin ordered the appetizer, then held his glass up and I did the same.

"To you. You have changed my life in ways I didn't think were possible."

A smile burst onto my face. "I couldn't have said it better myself."

A clink of our glasses, and I had my first taste of a red wine in ages. Instantly, I knew it was nothing like the wine I'd had in the past. A million flavors hit my tongue, from fruits to spices and hints of vanilla.

"Do you like it?" he asked.

I nodded. "It's very good. Much better than the wine I've experienced."

"Good. How is your job search going?"

"Okay," I said with a sigh. "I'm not sure if it will happen fast enough."

"I'm sure it will. Don't worry."

My brow furrowed. "Why wouldn't I worry?"

"Because I can help in many ways."

I shook my head. "I don't need your help."

"Not now, but you may, and I'll be there."

"Anyway," I cut in, trying to steer him away from using his connections for getting me a job or using his money to support me. I could handle myself. "I've got an interview scheduled after finals, and those are next week."

"Meaning?"

The wine seemed to get better with each sip that I took. "Meaning I probably won't see you for a little while."

His mouth turned down. "Can I come over?"

I shook my head. "I'm taking four days off from work. In all actuality, I shouldn't have said yes to tonight because I need to work on my final project."

"You should have."

I reached out and slipped my fingers between his. "But I couldn't. I just couldn't turn down a date with you, because I've been hoping for one for so long."

He pulled my hand up to his lips and kissed my fingers. "Then I'm happy I have this chance to show you how much you mean to me outside the confines of the hotel."

"By the way, when do you find time to shop for all of this?" I asked, motioning down to my dress.

"Lunch breaks for the lingerie, and I had my assistant help with the dress. I figured she couldn't go wrong with a little black dress."

"She could have."

He shook his head. "She sent me photos, and I told her which one."

"Did she model them for you?" I asked with a quirked brow. Really, I was teasing him.

"Of course not. I should clarify, she sent me the links to photos of the dresses."

"What were your conditions?" I was curious what guidelines he'd given her.

"Black. Sexy but not slutty. A classically styled black dress," he said.

"Well, Mr. Grayson, you, as usual, have impeccable taste."

The waiter arrived with our appetizer, refilled our glasses, and took our order. Before he left, I asked for directions to the restroom.

"I'll be right back," I said to Gavin.

A few minutes later I headed back to Gavin, weaving through tables and waiters when I heard my name.

"Emma?" My name came from the waiter beside me.

"Caleb!" I cried, my eyes widening in surprise.

"What are you doing here?" he asked.

"I, umm, I'm here for dinner. What are you doing here?"

Fuck. Fuck. Fuck.

My eyes scanned back toward where we were sitting, then back to Caleb. Bad. The whole situation was very bad.

"Dante is the head waiter. I work here sometimes when he needs help."

"Really? That's fantastic," I replied, plastering a smile on my face and wondering how we were ever going to get out of there unseen. How had I forgotten where Dante worked?

"Holy shit, is that Grayson?"

My eyes went wide, and I looked across the restaurant floor to Gavin, who was staring us down. Caleb looked between the two of us, to the way I was dressed, then back to the obvious open seat across from Gavin.

Panic pulsed through my veins as I tried to think of some sort of cover, but I was coming up blank. Caleb knew my situation and knew there was no way I could afford dinner there on my own. I braced myself for the impact as I watched understanding cross Caleb's features.

"But he's always yelling at you."

"Please, Caleb, you can't tell anyone about this," I begged.

He raised his hand and shook it in front of me, his brow furrowed. "Don't worry about that. I'm still stuck on how you two ended up here."

"His Audi."

"No, not *here* here, but on a date."

He had me so flustered that I didn't understand his meaning. "It's just something that . . . happened."

"And here I was team James."

"What?"

"I think I just switched to team Grayson. I mean, James is a good guy, but . . ." I watched as a shudder rolled through him ". . . Grayson is so domineering. By hotness factor alone, Grayson wins."

"So, you won't tell anyone?" I asked, not believing my luck. Then again, of all the hotel employees, Caleb was the easiest going.

He shook his head. "My lips are sealed. But when it all comes out, can we have a James and Grayson show-down for your affection?"

My brow furrowed while my heart still hammered in my chest. "What?"

He waved a hand in front of his face. "Never mind. Just go on. Have dinner with your man."

"Thank you, Caleb."

"No problem, boss, but I want details on our next overnight."

I nodded, agreeing to anything that would keep him silent. "Will do."

Gavin's eyes stayed on me the whole way back. "Who were you talking to?" he asked when I sat back down.

Even though Caleb promised he wouldn't say anything, the whole interaction had me shaking. Gavin noticed, his eyes shifting from narrowed to concerned as he sat forward and placed his hand on my arm.

"Emma, what's wrong?"

"That's Caleb, one of my employees."

Gavin looked back over, then to me. "I meant what I said earlier. If this causes you to lose your job—"

"No," I cut him off. "He said he's not going to say anything. It's just . . . I know I'm doing something wrong, and getting caught is hard for me to process."

"You aren't doing a fucking thing *wrong*," he growled. "Being with me is *not* wrong."

"Then what is it?" I asked.

His thumb caressed my skin as his expression softened. "Right. Fate. Serendipity. Kismet. I can continue on if you need."

"Need?" I sniffed and looked up. "The only thing I need is you."

He stared at me for a second before leaning forward and capturing my lips. "You have me. You've had me since the beginning. You're the reason I tripped, after all."

"W-what?"

"I was staring at you as I walked in and wasn't watching where I was going," he revealed.

I stared at him in stunned silence. "But you said the rug and . . . and the rug was . . ."

He pulled my hand up to his lips and placed a light kiss to the inside of my wrist. "I've been yours since the moment I walked into that hotel."

It was then I knew what I'd tried to fight in order to protect myself. I was open to it, to him, to everything.

I was in love with Gavin Grayson.

12th Floor

It had been three days since I had seen or heard from Gavin. Our only interaction was a few short texts, though I was still on a Gavin high after our date even as finals swallowed me up. In fact, I hadn't even worked for three days. I was locked in my apartment with a constantly running coffee pot, Chinese takeout boxes, and a few pizzas.

For three days I polished off my projects and worked on my accompanying speech. I went over and over the information to make sure I had it all memorized. I really wasn't all that worried, but the projects were what killed me.

I missed him so much in those days that I physically ached for him. He'd stayed away, but I worked right after my last presentation, so there was no celebration.

"Hey," James said as I walked into the back office.

"Hey, yourself."

"How did your exams go?"

"Good. Over." I couldn't keep the smile from my face. I was done. Years of sacrifice and long nights, and it was on to the next chapter of my life.

"Can I ask you something?"

"Sure."

"Where did you go?" James asked.

I turned to look at him. "What?"

"What happened, Emma? What changed?"

My heart fell. "James . . ."

"Don't feed me some bullshit, Em. You're distant. It's like you're a whole other person."

My stomach sunk. He was right. I'd avoided him ever since the first night with Gavin. We weren't together, weren't a couple, but in a way, I still felt like I'd cheated on him. Though at the same time, I contradicted myself, thinking there was no other man than Gavin. He'd completely taken me over.

Any thoughts of being with James were dead. It felt like another lifetime, and in a way, it was. My life before Gavin was another life, and as soon as I was out of the hotel, I would close the door on it.

"I don't know what to say. All I know is we aren't going to happen," I said. The air around us was heavy, oppressive.

"What changed?" he asked, his arms crossed in front of him, his jaw clenched tight.

"Me." It was the truth. I was changed. "It wasn't you, it was all me."

He shook his head, disbelieving. "Everything was fine, and then . . . you just pulled away."

The weight on my chest got heavier. "Things have changed, and I wish I could tell you something to make you feel better, but I don't think anything I say will make this better."

He shook his head, his face scrunched up. "You could say there are fifteen days left, or you got a job and that you would see me on Saturday night for dinner."

"I can't say any of that."

His eyes bored into mine, searching. "Three years of this, of flirting, of telling each other just about everything, of falling . . . all for nothing."

"I didn't mean for this to happen," I said, trying to offer up some sort of explanation. "Two months ago, I was excited about us dating."

"Two months . . ." He glanced over to me, our eyes locking. "Is there someone else?"

Why was it so difficult? Because I didn't want to hurt him.

"Is there someone else?" he asked with more force, causing me to jump back.

"Yes," I whispered.

His face screwed up while his hands combed through his hair. "So, I get screwed because we couldn't be a couple? Because I'm your boss?"

I nodded. "I'm sorry. I know that doesn't make it better, but I didn't want to hurt you."

"But you did, Emma. What I feel for you . . . you've fucking broken my heart."

I knew James liked me, but more than that?

I stared after him as he stormed out of the office and left for the day. A hand landed on my shoulder as the echo of the slamming door still rang in my ear.

"Don't be too hard on yourself, Emma. He'll be okay," Caleb said, having just entered from the lobby.

"Thanks, Caleb," I said. "I've just never broken a heart before."

"Does it make you feel better if I said I think the other one is the right one?"

I gave him a small smile. "I already figured that out."

"How?"

"Because he was able to win me over so quickly. It just showed that I care for James, but I'm not sure it would have ever been love."

"Still, that's a tough realization."

I nodded. "It really is."

"Don't dwell on it. You've got a hottie waiting to lavish you with lovin'."

I couldn't help but laugh at least a little at that. "Have a good night."

"See you tomorrow."

"Ready for an evening of fun?" I asked Jaqueline as I stepped up to the counter.

"As long as I get to look at that new bellhop all night," she replied while making an approving hum.

We both looked over to the new bellhop as he took some luggage from an incoming guest. He must have sensed it, because he looked up and shot a beaming smile at Jaqueline.

"I think you've got him hooked already."

"Oh, I will."

I laughed and shook my head as I ushered a guest forward.

I took Caleb's advice. While I hated to hurt James, it wasn't done intentionally. Gavin just wouldn't be denied, and I'd fallen hard and fast for him.

Jaqueline and I stayed pretty busy until a lull around seven. Her new love interested clocked out at six, so there was no more distraction there.

We were just contemplating a coffee run when the phone rang, the number burned into my brain and my heart, which had sped up.

"Front desk," I answered. The caller ID gave him away, and Jaqueline slinked back, not wanting to hear his voice.

"I need to see you," he spoke. I could feel the shiver run down my veins, pooling between my thighs at the urgency in his voice.

"The maid didn't leave you any fresh towels? Oh, I'm so sorry, Mr. Grayson. I'll bring some up right away," I lied into the phone.

I let Jaqueline know and set out to grab the standard set of towels from housekeeping. I could hear her mumbling something after I left. I laughed internally when I realized she was praying for my safe return and possibly adding a prayer that he would be swallowed up by the pits of hell.

The elevator pinged on the fourteenth floor, and I felt my panties already getting wet in anticipation of what was to come. As I approached, I took a deep breath before freeing one of my hands from the stack of towels, reaching out to knock.

The door flew open a short moment later; he stood before me with wet hair and nothing but a towel wrapped around his waist.

I stepped through the door and as soon as I was inside he turned my body, pushing my chest into the wall. The stack of towels fell to the floor while his hands pushed the hem of my skirt up to my waist. His fingers dug into my hips, pulling my ass back to him before he yanked my panties down to my knees.

In one smooth motion he thrust his cock all the way inside.

I cried out as he began a relentless pace. It was delicious and torturous at the same time, the force of his thrusts pushing me into the wall.

It was obvious he'd had a bad day at work, or maybe he felt the same as way I did and had missed me as much as I missed him.

"Baby, oh, fuck, baby," he grunted.

My legs were trembling, my insides tensing as he drove me to the edge. His need was a palpable force and just as much of a turn-on as the force of his thrusts.

I needed it just as much as he did. It was a way to wash away the tension, and he pushed me straight to the cliff as each press of his hips drove me higher and higher. My body was on fire, and it didn't take long before I tensed around his.

"Gavin!"

"That's it, baby. Shit!" he cried out, his fingers digging into my hips.

I almost came again from his grunts and groans; the sound of him coming made my whole body tingle.

He paused for a minute, calming down before he pulled out. He stepped away and in my periphery, I watched him remove a condom and toss it in the trash.

"Damn, baby, I'm sorry," he apologized. Dipping down, he picked me up by my thighs and walked us over to the couch to sit. "I hate not seeing you for so long."

We sat there for a moment, soaking each other in. Skin to skin, breath to breath—a connection I so desperately missed. I hadn't noticed how bad it was until his forehead touched mine, his arms tight around my waist.

His phone buzzed, and right away his gaze hardened and his jaw clenched. He leaned forward and picked it up from the coffee table, looked at the screen, then threw it back down.

"Fucking incompetent idiots," he grumbled. It was the first time I'd heard him use words like that to refer to someone besides the hotel staff.

"Bad day?" I asked, my fingers running through his hair. I found it was soothing to him and could calm him down.

"Shittastic," he growled. "One of those that make me question my decisions. Especially the agreement to take over Cates and to move to Boston."

My heart fell at his words, and I tried not to let my disappointment show. His fingers traced my cheek before moving under my chin, raising my eyes to meet his.

"But, then I remember that if I hadn't made those life-altering decisions, then I wouldn't have you, so all the shit I have to put up with is completely worth it."

My heart sped up, and I could feel tears welling. With school finally over, I realized just how much I wanted him. Every fiber of me begged for him. The desire to take his hand and never let go was overwhelming.

"Really?"

"Really."

"I missed you," I said, a tear falling free.

His thumb lightly brushed it away. "I had this fantastic date with a woman, then suddenly no calls, and only one-word texts. I was beginning to think I screwed up, but then I remembered I wasn't the center of her world, even though I want to be."

"Is that your way of saying you missed me, too?"

He nuzzled my nose. "I missed you an insane amount."

"Insane amount? That's a lot."

"It is."

As much as I hated to, I climbed off him.

"Don't go," he begged.

A groan slipped from my lips. "I have to."

"Quit and just stay with me."

I shook my head. "You're a bad influence."

"But I tempted you, didn't I?"

With a reluctant nod, I agreed. "A tiny bit." I straightened out my thong and skirt, then double-checked the rest of me.

"Before you go, happy graduation," he said as he pulled a small, robin's egg blue bag from the side table.

It was one of the most iconic, recognizable colors.

Tiffany and Co. He'd gone to *Tiffany*.

I stared at it, slack-jawed. "Gavin . . ." Inside there wasn't one box, but two. I pulled out the first box and opened it. Nestled in the matching blue was a gorgeous silver bangle. There were five interlocking bands that slid around each other and one of them was a string of what looked like diamonds. I slipped it over my hand, loving the way it changed as it slid down my wrist.

"It's beautiful," I whispered.

"There's another."

My heart slammed in my chest as I reached for the other box. The experience was surreal. Once, a boyfriend had given me a little silver necklace, but that was in high school. Gavin's gifts were beyond anything I'd ever even dreamed of receiving. Especially for something like a graduation.

The second box was a flat, rectangular shape, the hinge tight as I peeled it open. I drew in a sharp breath at the delicate, diamond-crested key pendant on a silver chain.

"Gavin, they're beautiful," I whispered in a reverent tone. "I . . . thank you. Thank you so much. You didn't have to get me anything."

"I did." He took the box with the necklace and slipped it out. "Lift up your hair." I slipped my hair up into a ponytail with my hand as he unclasped the necklace and laced it around my neck. "There," he said when he was done. "That's the key to my heart, Emma. Keep it safe."

My mouth dropped open. The key to his heart. He was showing me that he was mine.

Tears began to well in my eyes. My heart was so full. The wave building in my chest was overwhelming. I jumped up and wrapped my arms around his shoulders as I slammed my lips to his. Gavin might have moved me from my path, but I seemed to be forging a new one with him by my side.

"Thank you. I can't say it enough. This means so much to me, you have no idea."

He leaned down, his forehead resting against mine as his hands rested on my lower back, holding me close. "Tell me you're mine."

"I'm very much all yours."

"Why don't you come over to my place tonight?"

He grimaced.

"Gavin?"

"I have to get up very early."

"And? How is that different than any other day?"

"Your crone of a neighbor downstairs yells at me for making a 'ruckus.' It's like she sleeps by the door, ready to strike."

I let out a laugh. "I think the 'ruckus' is the bed slamming against the wall. You know, when you're fucking me so hard I can hardly walk the next day."

He smirked up at me. "Those are my favorite nights."

"How's the house hunting going?" I asked, my hands absently running across his chest and arms. "That good, huh?"

All of his movements stopped, and I was about to ask if he was okay when he spoke, "Do you work this Saturday?"

"Overnight."

"Will you come with me?" he asked, his head tilting up so his gaze met mine. "To see some places."

How could I say no? It was time with him outside the hotel, outside of my apartment. "Of course."

I gave him one last kiss and headed back to my post, excited for our upcoming outing.

Jaqueline's eyes were wide, expecting to hear the tales of my trial. I shook my head, rolled my eyes, and attempted to put a seething look on my face as I approached.

"He is such a demanding ass!" I hissed in a low tone when I got to the counter.

"It sucks that he's always picking on you," Jaqueline said with a shake of her head.

"Unfortunately, there seems to be something about me. Is there a sign on my forehead that says 'yell at me, I can make it all better'?"

"I gotta say, he must be one hell of a lover to some unlucky bitch, otherwise there is absolutely nothing redeeming about that bastard."

I felt my face heat at the remembrance of how good a lover he was. If only Jaqueline knew it was one of his *many* redeeming qualities. Then again, Gavin didn't open up to a lot of people. I was one of the lucky few who knew just what an extraordinary man he was underneath his gruff exterior.

14th Floor

Gavin stayed at my place Friday night, meeting me after my shift. It was an excuse so that he didn't have to get up extra early on Saturday. Really, it was an excuse for sex and cuddles, and I was not opposed to either.

"Why are we meeting your realtor at stupid o'clock?"

He chuckled, his hand reaching out to rest on my thigh. "Emma, it's almost ten."

"Yes, well, I worked second shift, then was kept awake by someone for another two hours." I turned and narrowed my eyes on him. "Why are you so chipper?"

"I'm used to five or six hours of sleep. Starbucks?"

"If you want me not grumpy, I need a venti quad vanilla latte stat."

"Who is the demanding one today?"

"Hey, about time you got a taste of your own medicine. Waking a woman up from a perfectly good sleep."

His hand disappeared from my leg. "You don't have to come if you don't want to."

I reached out and pulled his hand back to my leg. "Yes, I do."

"Why is that?"

"Because, the one thing I've been wanting for weeks is time with you outside the hotel. I'm just bitchy without my caffeine fix."

"I will buy you a Starbucks if it makes you happy."

I couldn't help but laugh at that. "That would make me very happy."

"Good, because that's all I want."

"What?"

"You happy."

I stared at his profile in shock. "Really?"

"You make me happy. Why do you think I put this off for so long? Finding a house meant not seeing you almost every day."

"You stayed at the hotel for me?"

He nodded. "I told you. From the moment I walked through that door, it was always you."

"But you were always yelling at me. Talk about the wrong signal."

"It was the only way I could think of to see you and not seem like some sleazy hotel guest."

"So you made my work life a living hell?"

He nodded. "I do whatever it takes to get what I want."

"That was underhanded and a huge headache."

"But it worked, because now I have what I want."

We were heading back into downtown, which surprised me a bit. Though, once he stopped and got me my coffee, I didn't care about where we were going anymore.

The first building we pulled up to I thought had to be a joke. It had to be. The high-rise condos in the building were known for starting in the millions.

"What is your budget?" I asked Gavin in a whisper as we walked through the parking garage and into the building.

"For Boston? Four million."

He pulled on my arm, but my feet were stuck as I stared at him.

"What? I spend eight hundred a night at the Cameo, Emma. The mortgage is actually quite a bit less."

"I just, I mean, I knew you had money . . ." I glanced down and stopped again in my tracks. "Are you wearing jeans?"

A chuckle slipped from a half smile while he shook his head. "You really do need coffee in the morning."

I was stuck staring at him. I'd never seen Gavin in jeans. Ever. And it was even better than my fantasies, but also freaky. He looked so laid back, but he also looked like he'd stepped out of a fashion magazine. I'd noticed the fitted sweater and the way it hugged him perfectly, but adding in the jeans should have been illegal.

"Damn, you're hot." I peeked around the back and about died. "Your ass looks so biteable."

He chuckled and we continued on our way in.

The one problem with being out with Gavin was the minute possibility of running into someone from the hotel. And even though the man behind the security desk didn't know Gavin, he did know me.

I'd met Shannon's boyfriend on multiple occasions, including bumping into him on campus a few times. I prayed he didn't recognize me, but I didn't have such good fortune.

His face lit up when he saw me, and I knew there was no getting out of it. "Hi, Emma! What are you doing here?"

"Hi, Brandon." I gave him a wave. "Just helping a friend look for an apartment."

"Oh, hi," Brandon said, his hand sticking out for Gavin to shake.

Gavin merely glared at the outstretched hand momentarily before ignoring Brandon altogether.

"Baby, what time is the realtor meeting us?" he asked, his hand moving to my lower back as he guided me away from the desk. "What the fuck was that, Emma?" His eyes were slits as he looked at me. Shit, he was angry.

"His girlfriend is Shannon," I said, but received no reaction. "One of my front desk clerks."

"So?"

"So? He'll tell her he saw me! I need my job, Gavin."

His jaw tightened, and he mumbled something under his breath I couldn't understand.

"And besides, I don't even really know where this is going."

His head snapped to look at me, and I could see hurt in his eyes as well as anger.

"Don't look at me like that," I whispered.

"Being my girlfriend isn't enough? What do you need me to say? Are my actions not enough?"

"I need something more, Gavin. Because most days I just feel like your girl on the side," I admitted, tears stinging my eyes, threatening to fall. I didn't want to be that to him. I wanted to be so much more. Even with the meaning of the necklace, I still didn't feel secure in his want for me.

"Oh, I am getting rid of that ridiculous notion right this moment," he growled before taking a deep breath. "I'm falling in love with you, Emma, and I want you to move in with me when we finally decide on a place."

My jaw went slack as I stared up at him, speechless. His hand moved up to my face, the back of his fingers gliding down my cheek. His eyes bored into mine, and I knew the truth of his words.

My arms flew up around his neck and pulled him down. I crashed my lips to his and he gave a startled sound, but it quickly faded. His hands wrapped around my body, drawing me closer, kissing deeper.

"But, what's so great about me?" I asked, still shocked that he really wanted me enough to move in with him.

He shook his head. "*You* are what's so great about you. I wouldn't have you any other way, Emma."

Suddenly, an image popped into my head of cooking dinner, but instead of being by myself, there was a little girl on the floor banging on pots and pans. Gavin would come in and scoop the little girl up before kissing me. It was a beautiful dream I hoped one day would become our wonderful reality.

It was only a few minutes later when the realtor arrived. The woman before us was so polished and put together that I felt strange being in the same space as her. My worn jeans, T-shirt, cardigan, and flats accentuated our age and status difference. I glanced over to Gavin and, of course, he seemed to match her, at least in aura.

Elite. Even in jeans.

"Diane, this is my girlfriend, Emma."

"Emma, it's a pleasure to meet you." She held out her hand, and I slipped my hand in.

"Nice to meet you."

She gave me a warm smile, then turned her attention back to Gavin. "Well, I've got a lot of houses lined up for you to look at today."

"I really hope the right one is in there, because I don't want to do this again," Gavin said with a grumble.

"I assure you, Mr. Grayson, there is something in here. Maybe not to the level of features and upgrades you are looking for, but those are easily changed."

"Please tell me there are some single family homes in your list."

She gave a rueful smile. "Unfortunately, to stay close to downtown, that isn't really an option. I found a few with a short commute for us to look at."

"Mostly condos, then?"

She nodded. "Mostly."

Gavin's lips formed a thin line.

"City life not agreeing with you?" I asked. He'd come from New York, but had mentioned once that it was too congested. No room to breathe.

"Everyone is on top of everyone," he said as we stepped onto the elevator. "If it has to be a condo, I want some square footage."

I shrugged. "A condo is just a more expensive hotel."

"That we can modify and make our own."

"True." I loved the way he said *we*.

"This first place is 1,975 square feet with three bedrooms and three bathrooms," Diane said as she unlocked the door.

The second we stepped in, I was blinded. The lights bounced off nothing but white. White walls, flooring, furniture, cabinets, and even white decorations.

"It's so . . . white. Do you think they are allergic to color?"

Gavin chuckled beside me. "It's possible. What color would you paint this?"

"Something light that is not white. Maybe gray or a robin's egg blue."

We walked through, but I could tell pretty fast that Gavin wasn't a fan. His expression was that maddening neutral.

"It's too small," he said to Diane. "Especially for nearly three million."

The next place was nothing but a wall of brick and windows. It was hard to tell any of them apart. The ground floor was wall-to-wall hardwoods. Some rooms were modern, while some were in a classic style with intricately designed wood walls. It was big. Over three thousand square feet big. Lots of rooms and plenty of space.

It felt like a home, and while it didn't have a private backyard, it did have a large grassy common area with lots of trees behind it.

"What do you think?" Gavin asked.

"I really like it. It has that room to breathe."

He nodded in agreement, but I couldn't quite read his thoughts. "It's nice."

The next option on the list was just a few blocks away, another high-rise. It was nice, with one problem.

"This kitchen is a cave," I whispered. It was beautifully done and modern and clean, but there was absolutely no natural light or sight to *anywhere* else in the condo. A single, small doorway that I wondered how they even got the appliances in was the only opening. Not only that, the ceiling was a little bit lower than the rest of the condo, accentuating the cave-like feeling. "This is the kitchen of a nearly four million dollar condo?"

"Diane, this is a no."

Half a dozen places later, we arrived at the last one of the day. It was an older townhome, which held some possibility until we got to the "back yard." If that was what you could even call three ten-foot-tall brick walls around a brick patio.

"This isn't a patio. This is a brick box with the top open," Gavin said as he walked out and straight back to the front door.

Diane and I followed behind to the front where he stood looking up and down the street.

"Everything is so . . . historic. Is there nothing newer?" he asked.

"Babe, this is Boston, not Ohio."

"I know, but isn't there at least a ten by ten patch of green in any of these places?"

"We can always go farther out, Mr. Grayson," Diane suggested. "In Newton and Needham there are some nice sized yards."

Gavin tilted his head back and heaved a sigh before looking at me. "What do you think?"

"What's important to you?"

"You."

My heart skipped, and I smiled and leaned into him. "I meant in a home."

"Besides you being there? Room to breathe, some green, but I don't want a long commute that will keep me away from you even longer."

"Then what about the Charles River home?" It was my favorite out of all of them. "It has a common green space between the buildings."

"It wasn't my favorite home, but I did like that green space."

"Lots of space, and it also had that big rooftop deck," I reminded him.

"It was also one of the most expensive, and there is no covered parking when it snows," he argued.

"Actually, there is now an app for that," Diane said as she pulled out her phone. "I've used it a few times myself. They come out and shovel the snow from around your car and clean it off for you."

Wow, I'd lived in Boston for twelve years and never heard of that. I looked back to Gavin who was deep in thought. "There is always that twenty-fifth-story condo with the balcony."

"Which is the same price as the house and more than I really wanted to spend." He groaned and turned to Diane. "What if we upped the budget?"

"Wait, you just said—"

"I'm willing to spend more to get what I want, I just don't want to," he said, cutting me off.

"Still, in this area, there will be rooftop decks," she said. "The Charles River house is a great location, a great size, and a great area."

He gave a nod. "I think I need to sleep on it."

"You have my number. Just let me know if you decide on one or if you want to look farther out."

"Thank you for your time," he said as he held his hand out.

We shook hands and said a final goodbye, then headed down to the car.

"You didn't like any of them?" I asked when we sat down.

"It's not that. There were a few I liked, and the Charles River home was one of them."

"It wasn't too far over your top budget," I said.

"Two hundred thousand. That's no small amount." His jaw ticked, and I watched as his mood switched. "My money isn't unlimited. You can't just spend it like it's never ending."

I pulled back, pressing against the door. My hackles were raised. "Why are you trying to fight? I never said anything about spending your money. I just meant when you're talking about millions, what's a few hundred thousand? I doubt Diane would have an issue negotiating a lower price."

His hand covered his eyes, his fingers pressing into his temple while his thumb dug into the other side. "I'm sorry. Sometimes I have to remind myself . . ."

"That I want you for you?" More of the Gavin Grayson mystery. Whatever or whomever it was, money was evidently an issue.

He nodded, sighing as he turned to me. "That was your favorite, wasn't it?"

I tried not to let it show, to smile, but I couldn't help it. "It was so pretty, and looking out the back windows, it didn't seem like it was in the heart of downtown. There's always looking in other areas, like she suggested. Lots of single family homes, but it's quite a commute."

He twined his fingers with mine and pulled them up to his lips, his demeanor back to normal. "I'll have Diane write up an offer when we get back to your place."

"Really?"

He nodded. "For us."

I crawled across the seat into his lap and wrapped my arms around him. "For us."

Never did I think when we met that I would one day live with him, but there we were, buying a house. Sure, we'd only been together a few months, but I'd never wanted anything more than to be with him.

15th Floor

Two days later Gavin stood at my door, plastic bags in one hand and a bottle of wine in the other.

"What's this all about?" I asked.

A huge smile broke out on his face. "We have a house."

The smile that grew on my face was almost painful. I jumped up and wrapped my arms around his neck, which made him laugh.

"We have a house!" I still couldn't believe it. The house was huge and beautiful and so much more than I ever thought I would have.

He chuckled as he kicked the door closed and continued to walk in with me wrapped around his shoulders, lips on his. I slid down when we got into the kitchen and began to inspect the bags.

"What do you have for us this evening?"

"I was in the mood for some Italian," he said as he started pulling containers out.

While I was thinking spaghetti with meatballs, Gavin pulled out chicken piccata and tortellini. It probably paired better with the wine than my idea. There was also some bread with an oil dip along with a large salad. Gavin popped open the wine and poured two glasses while I grabbed some dishes and silverware.

We sat at my dining room table that—for possibly the first time—wasn't covered with school work and papers. It had been many months since the last time it was empty.

"I've been meaning to ask; when is your graduation ceremony?" he asked as he put some salad on a plate.

"Tomorrow."

"You're not going?"

I shook my head. "I went to my undergrad, and that was enough for me. Besides, nobody would be there anyway."

"I would."

I stopped dishing out tortellini and looked at him. "You would?" He could make my heart melt with the simplest of gestures.

He nodded. "Of course. At least I get to give you your graduation present."

"Another one?" I asked as I pointed to the necklace around my neck. I'd only taken it off to sleep.

"That was my original."

I tore off a piece of bread. "I don't need another."

"Fine. When is your birthday?"

"July ninth."

"Perfect birthday gift, then." He took a bite of the chicken with one of the tortellini. "In around forty-five days, which is pretty close to the day. I spent a pretty penny on it."

I shook my head. "That doesn't surprise me." Considering I was pretty certain the amount of money he'd spent on my few gifts was more than I made in a few months. Our dinner date alone had been in the hundreds.

"A cool four hundred million pennies."

I blinked at him, finally understanding he meant the house. "Only?"

"Well, technically three-hundred and ninety-one million."

"Good job, Diane!" I held my hand up for a high five. He laughed as he slapped my hand.

"It comes complete with a man ready to serve you." He gave a little wag of his eyebrows.

I clapped my hands together, my expression wide and animated. "My very own pool boy?"

"Feel free to use him sexually whenever you need him." He winked at me.

"Oh, I plan on it."

It really was the perfect birthday gift. My lease ended in August, and hopefully one of my coming interviews would result in a job offering. The quicker I was out, the better. Especially with the fast progression of our relationship.

Moving in with Gavin after only a few months of a hidden relationship may have been a bit rash, but I couldn't find any reason *not* to. I'd fallen hard and fast.

"Is the asshole Mr. Grayson going to come out when we live together?" I asked. I knew how particular he was. Did he expect that level of perfection with me in our home?

He shook his head. "In my job, I have to scrutinize everything. I used that as a way to get close to you, but it will be our home. Our place to relax and be ourselves."

"That sounds like paradise."

"Agreed."

We finished dinner and moved to the couch for a movie. Gavin was flipping through Netflix, and I was curled against his side.

"Have you ever lived with someone before?" I asked as I looked up at him.

His expression dropped, and the warmth seemed to ebb from him, making me instantly regret I'd asked.

"Once."

"The one that didn't end well?" He'd made mention of it in the past, and I had a feeling she was the reason he got money defensive when we were looking at houses.

He nodded. "I suppose it's best I told you that I've been married before."

The news stunned me, and I stared up at him. "Oh? For how long? What happened?"

"Two years, and basically, she was a gold-digging whore."

Bingo. A lot of things began to make sense. "You didn't want to be attracted to me, did you?"

His eyes never left mine. "No." He pulled me closer, forcing me to straddle his lap. "I was angry with you and myself for those first few days, but each time I saw you, a little chip fell off my shoulder until there were none left."

"I think you still have a chip on your shoulder," I said. It reared its ugly head more than once.

"But not about you."

He reached out to touch my face. It was another one of those sweet gestures he did. His hand stopped momentarily before he spoke, "I have a charity auction to go to; will you accompany me? It's themed. I'm going as Zeus. You could be my Juno."

I quirked my eyebrow at him. "Zeus cheated on Juno. A lot."

A small smile graced his lips. "True."

"We'd be better going as Hades and Persephone."

"I'm the devil now?" he asked indignantly.

I nodded. "More believable than the leader of the gods. Just ask the people I work with."

"But I am a leader, and I feel like a god quite often. Besides, Persephone wasn't exactly happy with Hades. I think you're Aphrodite."

"Aphrodite? Me? Does that make you Ares or Hephaestus? If Hephaestus, she cheated on him and mostly with Ares. Though you do share similarities with the god of war." I smirked up at him.

"That I do." He hummed as he tapped his fingers on my hip. "What about Athena? She was very wise, just like you."

"And a virgin. I think you know by now that I am no virgin."

"No, I have made certain no virgin holes are left on you," he replied with a smirk. "Hmm, this is getting more and more complicated. I didn't realize you were so well versed in Greek and Roman mythology."

I pointed to myself. "Slightly more intelligent than the average hotel clerk."

He pursed his lips, not happy with my comment. "I'm never going to live that down, am I?"

I leaned in close, my lips barely an inch from his. "You can make it up to me."

His hands squeezed my hips and pulled me closer and down. "Yeah?"

There was a playful smile on my lips as I slipped my arms around his shoulders. "If you're *up* to it."

"With you, that is never an issue," he said as he flexed his hips and pressed his lips to mine.

One day we wouldn't be crammed in my small apartment, but in our very own home.

With my fourth interview in two weeks at a close, I walked out with a lighter step. Each interview was practice, and I was getting better and better at them. Every one was a stepping stone, a progression to my goal. I was very ready to be free to be with Gavin, not hiding like we had been forced to.

The charity event was fast approaching, and I still didn't have a costume. Gavin had told me not to worry about it, but we were only a few days away. On Wednesday, one of my first days off, I surfed the internet for anything I could get my hands on just in case.

We had plans for a little more casual night out, but knowing him, that just meant no dress code.

The buzzing vibration of my phone in my hand made me jump, and I had to swipe the screen a few times to answer. I couldn't stop the smile from taking over my face at his name, or rather his initials, popping up on my phone.

"Hey, baby."

"Meet me downstairs," he said, then hung up.

I jumped up from the couch and slipped on some flip-flops on my way out the door and down the stairs. Parking was always a mess around my apartment, and I hoped he could find a space.

Luckily there was one a few spaces down, and I walked over as he pulled in and climbed out of the car.

"Hi, baby," he greeted, leaning down to kiss me.

"So, what's this all about?" I asked, wondering why he had called me down.

He leaned into the car and pulled a large box from the back seat and handed it to me.

"My costume?"

"Your costume, Aphrodite," he confirmed, a smirk forming on his face.

I rolled my eyes at him. "This looks a little too fancy of a box for costume wrappings."

After he grabbed his overnight bag from the passenger's seat, we headed back up. There was a whole, wide-open table in my apartment, which still amazed me, to set the box on. Lifting the lid, I gasped at what lay inside.

What Gavin had purchased could by no means ever be associated with the costume image I had in mind—cheap, overpriced, flimsy material.

No, this was rich fabric and stunning glass crystals that formed the bodice. It was one shouldered, the fabric intertwining with the crystals.

"Gavin . . ." I trailed off, staring at the dress in awe.

He came up behind me and wrapped his arms around my waist. "Do you like it?"

"I love it," I replied. "But this is way too much."

"No, it isn't."

"Yes it is," I argued as I turned in his arms.

"Nothing is too much for my goddess," he stated, his eyes locked on mine.

A groan left me as I wrapped my arms around his waist. "You spoil me too much. I'm not used to it. I've worked very hard to get what I need and what I want."

He leaned down and kissed the tip of my nose. "Oh, I know how self-reliant you are," he said with a chuckle. "However, I like to spoil you. I want to spoil you because you deserve the world at your feet."

"And what did I do to deserve that?"

His hand moved to caress my cheek, his soft gaze making my chest ache. "You opened my heart, and that was no easy feat."

I touched the pendant around my neck, then ran my hands up his chest and into his hair. His eyes fluttered closed, and a moan escaped his lips and his arms pulled me closer.

His words solidified the certainty I felt that we belonged together. I loved him, and I hoped soon I would be able to tell him.

16th Floor

Two days later, my stomach was in nervous knots. Along with the dress, Gavin had purchased undergarments, shoes, and a long blonde wig. I had the dress on and was working on bunching my hair so that it would fit under the wig, which was also expensive and very fine quality.

I stared into the bathroom mirror of the hotel room, shaking my head as I pinned the wig on. Gavin had rented a room at the hotel where the event was being held. To me, it was incredibly ridiculous to have two hotel rooms when he wasn't even staying in one of them. I had tried to talk him into moving in with me since he spent half of the nights with me, but, in his direct way, he said my place was just too small for both of us.

Not that I could really argue with that statement—the bed alone barely held the two of us.

Out of the corner of my eye, I watched him walk up to my side. I turned to look at him and nearly died on the spot from internal combustion.

Gavin. In a toga.

"Need any help?" he asked.

I stood there, drooling at him. The cloth hung perfectly from his body and exposed part of his chest. "Yes, please. I need help out of this dress," I replied.

A cocky smirk formed on his face as my tongue swiped across my lips to wet them.

"Emma, we need to leave, but I promise that I will rip you out of that fucking dress before the night is over."

I reached up to lay my hands on his chest, my fingers flexing and one hand fisting the fabric that crossed his pec. "Promise?"

He leaned forward and nuzzled my nose, all the while his eyes never left mine. "I will worship you like the goddess you are before I fuck you like the slut I know you can be."

In one sentence, my panties were soaked. Gavin had a bit of a dirty mouth, but he'd never said anything like that before and I couldn't help my body's reaction. His lips met mine, and he pulled me tight to him.

With a groan, he stepped back, his hands raking up and down my sides, his lips against my neck. I finished getting ready as best I could in the state in which he had left me.

A few minutes later, we headed down to the event, and the butterflies returned. It was my first time out with Gavin at a professional event, and I hoped I wouldn't do anything to embarrass him. There was so much riding on his shoulders with the company, and I was a stranger to everyone.

When we entered, my mouth fell open as I looked around at the lavish decorations. The costume ball, I determined, was one that put all others to shame.

"What's on your mind?" Gavin asked, noticing my change.

"I'm confused and in awe. All the money they spend on this event, why don't they just use it?" I asked. It all seemed like a waste.

He leaned down to whisper in my ear. "Because what they spend is a minute fraction of what they will gain before the night is over."

We located our table where another couple sat; they were dressed as Julius Caesar and Cleopatra. Their costumes were also extremely detailed.

Gavin recognized them right away and introductions were made. We sat and chatted for a while as the hall filled with people.

"Gavin!" a man dressed as what I assumed was Henry the Eighth called out.

"Alexander!" Gavin stood and smiled as he held out his hand.

The two men shook hands and talked a bit while the woman with him and I just watched.

"Oh, I'm being terribly rude. Who is your guest?" Alexander asked.

Gavin pulled me to his side and gave me a calming smile. "This is my girlfriend, Emma. Emma, this is Alexander Cates, CEO of Cates Corporation."

I froze momentarily before reaching out to shake his hand. "It's a pleasure to meet you, Mr. Cates."

"Ah, no Mr. Cates's here tonight. I am 'Henry' and this is my wife 'Jane,'" he said, bringing his wife forward.

"It's a pleasure to meet you both," I said.

"You as well, Emma," his wife said. "It's not often we see Gavin in the company of a woman at one of these. He's usually just sulking in the corner."

"Sarah," Gavin groaned at Mr. Cates's wife. "I do not sulk."

We all laughed and moved to the table where our conversation resumed.

Dinner was served not long after, and I was amazed at the food. It wasn't your normal banquet spread. No money was skimped on the quality.

The announcer took over as we ate dessert, talking about the silent auctions, stating that the live auction would begin a little bit after the tables were all cleared, and the dancing would begin momentarily.

At the mention of dancing I looked to Gavin, who smiled and tilted his head. Just as he held out his hand, Alexander stood beside me.

"Emma, may I have this dance?"

"Of course," I said, then glanced to Gavin as I stood. He didn't look too pleased when I took Alexander's hand and moved to the dance floor with his boss.

"So, Emma, what is it that you do?" he asked as we began moving.

"Well, I just finished up my MBA, and am currently searching for a position," I replied.

"MBA? Hmm . . ." he trailed off. "You are quite the dancer, I must say."

"Thank you." I smiled at him. "I took ballroom dancing once upon a time."

"Very nice. I must say, you seem to have my successor making faces I've never seen before," Alexander said with a deep laugh as we swayed on the dance floor.

My brow scrunched, trying to understand his meaning. "Sir?"

"Please, call me Alex, Emma."

"Alex."

He grinned down at me. "That's sure to get his blood boiling."

"I'm afraid I'm a bit lost," I admitted.

"You, dear girl, have the next in line of my company completely smitten with you. I've never seen him act this way with a woman before. Just look at his face!" he exclaimed jovially.

I turned to find Gavin glaring at us as we spun around the dance floor. He wasn't just glaring, though, he was . . . sulking.

"He is very angry that another man is touching what is 'his,' even though it's a sixty-five-year-old man. He can't stand to be away from you, that much is obvious," he explained.

Gavin's hand rubbed at his face. It was clear he was agitated.

"Shall we really get him riled up? Enough that he will come and take you away from me?" Alex asked.

I laughed. "You're terrible! And yes." The curiosity of his reaction gnawed at me.

We put operation "make him take Emma away" in play and were soon a bit closer then we had been. The band switched to a tango and we were off.

We moved gracefully around the floor as if we had done it before. Alex was a wonderful dancer, and the tango was such a sensual dance, I knew it would infuriate Gavin to see us touching so intimately.

Unexpectedly, he turned me into a dip, his hand grasping under my knee and moving up my thigh.

"Forgive me for . . . copping a feel, Emma. Just trying to give the best show for our audience," he said with a wink.

I couldn't help but laugh. Poor Gavin. I was sure his head was close to exploding.

He righted me, and we spun once more before I felt two large hands wrap around my waist, and I was pulled back against what I knew was Gavin's large chest.

"Mine," he growled in my ear. A shiver ran through me, and I smiled up at Alex. Our operation was a success.

"If I could cut in, Alexander?" Gavin asked, though his body had demanded it.

Alex grinned at me. "Thank you for the wonderful dance, Emma. It was a pleasure meeting you, and I hope to see you again soon."

He took my hand and placed a kiss on it, his gaze looking past me to Gavin. I felt Gavin's grip tighten on my waist and his chest rumbled.

Alex merely smirked and turned to leave.

"That wasn't very nice, Emma," Gavin said into my ear.

I turned in his arms and smiled sweetly up at him. "Shall we dance?"

He glanced around the floor, then to me.

"Don't worry, I won't let you fall."

He let out a small snort. "I'm afraid you are a bit late on that." His gaze softened, his hand reaching up to move the hair from my wig behind my shoulder. "I've been falling for months, and it's entirely your fault."

I stretched up and wrapped my arms around his neck, bringing his lips down to mine. "Ditto, Mr. Grayson."

He beamed down at me. "And you really are mine and mine alone," he stressed, pulling me tightly to him.

I didn't think about what he had said and how he had said it. All I heard was that I was his, and that was the truth. Gavin Grayson owned me: mind, body, and soul.

Every day I fell further and further in love with him.

I gave him one last kiss before assuming the position for the remainder of the tango. I was shocked and surprised when he expertly did the same.

"You tango."

"Of course."

We finished up our dance and returned to the table where he let out a sigh. The auction took place then, raising lots of money for the local Children's Hospital. Gavin had even bid on and won a week-long vacation on Mr. Cates's personal yacht and promised to take me.

I was excited by the prospect of a week alone with Gavin with no disturbances.

After everything was over, we headed back up to our room. We were barely in the door when his arms wrapped around my waist, his lips kissing my neck and shoulder, a sigh of contentment escaping him. I had never felt so secure and as loved as I did in his arms. Did he have any idea? I wasn't sure, but I wanted him to know. I was ready for him to know.

I spun in his arms, gazing up at his face and the serene expression it held.

"I love you, Gavin," I said in a clear voice, my heart pouring out all of the emotion I felt for him.

His eyes widened, and he stared down at me. There was silence, and I suddenly felt very self-conscious.

All of the blood rushed to my face, and I had to look away. "I . . . I'm sorry, I just . . . I . . ."

He silenced me by pushing me against the wall, and his lips crashing to mine. I was momentarily stunned but quickly responded, my hands grabbing for him with the same hunger that his roamed my body.

When he pulled back, he was breathing hard. The look in his eyes set my being on fire. "I love *you*, Emma."

My world exploded when his lips met mine again. He loved me. Gavin loved *me*.

Our kisses grew hotter, heavier. My legs wrapped around his waist, and he groaned; his hard cock rocked against my wet center.

It was frantic, our need. Hands and lips roaming everywhere they could reach. I reached behind me and pulled at the zipper of my dress. Gavin's hand clamped onto mine, stopping me.

"Remember what I told you earlier? That's my job," he growled against my neck, sending shivers straight through my entire body.

"Yes," I replied, panting.

I removed my hand from under his and he moved the zipper down before roughly pulling the garment over my head and throwing it onto the floor. He pushed me back up against the wall, his lips attacking my neck.

My legs returned to his waist and his hand moved between us, freeing his cock from the toga.

He lined up and thrust his hips forward until he was fully seated inside me.

A tear escaped; my heart was unable to contain all that I was feeling. He leaned forward and kissed it away, whispering how much he loved me, all the while his body showing me how much he adored and needed me.

I cried out, my nails digging into his back as I clenched around him, coming undone. Gavin's thrusts became erratic, and I knew he was close. He reached between us and pulled his cock out, pumped it in his hands before he came, spraying all over my stomach and his hand.

His forehead came to rest against mine, his breath coming out in hard pants. "Mine."

"Always."

We fell asleep wrapped in each other's arms. For the first time in my life, I began to believe that fairy tales and Prince Charmings just might be real. Because I had found mine.

17th Floor

"Shit, shit," I hissed as I raced in from the parking garage. Traffic had been a bitch as it always was getting into downtown in the morning.

Racing through the hall to the employee break room, I clocked in at five after seven. As I exited, Gavin emerged from the elevator bay. His eyes scanned to the front desk and immediately away when he didn't find me. Almost as if he knew I was watching him, he looked again and my heart skipped when we locked onto one another before turning away.

When I broke away, I found Jaqueline staring directly at me. It didn't matter, I told myself, choosing to ignore her, and went to check in with the night shift.

I was just happy to get a glimpse of him before he left.

The morning check-out rush was the same as any other day, no hiccups and only a few minor complaints. When ten rolled around, Jaqueline's shift was over and she headed off to the break room, leaving her replacement, Caleb, and me out front.

"By the way, I've been meaning to tell you how much I love your bangle."

"Thank you," I said with a grin. The interlocking bracelet Gavin gave me was a perfect accent to my suit.

"May I?" Caleb asked as he held out his hand.

"Sure," I said as I pulled it off and handed it to him.

He looked at it in awe, his eyes narrowing in. "You know these are real, right?"

"Real what?"

"Diamonds."

The blood drained from my face as I stared at him. "Diamonds?"

He nodded. "Mm-hmm. Platinum, too. From Tiffany!" His eyes lit up when he saw the marking on the inside. "Wow, your man spent a lot on you."

He handed it back to me, and I stared at it in awe as I searched out the markings. "How much?"

"I'd guess around fifteen thousand, maybe twenty."

My eyes bulged from my head as I frantically put it back on my wrist. Thousands? Tens of thousands? Panic began to fill me. For weeks I'd worn the bracelet to work every day, not knowing it was worth so much.

I swallowed hard, then pulled the pendant from under my collar. "What about this?"

Caleb stepped forward, pulling on the chain as he scrutinized it, twirling between his fingers. "Same for the diamonds and platinum. Probably ten grand."

"Holy . . ."

He glanced up at me. "You didn't know?"

I shook my head. "They were a graduation present. I mean, I know *Tiffany* is expensive, but I didn't think to ask if they were real diamonds. Oh my God."

He stepped back and leaned a hip against the counter. "My sister works there, and I go see her a lot as an excuse to look at all the pretties."

"I was wondering how you knew," I said as I slipped the pendant back under my shirt.

"He's a keeper."

I nodded in agreement. "Definitely."

"Now I'm a little jealous."

"What about Dante?"

"Pfft . . . okay, I love him. A lot. Maybe I can get him to buy me something from there."

"The restaurant is doing good, right?"

"Sure is," Caleb said before turning his attention to a guest headed our way. "Good morning. What can I help you with?"

"Hi, I need to check out," a gentleman in a suit said.

"No problem. What's your room number?"

There was no need to watch over Caleb. He was always great with the guests, but management liked to have two people behind the counter at all times. It was strange that I hadn't seen Shannon yet. The clock on the phone caught my eye, and it was ten after. Where was she?

"I'll be right back," I said as soon as Caleb was done.

There was no sign of her in the office, so I headed back to the break room to check. A few feet from the door I heard her talking with someone else. What I heard made my blood run cold.

"Brandon said Emma was in his building with some rich guy checking out a condo. He said the guy was an ass and ignored him and was acting all possessive of her. What asshole do we all know that has her wrapped around his finger?" Shannon asked.

I knew when we had seen Brandon that it would come back to haunt me.

"You know, she was acting strange when she came back from Mr. Grayson's room the other night. I said that an ass like him had better be a good lay because that was the only endearing quality he could have, then she got very quiet and her face got really red," Jaqueline chimed in.

"And he's always asking for her, never anyone else."

"She doesn't get as pissed anymore either," Jaqueline noted.

"Housekeeping has made sure that his room is perfect so that he has nothing to complain about, yet he always makes something up," Shannon said.

They'd put it all together. Fuck.

"I can't believe she has been fucking him and no one has noticed!"

Gavin and I were on the verge of being found out, meaning I was on the verge of losing my job. My need to find a new job was now on the fast track. I needed out of the hotel sooner rather than later. I needed to be free to be with Gavin, without this cloud hanging over us.

Instead of going in, I headed back out to the front desk and waited for them to come out before I went in to retrieve my purse. A few minutes later I was sitting in the Starbucks with my latte and phone surfing through job positions when one caught my eye—treasury department, large company, MBA required. I was missing the experience, something I knew would make it difficult, but I had many of the skills and background they were looking for. My eyes scanned down the page and stopped when I read the company name—Cates Corporation.

I debated about applying. It was the company that was soon to be Gavin's, so I knew if I told him I wanted it, I would have it. But, that wasn't how I wanted to get my first job out of school. I wanted to do it on my own, without the help of his name or brand of bullying.

Finally, I decided to apply and not tell Gavin. I didn't know what the company's fraternization policy was, but Gavin being who he was, I didn't see it being a problem. Besides, what were the chances I would actually get the job?

After submitting my resume, I sipped on my latte and continued to surf, all the while thinking about what it would be like to work at Gavin's company, in the same building as him every day. We could carpool and have lunch together, and maybe try out some of those desk fantasies of his.

Lost in my daydream, I was almost late coming back from my break.

Yes, the sooner I was out of this hotel, the better it would be for both of us.

There was only an hour left, and James was due in any minute. I headed into the office to finish up a few things. My stomach was a nervous knot. Once upon a time, not so long before, it had been filled with butterflies, but ever since we'd talked, things changed.

He knew whatever we may have been was no longer an option. I hated hurting him, but it had to happen. Not the hurting him part, but the telling him things had changed.

A few minutes before my shift ended, the door from the hall opened.

"Hi," I said as James entered the office.

There was no smile to greet me. In fact, he'd been avoiding me for all those weeks. It was rare to be on the same shift anyway, but he made sure to stay away from me if we happened to be there at the same time.

"How did today go?" he asked, not even looking at me.

"Fine. Nothing to report."

"Good." With that, he headed to the door.

"James!" I called out.

"What?" he growled.

I felt chastised, and maybe he was right to lash out, but was it so much to ask to be civil?

"Have a good night."

He nodded. "Night."

There was a stinging pain in my chest, but as I rubbed absentmindedly, my fingers bumped over my shirt. Underneath laid the key to the only heart I wanted, and it was all mine. If I had to break a hundred hearts to get it, I would, because Gavin showed me what true love could be.

It had been a very long day, and I was looking forward to getting home and curling up on my couch and doing nothing. Gavin said he had to work that night, so I was on my own. Time for some Netflix. Sadly, without the chill.

James wouldn't even look at me when I went out to hand off the keys. When I turned, Caleb had appeared from the office and I gave him a smile and a wave.

"Have a good night, Emma," Caleb said as he stepped up behind the counter.

I yawned in response as I passed him. "Thanks, Caleb."

"You know, you should have that man of yours run a hot bubble bath and cook you dinner."

"Ha! I'm not sure he can cook anything," I said with a laugh.

"I can believe that! Most guys can't cook. I lucked out with Dante."

I caught James's eye, and my chest clenched. Never did I think my life would change so drastically and in such a short period of time. Or that there would be collateral damage when it happened.

Gavin had come in like a hurricane and wiped out my carefully laid-out plan. Claimed me so no other man could have me.

With all that I overheard, the only thing I wanted right then was to see him. Maybe I could convince him to come over for a little while.

As I stepped out of the hotel elevator and into the parking garage, I nearly stopped in my tracks. Heading right for me was the man himself.

"Hi," I said as I stared up at him.

His brow furrowed as he looked down at me. "Hello."

Popping my head to the side, I gave him a silent request to follow me. His Audi was about ten spots down, right after a large SUV, and I slipped between the two. Gavin was a few steps behind, but as soon as he was in front of me I slipped my arms around his shoulders and pulled him down, pressing my lips to his.

The simple feel of his large hands moving around my waist, pulling me closer, began releasing my tension. Being with him, embraced in his arms, was exactly what I needed after a rough day. His tongue lapped against mine as I ran his hair through my fingers.

I was ready to advance, to continue, when he pulled back. His warm hands cupped my face, clear blue and green eyes locked on mine.

"Are you okay?"

I let out a hard breath and relaxed further into his arms. "Yes . . . no."

"What's going on?"

"Jaqueline and Shannon figured it out. They know we're together."

"No, they *suspect*."

"Well their suspicions hit the nail on the head. You need to keep up the attitude, especially tonight when I won't be there."

His jaw ticked, his eyes flashing dangerously. "Did anyone say or do anything to you?"

I shook my head. "I overheard it. There were also some looks . . ." I trailed off. He wasn't supposed to be back, especially not so early. "Wait, what are you doing here?"

"My meeting got cancelled." He pulled me close, wrapping me in his arms. "I was going to change and then come over and surprise you."

My heart melted, loving his plan, but then it sunk. "You should stay here. Just for tonight."

His fingers brushed back my hair. "I don't like seeing you upset like this."

"I'm just freaking out."

"Emma, I am here for you. No matter what happens, I will take care of you." Leaning forward, he pressed his lips to mine.

The kiss was filled with promises of more, but he held back. But I needed more. I pushed harder, deeper. I needed settling, and only he could help.

I couldn't stop, didn't want to. Suddenly, I didn't care about anything else but his lips on mine. His tongue, his hands, every part of his body that was touching mine. I needed it all.

A growl rumbled through his chest as he backed me up against his Audi. We were both so worked up that I didn't want to stop.

"There aren't cameras pointed over here, are there?" he asked through panting breaths.

My eyes went wide as I glanced around. I couldn't believe I didn't even think of them before it got this far. I didn't see any, but that didn't mean there weren't any.

"I don't think so. We're in the middle and they're at the ends." We were also between two SUVs.

"Good," he said before returning to kissing me. His hands pulled at the edge of my skirt, drawing it up.

"Wait, Gavin," I whimpered against his lips.

"Nobody can see us."

A shiver rolled through me.

"Give me this," he said as his fingers brushed against my slit.

I nodded, my fear heightened, but there was an explosion in my lust. It sent reason out the window. All I could think about was him inside me.

With my right leg hitched about his hip, I heard the familiar sound of his zipper before I felt the hot tip bounce on my clit. His lips never stopped touching mine, never let me pull back as he pushed my thong aside and pressed into me.

His mouth captured my cry as he thrust forward. Pleasure enveloped my mind, shutting everything else out but the feel of him.

It was exactly what I needed.

His hips ground into me with each flex, pushing him deeper. It wasn't drawn-out sex—it was a quick fuck to release the tension we both held.

"Gavin," I moaned against his lips.

"Shh," he whispered before silencing me with his mouth.

Each thrust was fast, desperate, racing, and rubbed me just right. I tensed in his arms, whimpering into him until everything broke apart.

I was coming around him, squeezing him, each wave shaking me in his arms. His movements became less rhythmic and harder, signaling he was close. The squeal of tires rang out, and he dipped his head into the crook of my neck and stopped thrusting, his teeth digging into my neck. As soon as the car passed us, he started to move again, but cried out against my skin before frantically pulling out.

Almost before he was even out, cum splashed against my shirt as he groaned against me. His forehead rested against mine as he regained his breath.

"Fuck, baby."

"Thank you," I said, a small, content smile filling my face.

"Do you feel better now?"

I gave him a lazy nod. "Infinitely."

He tucked himself back away. "Are you still worried?"

"Are you beside me?"

He cupped my cheek. "Always."

"Then who cares?" I said with a sigh, though I knew the truth. I did care. I just cared about him more.

"Exactly."

He stepped back, and my eyes went wide. "Oh, shit." The droplets that landed on my shirt were pressed into his vest.

He glanced down and sighed before buttoning his jacket up. "I suppose it's a good thing I don't personally interact with the dry cleaner."

I couldn't help but laugh before doing up my own suit jacket. "Good thing."

"Are you good now?" he asked again.

I nodded. "Yes. You definitely have a way about you." I hated to leave him. I didn't want to.

"Sleep well, my love," he said, giving me one last kiss.

"Love you." I leaned down to pick up my bag that had fallen. Once out from between the cars, I stopped and turned back to him. "Come over tonight?"

"What about the plan to not come over?" he asked.

"I changed my mind."

His lips drew up into a smile. "I'll see you in a few hours."

I blew out a breath and continued my path. A few hours would allow me to apply for a few more jobs, and hopefully one would pan out. Then I wouldn't care what happened to my job at the Cameo Hotel.

18th Floor

Music filled my ears, rousing me from sleep. I reached out and fumbled for my phone as my eyes attempted to open. I managed to get the alarm turned off, but getting out of bed was another issue.

Hands pulled at my waist, moving me back down to the bed.

"And where do you think you're going?" Gavin asked, his fingers pressing against my clit, teasing me.

"I have to get ready for work," I said in protest, crying out when his fingers pinched my clit.

"Call in."

"Gavin," I groaned.

"I'm serious, Emma. That place is nothing but a headache for you. I'll just pay for everything until you find a job. Or you don't have to work at all."

"I have to work, babe."

He sighed. "If you insist."

I smirked back at him. "You like that I don't want to depend on you, but at the same time it makes you want to spend more money on me!"

"You got me."

"Besides, I didn't work my ass off for all these years to get a master's and not use it." With great difficulty, I pulled out of his arms and headed into the shower.

As I waited for the water to heat, I pulled out a few towels from the laundry basket. I'd folded them up the other day, but forgotten to put them away. The warm water felt refreshing as it fell over me, a great wake-up until I could get a cup of coffee. I'd barely started washing when the shower curtain pulled back and Gavin stepped in, his cock leading the way.

"Tease," I said as I ran the washcloth around my skin.

He grinned at me. "You're not the only one that has to work."

"And who was the one trying to get some morning nookie?"

His hand stroked down and then back up his length. "Always."

I shook my head as I rinsed off, then pulled the curtain back to step out. "All yours."

"I can't wait until we move in."

"Why's that?" I asked as I began wiping myself down with a towel.

"Do you remember the size of that shower?" he asked. I nodded. "I'm going to fuck you in it our first morning."

My hands stopped moving the towel around and I stared at him. "I've never had sex in a shower before."

He grinned at me. "What a way to christen the house."

"There you go teasing me again."

"Not a tease, baby, a promise." He reached out and grabbed my towel and pulled, yanking it from my hands. With his other hand, he pulled me closer to the tub until he reached down and picked me up, setting me back in the shower.

"Gavin, I really have to—"

His lips cut me off, stopping any protest. Finally he'd broken me down. I couldn't resist him, even when I needed to.

"Fuck," I cursed as I walked into the hotel. I was fifteen minutes late due to Gavin.

Really, it was all his fault. I was good, took a shower and got out before he got his hands on me, but his mouth got me. Next thing I knew, my back was pressed against the shower wall, his cock filling me.

The employee lounge was empty, and I threw my purse in and changed my shoes. I was about to head to the office when Caleb came in.

"Hi," I said with a smile.

Caleb's eyes popped wide, and he rushed over to me.

"The parking garage has cameras," he whispered.

I froze, my smile falling as utter horror washed over me.

"I know."

He shook his head. "It was on the upper level and pointed right at you."

I fell back against the lockers and leaned over. "Fuck."

"I tried to keep others from seeing it, but Barry, the compliance nazi, saw it before I could do anything."

"Why . . . why would you try and help me like that?"

He smiled. "I like you, Emma. We're friends . . . at least I'd like to think so. Plus, Dante was once a guest, so I know a little of what you've been going through. I wanted to give you a heads up, because I know they'll say stuff about you, but I know."

My brow scrunched. "You know what?"

"I've seen the way he looks at you. When you were at the restaurant . . . it's obvious he loves you."

I nodded. "He does." I took a deep breath before getting back into my locker for my phone. "An inquisition?"

"Yeah. Phillip was yelling in the office earlier. It was so loud the guests heard him."

"Thanks, Caleb. For everything."

"No problem at all." He leaned forward and wrapped his arms around me. "If this gets you fired, just know you were my favorite."

A chuckle sprang out of me. "Ditto." He pulled back, and I heaved a sigh. "Guess I should go find out my fate. See you."

I slipped my phone into my jacket pocket and headed down the hall. When I entered the office, it was silent. James's head popped up at the sound of the door. His brow was furrowed, and he looked beaten down.

"Miguel wants to see you in Phillip's office," he said, his voice low.

"Oh?" Shit. It was over. I lost the race to find a job first.

"Tell me it isn't true."

"What?" I asked, feigning ignorance. I wasn't sure what he knew.

"Tell me you aren't fucking Grayson," he growled.

I shook my head. "I can't."

The pain that crossed his face clawed at my chest.

"It was our time, Emma." His face screwed up, teeth bared. "You were going to leave and we could finally be together. Finally have an honest chance at something."

"I'm sorry, James," I said. There was no way he was going to understand how truly sorry I was. "A few months ago that was what I wanted, too, but things have changed."

"Now it's him?" he asked.

"I love him."

He scoffed, a harsh laugh coming out as he locked eyes with me. "When he's finished with you, don't come crawling to me," he spat.

With that he pushed past me, leaving me alone. I heaved a sigh and pulled out my phone to type a quick message to Gavin.

About to be sacked. There was a camera pointed right at us. I didn't see it.

After sending the message, I took a deep breath and walked down out into the lobby. Shannon's mouth dropped as she stared at me, but I didn't stop. I continued across the lobby, my head held high. Entering into the central offices, I made my way down to Phillip, the hotel manager's, office and knocked on the door.

"Please, come in, Emma," Miguel called.

"You wanted to see me?" I tried to play naïve, though I knew exactly why they were calling me. Based on my conversation with James, probably everyone knew.

I stepped inside and closed the door behind me. Miguel had a somber look on his face while Phillip scowled at me, his skin turning red.

"Emma, it has come to our attention that you have been engaging in conduct with a guest that is strictly prohibited," Miguel said, cutting to the chase.

"This is not a brothel, Miss Addison!" Phillip chided.

I flinched slightly at his words, and I was glad Miguel was with us as he had a level head.

I'd never really dealt with Phillip and only saw him in passing. Some hellos and goodnights, and the occasional conversation, but mostly he talked to Miguel, James, Valeria, and the other managers. He always had an air of superiority around him.

"Phillip, please," Miguel begged. He turned back to me. "Emma, we have evidence to back up speculation that you have been in a relationship with Mr. Grayson that goes against our policies. I know that you are aware that we have a policy against fraternization with current guests. As Phillip so crudely pointed out, this is a hotel, not a brothel. We cannot allow this to happen. We cannot gain a reputation that suggests that guests can call upon our staff to . . . service them. This policy was put in place to protect you, protect the guests, and, above all, protect the hotel."

"The legal ramifications . . . if someone even thought we allowed or encouraged this, the hotel could be shut down!" Phillip cried out again. He really didn't seem to know how to handle his anger very well. The few times I had interacted with him, he had been very brash and abrasive.

"Emma, is all that I have said true? Have you, against company policy, been in a relationship of a sexual nature with Mr. Grayson?"

I nodded. "Gavin Grayson and I are dating."

"It's not dating, Miss Addison. You are nothing but his hotel floozy! Don't you realize that once he is gone, he won't want you any longer?"

"It is not like that, sir," I argued.

"Of course it is like that! Do you honestly think you two will ride off into the sunset together? You are a hotel clerk, and he is the vice president of a multi-billion dollar company!"

It was a good thing Miguel was there as mediator, otherwise I think I might have punched Phillip. His crude words painted me as nothing but an idiot whore who thinks she's Cinderella.

"Phillip, please remain calm," Miguel said with a sigh. "I'm sorry to have to ask this, Emma, but has Mr. Grayson ever given you any type of . . . compensation?"

"My boyfriend has purchased me a few gifts, but they are far from 'compensation,'" I replied, trying not to let my disdain through.

Miguel nodded and sighed, his expression full of agony. "It pains me to say this, but Emma Addison, you are hereby terminated from employment with the Cameo Hotel. I'm sorry it had to end this way. You have truly been a great employee, but rules are in place for a reason."

I nodded. "I understand, Miguel."

"You have to be escorted off the premises," Phillip grumbled, his face still scrunched up.

Again, I nodded.

Miguel held the door open, my eyes catching his. "I'm sorry."

"It's okay," I said, even as I felt my eyes begin to water. It took every ounce of strength to maintain my composure.

Once out of the office area, Miguel took a position on one side of me, Phillip on the other. It seemed like most of the hotel staff on duty was in the lobby, watching. I felt all of them staring at me. Embarrassment flooded my face. I didn't like the attention, especially since I knew their thoughts were not favorable.

I kept my head down and tried to shut off the voices, the murmurs. The intricate tile work of the hotel's namesake came into my lowered view, which meant we were halfway across the lobby. Just outside the design there was a pair of highly polished black shoes and black slacks heading straight for me.

Electricity shot through me as a hand cupped my jaw and forced my head up. Gavin's beautifully different eyes stared back at me.

"Mr. Grayson?" Miguel started, but was cut off.

"Shut up," he said, his gaze never leaving mine. "Are you all right?"

I nodded as I fought the tears in my eyes. His thumb caressed my cheek before he leaned in and pressed his lips to mine.

"Come on," he said as he took my hand and headed toward the elevators, making me spin around to follow behind.

"Mr. Grayson, where are you taking her?" Phillip asked, clearly surprised.

"I'm taking my *girlfriend* upstairs where we will pack up my belongings and I will check out of this damn hotel. The *only* reason I am still here is Emma. That, and *we* are currently in escrow of *our* new home and closing is still weeks away."

There was a cacophony of gasps, the murmurs picking up. I looked over to the desk and found a shocked Shannon and a distraught James. Any last strings of hope he may have had, Gavin destroyed in a few seconds.

"So, if you would check me out and cancel my reservation, we will be gone." Phillip was in a panicked shock, his eyes wide as he kept trying to get a word in, but Gavin rolled right over him. "Also, I require the tape and any copies. If I do not receive them all and I find out down the line there was another copy, I want you to know I will then own this hotel as my lawyers will eat you for lunch before you are all fired."

"We need to escort Emma off of the premises, Mr. Grayson," Phillip argued.

"The only thing she *needs*, gentlemen, is for me to remind her how much I love, adore, worship, and need her. That is all that matters. Now, if you'll excuse us, we need to get home."

Miguel only looked at us and smiled. It was company policy, and I broke it, but by his look, he was happy to have Phillip proven wrong and put in his place.

As we stepped onto the elevator, Gavin pulled me against his chest, his arms protectively cocooning me.

"I want the tapes in thirty minutes," he said as the doors closed.

"Thank you," I said into his chest, my arms tightening around his waist.

"Their parade was completely unnecessary and uncalled for. What ever happened to discreet?" His jaw ticked.

"They were making me an example."

"It was a shitty example," he hissed. "I couldn't abide by their disrespect. Thankfully my timing couldn't have been more perfect. Now that blond guy will stop looking at you."

My brow scrunched. "James?"

"Yes. I've seen the way he looks at you."

"He has feelings for me," I said. There was nothing to hide about James, but I realized I'd never really told Gavin.

"I could tell. What about you?"

"I did, but then you came barreling into my life and gave me feelings I didn't know existed."

He smiled down at me and kissed my forehead. "I know exactly what you mean."

As Gavin opened the door to his room, the elevators opened and a very red-faced Phillip stepped out.

"Shit," I said as I pushed into the room. I wasn't sure what Phillip was capable of, especially away from prying eyes.

"Emma! Emma, get out here!" he yelled, but Gavin held his hand out, stopping Phillip from getting any farther.

"You have twenty-five minutes. One more than that, and I will own you. Do you understand?"

"It's not possible. You're just using your weight and money to manipulate me. She needs to go. Now."

I shook behind Gavin as I tried to understand why Phillip was so irate. Company policy dictated that I needed to be escorted out, but Phillip acted like he would drag me out if Gavin wasn't so intimidating.

"Twenty-three minutes. I know the president of Cameo. In fact, we're working together on a deal as we speak. I've had drinks with him twice this week. If I asked, he would not hesitate to fire you or sign this place over to me."

Phillip was vibrating in anger. "You don't scare me like you do them, Mr. Grayson."

Gavin leaned in closer, his eyes slits. "Twenty-one." Then he slammed the door in Phillip's face.

"Do you really know the president of Cameo International?" I asked as he pulled his suitcases from the closet.

"Yes."

"Would he really do all that?"

He tossed the large one onto the bed, then worked on opening his garment bag. "I use force, not lies. Richard Hayes is a good friend."

It took us about fifteen minutes of speed packing to get everything into his luggage. It helped that he was very tidy.

"You don't have anything in laundry, do you?"

"Besides my missing suit? No."

I rolled my eyes. Laundry never did find the suit that I paid for in a kinky way. "I think someone stole it so they could be closer to you."

"I can't convince you to move into another hotel with me, can I? We could get a bigger suite."

I smiled and shook my head. "It's unnecessary. I have an apartment, you just bought a place, so why do we need a third?"

"We could end your lease."

"My lease ends on August first. Let's just finish it and be cozy for a little while."

He smirked.

"What?"

He shook his head. "You're crone neighbor is going to love us. She'll probably come stomping up, banging on the door telling us to keep it down."

Gavin attached the garment bag to his suitcase, and we took one last look around.

"I'm going to miss this wall," he said.

"You are?" I asked, my brow quirked.

"Of course. It's where I first had you. I was hooked after that and knew I had to have you in my life."

I bit my lip and stepped forward, my arms wrapping around his waist. "I think it's sweet that you're sentimental over a wall."

"It's hard to say goodbye to this whole room." He sighed as he looked around one last time. "This is where I scrambled every day to find something to get you up here, just to see you. This is where *we* began."

I reached up and cupped his face, bringing it down to mine. "I love you," I said before pressing my lips to his.

We headed back to the lobby, and with each floor that passed I grew more anxious of what would be waiting for us when the doors opened. When the lobby came into view, there was no Phillip, but Miguel and James stood in the spot Gavin had pulled me from.

As we drew closer, Gavin looked down at his watch. "One minute."

Miguel held out his hand, and a thumb drive sat in his palm. "It's all here, Mr. Grayson."

"Where is your manager?" Gavin asked.

"We do not want this escalated, sir, so he is staying away," Miguel explained.

Gavin gave a nod. "Smartest thing he's done all day."

Miguel nodded. "Agreed. Also, here is your final folio. I've cancelled the rest of your reservation."

"Thank you."

"I cleaned out your locker," James said as he held out a shopping bag for me.

"Thank you," I said as I took the bag from him.

He turned away from me, his gaze locked on Gavin. "I hope you understand what you have."

"Undoubtedly," Gavin said.

With a last glance, we said goodbye to the first part of our story and took our first step to our future. Who knew what was ahead of us, but with each step we would be side by side.

19th Floor

I kept myself together on the way home. I had to, because I was driving. Gavin was in his own car. When we had parked, I held open the door into my building for him since he wouldn't let me help carry anything.

Once we got inside, I broke.

Sobs took over as rivers of tears streamed down my face. It felt like my whole body was splitting apart and falling to the ground. I couldn't remember ever having a reaction like that before. The whole situation was an overwhelming emotional experience that needed an outlet.

"Hey, hey." Gavin directed me to the couch where he sat and pulled me down onto his lap.

I cried into his shoulder as his hands made soothing strokes on my back and legs. I could manage nothing but tears against his suit as I clung to him with one arm.

"It's okay, baby," he whispered.

Was it? I'd just been fired in a horrific display by the hotel manager. Everyone had stared at me as I was being escorted out before Gavin got there. Then Phillip followed us upstairs. The things he said to me, about me . . . Thankfully Miguel was there, or I might have slapped the expression from his face.

At least with Miguel I knew he truly hated letting me go, but that was his job. Plus, once Phillip knew, there was no stopping my firing.

But what had he done or said when he'd gotten back to the lobby? What were people whispering about me? What awful things were they saying?

It took a while for me to stop sobbing, and nearly an hour to calm down.

Gavin wiped my tears away, his brow furrowed as he cared for me.

"I hate to see you like this," he said. "I feel so helpless."

"I can't believe I got fired. I mean, I can. What I did was wrong."

A growl vibrated in Gavin's chest and suddenly I was on my back, his arms slipping under my shoulders.

"Do you need me to say it again?" Gavin asked, hovering over me as his fingers toyed with my hair.

I nodded.

"You did absolutely nothing wrong. You know how I know?"

"How?"

"Because loving me isn't wrong. Yes, it was against their policies, but fuck them. I wasn't some John looking to get my rocks off and using you. I wanted you, and I went after you."

I nodded. "I know, but it still doesn't make it an easy pill to swallow. I've never been fired before."

"Everything will be fine, and you'll realize it was for the best."

"Yeah, but it's not going to help me find a job." I was pretty certain being fired was not a good thing for a resume.

"If you explain to them."

"Explain that I was fucking a guest?"

"Not crudely." He sighed. I knew my attitude was making it hard to talk to. "I was there for three months, Emma. Basically a resident."

He was right, in a way, and if I was asked, I'd find a way to explain it.

Once I was settled, Gavin changed into another suit; my tears and makeup were all over the one he was wearing.

"I hate to leave you," he said as he pulled on his jacket.

Me too, but I knew why he was leaving. It was late morning on Friday, and he had work to do. "It's okay."

"No, it's not. But I'm only going to go in for a few hours and wrap some things up for the weekend. I'll have my assistant cancel my afternoon appointments." He leaned down and pressed his lips to mine, drawing me up into his arms. "Let's go to dinner tonight. Your choice."

"There's a Ninety Nine not too far in Waltham."

"A what?"

"It's a restaurant. Huge menu. Casual."

He gave me a quick kiss as he reluctantly pulled away. "Perfect."

With the promise to be back soon, he left. It took me a little while before I was able to pick myself up off the couch and go change my clothes.

It all felt surreal, but it was the truth. For the first time in my life, I'd been fired.

All in the name of love, and it was a sacrifice I'd make again and again.

I sat on the couch in some jersey lounge pants, a tank top, and my hair in a messy, not cute, bun. Over the past three days, I'd binged almost three full seasons of The Walking Dead. People had raved about it for years, but I hadn't had cable or time.

Day four without a job, and I had plenty of time. The first few days were a mixture of miserable and relaxed. It was like a mini vacation, in a way. I spent the days binging Netflix and searching for jobs, and spent the nights with Gavin.

I was paused for a bathroom break when I heard the door open and Gavin stepped in.

"Welcome home." I loved saying that to him, even if our current home was my tiny-ass apartment. I reached up and pressed my lips to his. "How was your day?"

His gaze scanned down and then back up. "Fine. Yours?"

I shrugged as I headed back over to my nest. "Eh." I plopped back down in my spot and pulled my laptop onto my lap as I reached for the remote.

"If you're not careful, Netflix is going to tweet about this obsession," Gavin said.

I just shrugged. What did it matter? It kept my mind off losing my job, though the depression still sat there, waiting to strike.

Gavin sighed and suddenly, the TV was off.

"What?" I looked up to him.

Next, my laptop was gone from my lap and Gavin was looming over me, his hands resting on either side of my head, his brow furrowed.

"Enough. It's been three days, and wallowing in this feeling isn't going to make anything better," he said.

That got me going. I had to look away as tears filled my eyes.

He straightened out, then moved to the spot next to me, his hand resting on my knee. "I know you're depressed, but this isn't helping anything."

"What else am I supposed to do? I have no money and one task. No interviews and no calls. This is all I have."

"Then I have an idea. Something that will get you out of here for a little every day."

"Hmm? What's that?" I asked.

"Why don't you pick out furniture for the house?"

My brow scrunched. "Isn't that something we should do together? I was looking forward to shopping with you."

He nodded. "We can still do that, but we can make you the scouter and go together on the weekends. Money isn't really an issue, but there are four bedrooms and nearly five living spaces."

My eyes went wide. "Oh my God. I totally forgot that we'd need to furnish that whole place."

He chuckled and nodded. "There are a lot of rooms. Look at the pictures online, figure out any paint colors you want to change. You can go get paint swatches you like."

"I think you're just trying to keep me busy."

"Anything to keep you upbeat and positive," he said, then took my hand in his, our fingers intertwining. "Look at what we have, not at what you lost."

He was right, and it wasn't a bad idea, especially when shopping for so much. It wasn't just furniture, but a whole house that was ours. I would live in it with the man I loved. Maybe for once it was okay to not do everything on my own. After all, we were a couple, a partnership.

"One thing . . . that suitcase can't be all of your stuff."

He chuckled. "No. It's in storage, waiting for the house."

"So you have furniture?"

He nodded. "My assistant in New York took photos of everything before they loaded it up. I'll send them to you. I'm not attached to any of it. If you like it, we'll keep it. If you don't, it goes."

I gave him a small smile. It was a combination of the depression and the happiness that came with thinking about our home.

"Are you going to want to take any of this furniture to the house?" he asked, patting the sofa.

My gaze bounced around the items in the room. It was all secondhand stuff off Facebook Marketplace and Craigslist. The bookshelf was cheap, the shelves bending from the weight of my books. There was a cover on the couch, and I couldn't even remember what the print underneath was.

The dining room set was a simple, rectangular table with four chairs. In the bedroom, the bed was a cheap mattress with a memory foam topper to make it somewhat comfortable and a cheap frame.

The apartment was just a place to study and sleep. I didn't do much else there.

"Maybe a lamp or two, and that's about it," I said. "Oh, and the TV." That had been my one splurge over the years, besides my laptop. I'd been one of those Black Friday stalkers a few years back.

"Then you have a lot to shop for. Take lots of pictures and send me stuff you like and where you are."

I nodded and started making a mental list. "There's so much . . ." Excitement coursed through me, and a genuine smile formed on my face. "Let's make a list. Together."

"That sounds like a great idea."

I grabbed one of my leftover notebooks and a pen and had Gavin pull the house up. We ended up ordering food as we went through each room, talking about what pieces we needed.

In the end, he pulled me out of it. Gavin was right. Looking to our future was so much better than wallowing in the past.

20th Floor

Gavin

Soothing Emma was second nature. I held her in my arms, her body shaking as tears streamed down her face. Losing her job hit hard. While she grieved, I stewed in a quiet anger. It was my actions, my affections that had created the situation that were the grounds of her termination.

I had sacrificed her job to have her, and I would do it again.

But that man . . . The hotel manager would be fired within a week. I was going to make sure of it. I wanted to rip his face off. Maybe slam the fat bastard into something. The anger that consumed me when I saw the man, saw how he treated her. A man I had not seen in *months*.

My threat would not be empty, nor glossed over simply because I had the recording. My instructions were followed, but they weren't followed by him, and I intended to carry out my word. *He* was not there to deliver it. While I commended Miguel, whom I considered the true manager of the hotel, for his decision, I still couldn't let what Phillip did stand.

We shopped for groceries on Saturday, stocking up for Emma being home all week. I refused to let her pay for anything. She didn't have much money, and it was the least I could do.

When we entered her building, her downstairs neighbor was standing her doorway. She was older, curlers in her hair, wearing what appeared to be a small circus tent. A little yippy dog sat at her feet. The woman had chastised me in the past, which only made me want to piss her off.

"Good morning, Mrs. Carrow," Emma said, plastering a fake smile on her face. She was always trying to be pleasant.

"Harlot!" the crone yelled.

My jaw ticked as I narrowed my eyes at her. The woman was insufferable.

Emma stopped mid-step and turned back to her. "Excuse me?"

"You have men going in and out of your apartment all the time," she sneered.

What? A chill ran through me at her words, settling in the pit of my stomach.

"I think you need to get your eyes checked, Mrs. Carrow, because there is only one man."

I followed Emma the rest of the way up, but I couldn't shake the darkness that flooded in. What I hated most was the doubt.

"Ugh. I can't believe her. She was calling me a whore!" Emma seethed as she dropped the bags onto the counter.

"Don't worry about her," I said, though it was strained. I reached up and massaged my temples. Part of me wanted to ask her what the fuck the old woman was talking about. The other part reminded me that I trusted Emma.

"Gavin?" Emma walked up to me and rubbed her hands up my arms to my chest. "What's wrong, baby?"

It was warm, soothing, but something stung. My eyes snapped open. "I just have a headache. I think I'm going to go lie down."

"Oh, okay." She stood on her toes and cupped my face, pulling me down until her lips pressed against my forehead. "Feel better."

I nodded before heading to the bedroom, closing the door behind me. After pulling off my sweater and kicking off my shoes, I fell onto the bed.

I was used to Emma's crone of a downstairs neighbor, but her accusation . . . I knew it wasn't true, but it still hit me wrong. I stretched my neck, trying to loosen the growing tension.

I had told Emma I had a headache, but instead I stared up at the ceiling, questioning what she said. The woman was old, senile, but was there something to her words? Was there someone else Emma was seeing?

"Stop being ridiculous," I chastised myself.

Emma had never given me any indication that she wasn't as deliriously happy as I was, but still . . . doubts crept in. When my ex-wife had been cheating on me, we were barely speaking. That should have been my first indication something was wrong, but I let her make a fool out of me.

Emma liked the attention, the gifts, but she never expected them. Levelheaded and grounded, she was everything my socialite ex-wife wasn't. Emma was also independent—a trait I both loved and hated.

I hated my reaction.

I loved Emma. I was happy with her. The truth was, there was still a lot I didn't know about her.

Perhaps it was strange to say that I didn't know her and I loved her in nearly the same thought, but there was always the doubt in the back of my mind.

What if she was just like Katrina? When I met my ex-wife, she was similar to Emma—strong willed. I always had to remind myself of their difference. Katrina always asked for me to buy her things, while Emma graciously accepted gifts with honest surprise. Never once did she ask for anything but my time.

It was an unfair comparison, but it was what I had been left with when the divorce was finalized.

The doubts, the darkness, ate at me. It was a distrust I didn't want to have, a leftover from a scar so deep I never dealt with it. That alone was why I'd never dated after my divorce, the entire reason I was such an asshole to Emma in the beginning.

One look from her, and I was hooked.

"Of all the women in all the places . . ." I whispered with a small chuckle.

Emma wasn't Katrina. She was caring and kind and intelligent.

When I felt I had a handle on my emotions, I stepped out of the bedroom.

"What's that smell?" I asked.

Emma set her phone down and jumped up from the couch. "I made you cookies."

I blinked at her in surprise. How long was I in there? "You made me cookies?"

I followed her into the dining room, and to the cookies that were cooling on a rack in the center of the table.

"Yeah, I thought . . . I don't know, that it might help you feel better?" she said, though it sounded more like a question. "Silly, I know, making cookies for a headache."

"My mom used to always bake me cookies when I was down or sick," I revealed before I bit into one.

The flavor burst on my tongue, a flash of memories, feelings, and family. Home—that was what the cookies represented. I hummed from the chocolate that was still melty goodness, then reached out to brush my fingers against her cheek. My Emma. She didn't know the dichotomy that brewed inside me. The desire for all of her, while my past experience sowed doubt.

I leaned down and pressed my lips against hers. "Thank you, baby."

She smiled up at me, her fingers slipping between mine. "You're welcome."

The warmth was Emma, not the cold—something I needed to remember. More than once I let the anger gain control, and it was an emotion she didn't deserve.

We spent the rest of the day surfing Netflix with a plate of cookies between us, and then nothing between us at all.

Emma's deteriorating mood over the following week only served to flare the hatred I had for Phillip. By the end of the week, I had the president of Cameo International on the phone. My threats were not hollow things, and that pig of a manger was going to find that out first hand.

"Gavin, how are you this fine morning?" Richard said as he answered.

"Good. How are you?"

"Can't complain. I spent the weekend babysitting my granddaughter." I could hear the happiness in his voice.

"How is she?"

"Absolutely adorable. I'll shoot you over a photo later. She looks just like Everly, but with her father's eyes."

"I can't wait to see as soon as I get you off the phone."

He chuckled. "What can I do for you?"

"You know how vindictive I can be?" I stared at my computer, at the calendar and my meetings list for the day.

There was a chuckle on the other end. "Are you calling to complain about your stay?"

A small laugh left me. "One person. The manager. I believe his name was Phillip."

"Phillip? Really? What happened?" he asked. He seemed concerned, but not unresponsive to the idea.

Time to end a career. "Remember how I told you about my girlfriend, Emma?"

"The reception supervisor."

"She was fired last week for her relationship with me," I said. "And before you start in on your spiel about company policy and such, I'm not calling to ask for her job back."

"You want Phillip gone," he said. "Why?"

Because he deserved what was coming to him.

"What he did was unacceptable. The things he said to her, about her, about me. He chased us to my room, Richard. He was wild, acting like he wanted to drag her out by her hair and throw her into the street," I hissed. Blood pumped through my veins at an increased speed as my anger rose.

"That is not how he should have handled the situation at all," Richard said. "I don't like that he's representing our company that way."

"I was there for three months, and I never saw him." I'd never even heard his name. "All of my complaining, never a word. Not exactly a manger's response."

There was a humming sound on the other end. In the years I'd known Richard, I knew that meant he was mulling over the information I'd given him. "Well, that's interesting."

"I thought Miguel was the manager," I said, initiating part B of my plan. "He is *a* manager, but not the overall hotel manager. He and I spoke many times, and I was very impressed with him." Miguel was also highly regarded by Emma.

"But not impressed enough to stop being a nuisance," Richard said with a chuckle.

"All to keep up my pretense."

"All so you could have one of my employees."

"An employee I plan to keep."

"Good," he said. "I'll get some information on the hotel and Phillip, then remove him by the end of the weekend and have Miguel take over."

"You read my mind. Lunch next week?" I asked. "You can fill me in on how it went. I want all the details."

"Sounds good. Have your assistant set it up."

"Thank you for your help."

There was a deep chuckle. "You're a good man, Gavin, but I would never want to be on the receiving end of your anger."

I couldn't help but smile. "Have a good day."

As I hung up, one part of my plan was done, and I pushed away from my desk for the second part. For my lunch break, I had set up an appointment for a very special reason.

"Welcome back to *Tiffany*, Mr. Grayson. What can we help you with today?" Jeremy, the sales manager, asked as I stepped up to the counter.

"I'm looking for an engagement ring," I said.

Maybe I was being rash, but I'd never felt so strongly about anything in my life. I wanted Emma to be mine forever. Months were all it took for her to open my heart up and completely consume it. Even with how my last marriage ended, I wanted Emma as my wife.

21st Floor

A few days had passed, and I was feeling better. I was still curled up watching Netflix, but with my laptop in my lap as I researched furniture stores. I was making a list of stores to visit, looking at their reviews and quality as I narrowed it down. Gavin had said money wasn't something to worry about, so I tried to curb my discount ways to look for the higher-end furniture that would suit our very expensive home.

Just as I scratched a name off my list, noting beside it the lack of quality, my phone rang. It'd been silent for days, and when I looked at my phone, it wasn't a number I recognized.

I hit the green button to answer. "Hello?"

"Hi, may I please speak with Emma?"

"This is she."

"Hi, Emma, my name is Amy from the HR department of the Cates Corporation, and I'm calling about your resume."

I sat straight up, my hand frantically maneuvering the remote to pause the show. Inside I was freaking out because I knew they were calling for an interview.

"Yes, hello, so good to hear from you." I tried to sound casual and hide my excitement.

"We wanted to see if we could set up a time for you to come in for an interview," she said.

"I am available whenever you are."

There was a pause. "Hmm . . . it looks like the hiring manager has an opening tomorrow at one."

I wasted no time in agreeing. "I'll take it."

"Oh, wait, I'm sorry, that's today."

"I'll still take it if it's available." I glanced at the clock. It gave me just over an hour to get ready.

"Hold on a moment, let me check with her."

While on hold, I stood up and ran to my room, shifting through my closet for something to wear. Unfortunately, my suits for Cameo really were the best interview attire I had.

"Emma?" Amy's voice came back on the line.

"Here."

"She said that was fine. Do you know where we are?"

"Yes."

"Okay. When you get here, go up to the eighteenth floor. I'll be waiting to take you to her."

"Thank you so much. I'll see you soon."

"See you."

I hung up, was naked, and in the shower in less than thirty seconds. I didn't even let the water warm up before I started scrubbing. Luckily my hair didn't need to be washed, but it did need to be dried and styled. That alone would take thirty minutes.

"Shit," I hissed, suddenly regretting getting my hair wet.

Too late to worry about it.

An hour of drying and primping, and I was out of time. One last look, and I headed out.

When I arrived at the building, I waited for the elevators, which were crowded with everyone coming back from their lunch breaks. I hoped I wouldn't run into Gavin, so I kept a sharp eye out. When I got to the eighteenth floor, a short brunette was waiting in front of a reception desk with the Cates Corporation logo behind her. She smiled as I stepped forward.

"Emma?"

"Amy?"

She nodded, then gestured back to the elevators. "We need to go up to twenty."

Another elevator ride, then through an ID-locked glass door and into what I could best describe as a cube farm. Row after row of cubes filled the space, the outer wall lined by individual offices. We stopped in front of one, and Amy knocked.

"I have your one o'clock," she said.

"Thanks, Amy."

"Good luck," Amy said before moving aside to let me in, then closing the door behind me.

A beautiful blonde walked around her desk and held out her hand. "Hi, I'm Julianne Landon."

I took her hand and smiled. "Pleased to meet you. Emma Addison."

"Are you nervous?" she asked as she sat down and motioned to the chair opposite her.

I let out a small chuckle. "I'd be lying if I said no."

She smiled at me. "Good answer. Okay, so let's see. You have a BA in accounting and an MBA, but you've never worked in finance or accounting?"

I nodded. "That's correct. In order to be able to go to school and have a place to live, I had to keep a job that paid more. Most of what I was finding in my field was unpaid full-time internships. I know this hurts my experience."

"Some things experience can't teach you. Like sensibility. You took the economically rational route. I see that as a path." She looked back down to the stack of papers in front of her. "I see here you work at the Cameo Hotel. Tell me about that," Julianne requested.

I squirmed in my seat, my lips forming a thin line. "Well, as of a few days ago, I am no longer employed with the Cameo Hotel."

Her brows shot up in surprise. "Okay, could you please elaborate for me?"

"I was . . . let go."

She nodded. "Fired?"

"Fired," I relented.

"All right," she began, giving a small sigh before leaning forward, her arms crossing on the table. "By the look on your face, I have to hear this story."

"My boyfriend was a guest there."

Her brow scrunched. "So?"

"Well, he'd been staying there for a while, and that is where I met him," I explained. "Fraternization between current guests and employees is prohibited."

"Fraternization, huh?" She smirked at me. "Well, that's not an issue here unless one of the parties is a direct superior."

I laughed with her, partially at my secret.

"Besides your relationship with a guest, tell me what you did."

I went into my past with the hotel, my grades, my work ethic, and so many more questions. Before I knew it, an hour had passed.

"Oh, shoot, it's already two," Julianne said suddenly. "I am so sorry. I'm going to have to cut this short, though it was actually quite long."

"No problem." I was a bit stunned by the abruptness.

"I really am sorry." She stood and grabbed a stack of files and waved at me to follow her. "I have a financial meeting with the vice president in two minutes, and he really doesn't appreciate lateness."

"I completely understand." She had no idea how much I understood how demanding Gavin was.

We walked back through the cube farm to the elevators. "Thank you so much for coming today. I really enjoyed talking with you, Emma."

"Thank you so much for seeing me today."

"Oh, one last thing. I'm looking to have all the interviews done by the end of the week."

"Hopefully I'll hear from you."

I decided I wasn't going to tell Gavin about the interview. If I got the position, it was going to be because I earned it.

An hour after I returned home, I heard the key in the door before it popped open. Voices flooded up from down the stairs. Mrs. Carrow was once again complaining. I jumped up to meet Gavin at the doorway.

"I don't care, woman! Go back into your home," Gavin grumbled as he stepped in.

A giggled slipped out. "Hey, love stud."

Gavin's frown twitched up into a lopsided smile. "I'm about to throw you on that bed and show you my studliness."

"Just to rile her up more?" I asked as I stood and wrapped my arms around his shoulders to pull him closer. "Hi."

"Hi." He leaned forward and pressed his lips to mine, igniting the fire that burned every time he was close.

"How was your day?" I asked as I reluctantly pulled away.

"Productive. Yours? Any new interviews?"

"No. I did apply for a few more positions," I lied as I heaved a sigh. It was a small lie, just until I heard something. "I stayed at the hotel because it paid the bills, but it may have hurt me in the long run."

"Emma, all you have to do is—"

I pressed his lips shut with my fingers. "Don't finish that sentence. I love you, Gavin, but I need to do this on my own."

He leaned forward and pushed his lips that were still trapped by my fingers against my own. It made me laugh and let go.

"I love that you are independent, even though it drives me crazy sometimes."

"What? You want to swoop in and save me?" I asked.

"Yes." He nodded. "Isn't that what all knights do? Save the damsel in distress?"

I shook my head. "You get brownie points for the sentiment."

"I think I can deal with that, but can I add something to it?"

I tilted my head. "What?"

His eyes locked onto mine. "If you don't find anything by the time we move out of here, you let me help."

We still had a month, and it worried me that I might not be able to do it on my own with the previous experience requirement many companies were looking for. It was hard to do, but with a sigh, I agreed.

"Okay."

"I just want you happy, baby." He ran his hands up and down my back as he held me close. "And every day you're stuck in this tiny apartment, I see you get more and more down."

"I know. It doesn't help that I've got some weird depression from being fired. I've never been fired before, and it hurts more than I thought it would." It stung a lot, even though I knew I broke the rules and that what they did was what they should have done.

"You gave them many good years. Put up with assholes like me. Then you had to go and fall for my nefarious advances."

I quirked a brow at him. "Nefarious?"

"Yes. Didn't you know it was all some evil plot to get some extra-special, happy-ending service? I was just going to leave after that," he joked.

I smacked his chest and glared at him. "Not funny."

"No, but that is what the men who fired you thought. And instead, here I am, sharing this tiny, dingy apartment with you instead of living the life of luxury, having fun making their lives miserable."

"You're horrible."

"I get what I want," he said. It took no effort for those few words to exude every bit of confidence the man had.

I tilted my head as I looked up at him. "What if I didn't fall for you? I mean, you were very mean to me."

"You would have, because you can't help it."

"Why is that?"

The back of his fingers lightly caressed my cheek. "Because soulmates are drawn to each other. We may fight against it, try and disbelieve it, but you can't win against it."

"Soulmates? You think?"

"I know."

His lips were soft against mine, sensual. There was no rush when his lips parted, his tongue lapping against mine. Low moans, slow gropes, and his hard length pressed against me.

"You know," I said as I pulled back. "I love the take-your-time sex, but I have to admit, sometimes I miss the quickies."

"The quickies?"

I pinched my bottom lip between my teeth while I ran his tie between my fingers. "When I would come into your room and you would bend me over and fuck me like your life depended on it."

"Are you suggesting I've gone soft?"

"Soft? Not at all." I shook my head and looked up at him through my lashes.

His eyes darkened as his hands moved to my waist. "According to your neighbor, I've been fucking you pretty hard."

"And you do. But there's a difference between taking our time and the desperation you had to get inside me."

"Ms. Addison, do you not feel desired? Is that what you're saying?"

I shook my head. "What I'm saying, Mr. Grayson, is I want you to bend me over the couch, pull my pants down, pull your cock out, and *fuck me*."

A growl left him as he spun me around. He pushed hard on my back, forcing me over with one hand while the other yanked at my waistband.

It was exactly what I wanted, what I needed. That primal energy.

I barely heard his zipper before he slammed into me, filling me.

I cried out, my eyes rolling back as every nerve exploded. He pulled out, then thrust back in, bottoming out. Another loud moan crawled out of me. Only two thrusts, and I was on edge.

His hand wound in my hair, then pulled back, his breath hot against my ear. "Is this what you wanted, Emma?"

"Yes," I cried as he pulled out again and began a hard, steady pace.

Every thought left me, consumed by the pleasure of each thrust. I was lost, completely drunk on him.

"Fuck, baby," he groaned. "So tight, so fucking wet."

Every muscle tightened with each hit, and a whimpering sound filled my ears, turning into a high-pitched cry. I was shaking, spasms wracking my body, and I was barely able to hold myself up as my orgasm washed through me.

"Baby . . . fuck, baby." He continued on as I rode it out, my walls pulsing around him. "Shit," he hissed. He released my hair and pulled out.

Grunts and groans filled the air, sending shivers through me. Warm droplets fell against my skin, a few shooting up into my hair.

Harsh breaths sounded behind me, but I didn't have the strength to look back at him. The sudden sting of his hand against my ass made me jump.

"Feel better?"

A smile formed on my face as I nodded. "Yes, sir. Very much."

The weekend came and went, and I continued on my furniture quest. By Wednesday I was losing hope that Cates would call back, but at just after five, my phone rang.

"Hello?"

"Emma?"

"Yes?"

"Hi, this is Amy from Cates."

My heart slammed in my chest, eyes wide. "Hi, Amy!" I said a little too cheerfully.

"I am calling because you made a good impression on Julianne, and she would like you to come join her team."

It felt like I was on cloud nine. I was so excited that tears pooled in my eyes.

"Oh my God, that is so great."

"It pays sixty-five thousand dollars a year, with full benefits after thirty days, including two weeks of vacation."

I nearly choked, frozen as the amount sunk in. In my position at the hotel, I made pretty good money, but I could actually do things with the extra fifteen grand Cates paid.

"Emma?"

"Yes. Here. Sorry. Where do I sign?"

There was a chuckle on the other line. "Can you come down Friday afternoon to fill out some paperwork? She'd like you to start on Monday, if that's possible."

"Definitely. I would love to start Monday. Thank you so much, Amy."

"Welcome to the Cates Corporation. See you soon!"

"Thank you!" My hands were shaking as I hit the button to end the call.

I had a job. I had a job at Gavin's company, and I had done it without his help.

I began bounding around the room, unable to contain my jubilation. The handle to the door jiggled, and in stepped Gavin.

"Baby, I'm home," he called out. His eyes widened when he took me in his sight. "Hello, madwoman, have you seen my girlfriend around? Looks a bit like you, only she's been a bit sulky lately."

"I got a job!" I cried out.

A smile broke out on his face as he rushed forward and scooped me up in his arms, his lips crashing to mine. "I'm so happy for you, baby. Where at?"

I bit my lip and studied his expression, a bit unsure of his reaction. "Cates Corporation."

He blinked at me for a moment. "You applied at Cates?" he asked. I nodded in response. His expression became somewhat hurt. "You applied at Cates and didn't tell me? Why?"

I sighed. "Because I know how you are, Gavin. You like to throw your weight around, and I wanted to get this job because *I* deserved it, not because I'm the vice president's girlfriend."

He mulled that over for a moment and nodded. "Solid point. I can very much understand and appreciate that."

My brow hitched. "You do, do you?"

"You worked hard for it. You deserve it." He leaned down to press his lips to mine. "And you are correct in thinking that I would have thrown my weight around if you had told me."

"I'm getting to understand you a great deal, Mr. Grayson."

"How should we celebrate this momentous occasion?"

"Ninety Nine?"

He shook his head. "You love that place."

"Duh! Buffalo dip."

He nodded. "Buffalo dip."

"I've been craving it for a week."

We moved into the bedroom to change clothes. Another reason to go to Ninety Nine was Gavin in jeans. It was a place we could relax.

"Can we . . . keep us on the down low for a few weeks?" I asked as I stripped out of my shorts and tank.

He quirked a brow. "The 'down low,' Emma? Why ever for?"

"I want to come across as a credible hire."

With his suit hung up, he worked on undoing the buttons. It made me wish I'd asked for a strip tease.

"But I didn't help," he argued.

"I know that, you know that, but they don't know that."

"Then tell them."

I shook my head. "They won't believe me."

"I'm tired of creeping around, hiding my love for you," he said with a sigh.

After pulling on some jeans, I stepped over to him and wrapped my arms around his waist. "Just a few weeks to prove myself. Please, Gavin?" I begged, reaching up to kiss down the length of his jaw.

He let out a hum in response. "A few weeks. Then I'm sending out a company announcement."

I sat back with wide eyes. No, he wouldn't.

His face was completely serious before a smile cracked, breaking out into full out laughing. I swatted his arm. "Not funny!"

"So funny."

I shook my head. "Not."

"Yes."

"No!"

"Si!"

"No, no, no!" I cried.

Suddenly he grabbed my waist and backed me up until I fell onto the bed with him hovering above me, pinning my arms above my head.

I gasped at the look in his eyes, my whole body lighting up, bursting into flames. "Hello, Mr. Grayson."

"Emma, you're being naughty."

I smiled. "Yes, sir."

He dipped down and took my exposed nipple into his mouth. I drew in a breath, my back arching.

"Naughty girls get punished."

I moaned. "Yes, sir."

My stomach chose that moment to rumble, breaking up our sexually charged moment.

A huge sigh left him. "But first, food."

With great reluctance, he pulled away and we continued getting dressed. I couldn't help loving the routine we'd fallen into as a couple.

Even though the space was tight, I loved living with him.

22nd Floor

On Saturday morning I sat at the table with a notebook, coffee, and a plate of eggs with turkey bacon. I'd already checked my bank account, and my last check was in. It was for a whole pay period, but still, it was all the money I had for probably another month, and I had to make it stretch.

"What are you doing?" Gavin asked when he saw me. He headed straight for the coffee pot and the plate I'd made for him.

How did he still look so incredibly hot wearing pajama bottoms and an undershirt? Even his hair was a mess, and all I wanted to do was jump him.

I cleared my throat and took another sip from my mug. "With my first day on Monday, I need to make sure I'm ready."

"Ready how?"

I tapped the pen on the paper. "That's what the list is for. I need clothes, maybe some shoes." I wracked my brain, trying to figure out what I needed.

Five items made up the list: slacks, light sweaters, dress shirts, cardigan, heels?

Heels were questionable. I had a few pairs, but they had some good miles on them thanks to the hotel. They weren't in bad shape, but they were definitely beginning to show their age.

A few hours later we found ourselves in the women's department of Macy's. While I was happily plucking possibilities from racks, Gavin was grumbling.

"Why are we at the clearance rack?" Gavin asked.

"Because you can find great things at a great price," I said as I pulled two shirts from the rack and threw them over my arm.

"Don't worry about the price."

"Yes. You may have paid the rent, but Friday was my last check and that's all I have for probably four more weeks."

The dress code for my position was business casual and didn't require the skirt suits I wore at the hotel. Thus, I was having a major wardrobe emergency.

"Ooh, cardigan." It would probably be chilly at times and for seven dollars, it would help.

"I'm going to pay for your clothes," Gavin said. "You don't have to resign yourself to clearance."

I shook my head as I moved to a rack full of pants. "I'm not resigning myself to anything. There is nothing wrong with any of this stuff. It's a great deal. And no, you're not paying."

"Yes, I am."

"No." I locked eyes with him. His jaw was locked.

"Half."

If I continued on, we were going to blow up into a full-fledged argument over something stupid. Him paying half was a compromise we both could live with.

"Half," I agreed.

"I never give in to anyone."

"You just did to me. Even if it was a compromise."

"Do I get a reward?"

"Maybe if you're good, we can come to an arrangement in the dressing room," I said with a wink.

His brow shot up, and he gave an approving nod.

I took a deep breath as I looked in the mirror. Time was running low, and I was getting nervous.

"How do I look?" I asked as I stepped out of the bathroom. Gavin was still working his cuff links when he looked up.

A smile grew on his face. "Beautiful, as always, and perfect for your first day."

"Thank you." I reached up and gave him a peck on the lips, careful not to mess up my lipstick. "And thank you for your help shopping."

"You're more than welcome, though I wish you'd have let me buy you more."

"I let you pay half." I knew he wasn't happy about that.

"Yes, well, it is my fault you needed them."

"I was going to need them anyway," I pointed out.

He pulled his jacket on and straightened the collar. "You won't let me win this one, will you?"

"No, Mr. Grayson. It's called compromise. Get used to it because you don't always get your way."

He stepped forward and smacked my ass before grabbing it with both hands. "I'll just take my frustration out on you later."

Heat spread through my cheeks, and I bit down on my lower lip. "Promises, promises. Now come on. I don't want to be late."

Our cars were parked a few spots from each other and I could hear him grumbling, the muscles in his jaw tightening. He'd also lost the fight about driving together.

It was a traffic-filled drive, but not too bad. When we pulled into the parking garage, Gavin followed me to a spot instead of taking his reserved spot near the door.

He came around his car and pulled me close, his arms wrapped tightly around me. "I don't like not driving with you. We're going to the same place. This is ridiculous."

It was, but it was necessary. I understood why he was against hiding our relationship, and I agreed, but I didn't want to start out with whispers about getting the job because I was fucking the boss. Especially not after how I was fired from my last job because I was fucking him.

"We are, but give it a few weeks and we can go together."

"Fine, but I still don't like it," he grumbled.

My eyes widened as I looked at him. His bottom lip was jutted forward, his lips downturned. "Are . . . are you pouting?"

He pressed his lips together, removing the pout. "No."

"Oh my God, you are!"

He shook his head. "Good luck," he said with one last kiss before we separated.

It was hard to pull away from him, but I did. I stepped out from between the cars, and Gavin followed about ten steps behind. All I wanted to do was turn around and smile at him, to show him how excited I was, but I couldn't.

The elevator ride up to the lobby was excruciating and jammed with people. His fingers brushed against mine, and I linked my pinky with his.

Upon entering the lobby, I spotted Julianne in the distance near the elevators. The closer I got, the more Gavin began to slowly move to the side.

"Emma, welcome," Julianne said with a smile.

"Good morning." I couldn't keep the returning smile from my face if I tried.

"Good morning, Gavin," she called out.

"Good morning, Julianne," he said as he glanced at me, then continued on.

"How are you this morning?" she asked. "Ready for your first day?"

I blew out a breath. "Nervous and excited probably describes it best."

"Well, let's get going. Lots to acquaint you with."

We headed to the elevator bay where Gavin was waiting. When the doors opened, around ten waiting people crammed in. I ended up right in front of Gavin in an overcrowded car. It was an opportunity he took to touch me, his hand resting on my hip, his thumb caressing.

"How are the monthly figures coming?" he asked.

His voice near my ear shocked me, making me jump a little.

"I will have them for you this afternoon," Julianne replied before gesturing to me. "As soon as I get Emma here set up, I'll finish them."

"Good," he said. "I have a meeting at three with Tom."

"You'll have them by two." The elevator doors opened, and Julianne gestured to it. "This is us."

Gavin gave a quick squeeze to my hip before I stepped away from him. I couldn't help but glance back as I stepped out, and our eyes locked.

"That was our VP, Gavin Grayson," Julianne said as we walked down the hall. "Don't take any offense to him not introducing himself. That's just how he is."

"Rude?" I asked, trying to play it off. It didn't surprise me, knowing him.

That got her to let out a small laugh. "That's one way to describe him. Brilliant business man, great with customers, but he lacks some finer finesse with . . ."

"The worker bees?"

"Ah, you got it again."

After a trip to HR to get my ID and fill out paperwork, we headed up to the twentieth floor. For the first hour, I went over a training manual and an overview of what I would be doing before she took me to whomever I would be shadowing.

"This is Josh. He'll be the one training you today."

"Hi," I said as I held out my hand.

"Hey." Josh had a soft smile and the most brilliant pair of blue eyes framed by a pair of chunky black eyeglasses.

"I'll connect with you later," Julianne said as she stepped away. "I have IT coming to set everything up. With the short notice, they are a bit behind, but Josh will be able to start showing you were things are."

"Thank you."

She smiled at me, then headed off toward her office.

"Ready to learn?"

I nodded. "Oh, yeah."

After a few hours my brain was bleeding with all the new information. I was exhausted, scared, freaking out, and wondering what I'd gotten myself into. It all seemed so foreign, but I had to remind myself that it was just because everything was new to me.

"Do you want to go to lunch?" Josh asked just before noon.

I nodded, greatly appreciative of the break. "Sure. I'm not really familiar with what's around here." While we were downtown, the Cameo was over a mile away and everything was different.

"There's a lot of great places, tons. Sandwich shops, Italian, American, bars, Chinese, Thai . . . really, just about anything."

"Any good salads? I think I've been emotional eating too much lately."

He chuckled. "There's a place in the building across that makes your salad right there. Loads of ingredients."

"Perfect."

There were so many ingredients that I had a hard time choosing, so I had them throw in just about every vegetable they had and topped it with a raspberry vinaigrette.

"How is your first day going?" Josh asked as we sat down.

"Overwhelming. I'm not sure my degrees prepared me for practical use."

He let out a chuckle. "You'll see it more later, once you get the hang of things."

"Thank you so much for helping me today."

"No problem. I'm the resident training guru. Julianne always has me show people the ropes."

"That just proves how good you are at your job." Not only was he friendly, but I could tell as he showed me things just how good he was at training. He wasn't getting irritated that I was interrupting his workload and happily answered all my questions.

"Thanks," he said with a grin.

I took a couple bites of my salad, loving all the toppings I'd chosen, especially the dried cranberries for the hit of sweetness. "How long have you worked for Cates?"

He finished his bite before replying. "Six years."

"You must like it."

He nodded. "The company is great. One of the few that knows their employees work better and harder if they feel appreciated and compensated."

"That's really good to know."

"Where did you work before?" he asked.

"I worked over at the Cameo Hotel. I was a reception supervisor," I said, hoping he wouldn't ask why I left.

"Oh, wow, that place is swanky. My wife and I looked into getting married there, but it cost too much."

It felt like I'd eaten a ton, but my salad was only half gone. "How long have you been married?"

"Three years. We just had a baby girl, April, three months ago," he said as he pulled his phone out of his pocket.

On the screen was a chubby, smiling, pink-covered little girl. "Aw, she's so adorable!"

My heart melted at the sweet sight. Maybe one day Gavin and I would have that.

We returned to work shortly thereafter. The rest of the day continued on with more head-splitting knowledge. I'd written pages and pages of notes and only hoped I'd be able to decipher them. I knew I greatly slowed down his work speed, but he didn't seem to mind it or my millions of questions.

"How was your first day?" Gavin asked when we got home.

"Great. Tiring, though." I kicked off my shoes and pulled my shirt off. I was more than ready to get into some vegetating clothes and become a bump on the couch with a takeout container in my lap. "Julianne was great. Josh was amazing."

"Who's Josh?" Gavin asked, his brow furrowed.

"Don't you know your staff?"

"There's a lot of people. Tell me about him."

"We went to lunch, and he couldn't stop talking about his wife and new baby. She was soooo adorable."

"Hmm," was all he said, his lips pursed.

"You're not jealous, are you?" I asked, fighting a smile.

"We just left a place where there was a man who thought you were his, and now you're crammed in a cubicle with another man."

I rolled my eyes. "A married man. And you're the one who stole me away, remember?"

"Yes, because there's one thing they all need to know," he said as he wrapped his arms around me and pulled me close.

"What's that?"

"You're all mine."

I smiled up at him and squeezed him closer. "All yours."

The days got better, and my fears and insecurities began to slip away. By the end of the week, my computer was up and running and I had my own accounts. There were still thousands of questions, but at least I felt like I was actually doing work.

"What's the grand plan for the weekend?" Josh asked as he helped me with trying to figure out a discrepancy between a bank statement and the corresponding general ledger.

"Going furniture shopping with my boyfriend. You?"

I was looking forward to the weekend with Gavin, relaxing. We'd planned to do some furniture shopping based off the stores I'd selected.

"Sounds like fun. I'll be taking my lovely ladies to the beach."

"It's warming up."

"You should come. Does your boyfriend like the beach?"

I shook my head. "Not the cold ones."

While it sounded like fun, I couldn't exactly accept the invitation. At least not until we came out to the company. Only a few more weeks. By then, we would close on the house, which meant I'd have to update my address with HR.

"I'm going to go get some more coffee," I said with a yawn. "Want one?"

"No, thanks. I'm good." He pointed to the giant can of Monster on his desk.

I'd barely gotten through the door of the break room when my stomach turned. It was so intense my arm had crossed over my waist and my mouth began to salivate—the warning bell that I needed to find a trashcan ASAP.

I drew in a breath through my nose, then instantly blew it out. Whatever it was smelled awful.

"What is that?" I asked Jan as I peered down at the container in her hands.

"Chili," she said. "Are you okay?"

I nodded, then immediately backed out without my coffee.

"Change of plans," I said to Josh when I got back to my desk. "I'm going to take a break and go get some tea." I loved that there was a small coffee house in the building. It may not have been Starbucks, but it was better than nothing.

"Everything okay?"

I nodded. "Yeah, my stomach is a little upset."

The tea helped, and the nausea let up. Not entirely, but I was able to finish work, leaving at my regular time.

The drive home was brutal, and when I arrived, I'd beaten Gavin. As I climbed the stairs, my phone chirped in my purse.

GG: I have a late meeting, be home soon

The words seemed to make me float. I loved how he said home. Something simple, especially knowing how much he hated my apartment, but it singled me out as his home.

After changing, I peered into the fridge, but nothing was appetizing. Maybe by the time Gavin got home, I'd have a craving for something.

Netflix was my go-to relaxation of choice, and I pulled up a movie I'd seen a hundred times—*Sing*—and lay down.

Before I knew it, I was being jolted awake by the slamming of the door and Gavin calling out.

"Hey, baby."

I stretched and let out a yawn. "Hi."

"You okay?"

"Yeah," I said as I sat up. "Felt a little off today. Guess I was tired too because I don't even remember falling asleep." By the time on the clock, I'd been out for about an hour.

"What's going on?" Gavin asked, his brow furrowed.

I shook my head and rubbed my stomach. "I don't know. My stomach doesn't feel good."

"That's not good."

I shrugged. "It's not bad, just some nausea."

He leaned down and pressed a kiss to my forehead. "Let me go change, and we'll look at ordering something it likes."

"How was your meeting?" I asked as he walked to the bedroom.

"It went longer than I anticipated," he called from the other room. My apartment was so small he barely had to raise his voice. "In a way, that wasn't so bad since the traffic seemed lighter."

"It was a bitch when I was in it."

"I can't wait until we live closer."

"Me either."

He came back in wearing gym shorts and a T-shirt and sat down next to me, pulling my legs across his lap and making me giggle.

"Okay," he said as he settled and pulled out his phone. "Should I just go through the list to see if anything strikes you?"

"Perfect."

His free hand absently move up and down my calf.

"Let's see . . . we have some Thai?"

I pursed my lips. "No."

"Mexican?"

"Uh-uh."

"Chinese?"

That made my stomach turn even more. "No."

He hand stopped, his caress a gentle whisper of his thumb across my skin. "What sounds good to you? We'll do that."

Chicken and cheese and Frank's Red Hot popped into my head and instead of nauseous, my stomach growled hungrily.

"Don't hate me."

"You're going to say buffalo dip, aren't you?"

I nodded vigorously as he rolled his eyes.

Gavin just sighed and pulled up Ninety Nine's menu. "Anything else?"

I shook my head. "I might have a bite of whatever you have."

He quirked a brow at me and slowly turned his head. "My bacon cheeseburger?"

A giggle left me. "Not that, but maybe some of your fries." I shook my head. He was possessive over his burgers, though he did have to get a gym membership until we got into the house. Sex wasn't burning enough calories, especially when we were eating out a lot.

The next few days I continued not to feel well. It wasn't much, but a constant state of nausea. It was enough to curb furniture shopping, so we surfed from the couch.

I credited my ill feeling to my new job, as the prior week had been quite stressful in learning everything. That, and I swore the building was moving. I did learn that the building wasn't moving, but the floor was. Apparently Sean in the row next to mine bounced his leg constantly and due to where he was, the movement traveled. That didn't help.

All of the new information they were throwing at me, as well as the systems, made me wish that I had taken a job more in my field of study while in school, but the problem was they just didn't have the flexibility, nor the pay, that the hotel could provide.

Due to my job at the hotel, I was able to pay for everything I needed while I went to school full time. I had a small savings, one that would have been wiped out entirely if Gavin hadn't paid the bills two months in advance when we left the Cameo. Not that it was much to him; all of my bills for two months equated to about three to four nights at the hotel for him.

I was sitting at my computer sometime after lunch when another wave of nausea washed over me. It was so strong I found myself in the bathroom heaving up the contents of my lunch. As I rinsed out my mouth, I looked into the mirror. A bone-chilling thought raced through my mind briefly before settling in. It made some sense.

I whipped out my phone and pulled up the calendar. My eyes scanned back and I counted the days. Forty-two.

I froze, standing there in front of the mirror. I was regular, twenty-eight days, never deviating. I tried to convince myself that it was just the stress of losing my job and gaining a new one, but deep down I knew.

I took a few steadying breaths, convincing myself it did no good to freak out when I didn't know for certain. Returning to my desk, I sat down and resumed my work, all the while my theories nagged at me.

As soon as it was five, I was out the door. I stopped by a pharmacy on my way home; my hands were shaking the entire time.

I returned to my apartment building and ran inside. I didn't have much time. Gavin would be home soon. Taking my bag from the pharmacy into the bathroom, I opened up the box that contained two pregnancy tests. I removed them from their packaging and set them on the counter before stepping back. I stared down at them, folded my arms over my chest, and paced for a moment.

Realizing my time was limited, I pulled my pants down and went at it. Once completed, I set the tests on the counter and washed my hands. While waiting for the results, I returned to the bedroom and changed out of my work clothes.

After changing into some shorts and a tank top, I cautiously walked back into the bathroom. My eyes avoided the tests and went straight to the box as I read and reread the results signs and their meanings. It wasn't rocket science; plus symbol or minus symbol. I knew I was stalling and couldn't let it continue. My stomach was tied in knots, and my hands were shaking again.

I took a deep breath, and set the box back down on the counter and looked over at the tests; each showed a pink plus sign.

My eyes scanned back and forth between the tests and the box, hoping that I was somehow reading it wrong and the plus sign somehow meant not pregnant.

In a daze, I moved back into the bedroom and sat on the edge of the bed before slipping down to the floor, staring off into the distance. Tears began to well in my eyes. How would he react? Would he be happy? Angry? God, I hoped for happy.

I tried to ask myself how I felt, but I was just . . . numb. In disbelief and full of anxiety. I mean, I wanted kids, but I also had wanted to be married and for it to be something we decided as a couple to do. This was unplanned.

I was so trapped in my own head that I didn't even hear Gavin enter.

"Baby, what's wrong?" he asked, entering the bedroom and kneeling in front of me.

I pointed to the counter in the bathroom where the decider of our fate sat. He walked over, and I watched his back tense as he froze.

"How did this happen?" he asked, his voice flat, empty of emotion. "How did this happen, Emma?"

"I don't know," I responded, my tone much like his; lifeless.

He shook his head. "Are you fucking kidding me?" he growled. "Not this again."

"What are you talking about?" I asked. He wasn't making sense. "Again?"

He turned back to me. "We're about to move, you just started a new job, I'm about to take over as CEO. We don't need this right now."

It wasn't the reaction I was hoping for. "Well whether we need it or not, it's happening." My chest flared up, tears filling my eyes.

His eyes became slits, and I felt the warmth drain from him. It reminded me of his earlier days at the Cameo. Mr. Grayson had returned, and nowhere in his features could I see my loving Gavin.

"Is this what you planned? What you wanted all along?" There was no life in his voice. It was cold, thinly veiled anger.

I pulled in a sharp breath as I stared at him. "What the fuck are you implying, Gavin?" What was going on? Why was he so angry?

"Was this all about money?"

Shock and confusion bathed me. Money? Did he think I was some gold-digging slut?

"Why, Emma?"

"Condoms aren't infallible, Mr. Grayson," I spat. "Neither is pulling out."

"Is that why you gave in so easily to my advances?"

"What the fuck are you talking about?"

"Answer me!"

Anger vibrated through me. I wasn't going to continue listening to the shit he was spewing.

"Get the fuck out of my apartment."

"Did. You. Plan. This."

He stood there, staring at me.

"I just wanted you. I wanted *you*. Now, after what you just said, I want nothing to do with you. I don't need you or your money. Now, get out!" I fumed, the tears streaming unbidden as I pushed on his chest.

My dreams of a life with Gavin were crumbling apart.

23rd Floor

Time passed at an agonizingly slow pace. I waited and waited for him to come back. To apologize. To say he didn't mean any of it.

Every hour without him made the hole inside my chest bigger. Every minute I curled deeper and deeper into my blankets in hopes that it was all a bad dream and I would wake up.

Saturday came and went as did Sunday, with no word from Gavin. I'd hoped he would come back, try and work it out, apologize, but he hadn't even sent a text.

I tried texting him, to see if he'd calmed down, to see if he was ready to talk, but there was no response. When I called, it went to voicemail.

By Sunday night there'd been no response and I had my answer—we were over.

In five minutes, our relationship ended, cold turkey.

When that realization hit, agony enveloped me. I was so confused, so hurt. There was no answer as to why my loving boyfriend flipped out.

Everywhere I looked, there was the evidence of him, making the pain unbearable. His clothes were still scattered around my bedroom, in the laundry basket on the table. The bathroom was filled with his toiletries.

But he was gone.

I couldn't even comprehend how things had so suddenly changed.

The flame which burns the hottest and brightest is fastest to burn out, right?

Somehow, I managed to get up for work on Monday, but as I walked up to my apartment that evening, I couldn't remember a single thing that happened. The only thing I knew was that I didn't see him at all.

Upon entering, there was something wrong. Someone had been there, but the only things they took were Gavin's. Everything. All of his stuff was gone.

The weight in my stomach sank even further. I wrapped my arms around my waist as my knees buckled and I slipped down to the floor. My whole chest heaved in sobs, tears bouncing on the hardwood floors.

He really was gone. He didn't even want to see me, so he made sure to come when I wasn't home. It was over. Our wild ride ended in a huge explosion and left me with a parting gift.

He didn't want us.

What I couldn't stand to remember was the pain. Gut-wrenching pain I saw in his eyes beneath his anger and wrath.

It confused me.

I watched as my dreams shattered when the door slammed behind him.

Gone.

He didn't want a child, our child, and we didn't need him. I'd done everything on my own thus far. I could raise our . . . my child without him.

I really was nothing more than a passing fancy to him. I just wore out my shiny, now an old toy.

My heart fractured a final time before bursting into millions of pieces, the last bit of hope dying.

They were right. They were all right.

It took two hours to peel myself up from the floor. Another two when I decided I needed to figure out what I needed to do to get ready for a baby.

With or without Gavin, in roughly eight months I was going to have another life to take care of. I needed a clear plan on how I was going to accomplish that.

Tuesday I was in a clearer mindset, once I had a task to handle. My heart hammered in my chest as I fidgeted with the hem of my sleeve. Insurance wasn't available for thirty days, and I was still a few days shy.

I arrived early, hoping Julianne was in her office and could talk to me before everyone got in. Luckily, the light was on and I saw her figure sitting at her desk as I stepped up to her open door. I knocked on the frame and her blonde head snapped up, a smile forming as she looked at me.

"Trying to get brownie points by coming in early?" she asked.

"Can I talk to you for a moment?"

Her smile faltered, and she waved me in. "Come on in and shut the door."

I walked in and sat in the chair opposite of her.

"What can I do for you?"

"Well, I was wanting to get some information on short-term leave," I said, sitting down in the chair across from her desk.

"Is everything all right?" she asked, and I could hear the genuine worry in her voice. "You weren't looking very good yesterday, and now this? It worries me."

I didn't know if it was the hormones, the stress, my depression, or a combination of all, but her kind words opened a flood gate and everything began pouring out.

"I found out I was pregnant on Friday, and when I told my boyfriend, he flipped. I kicked him out, and I haven't heard from him since."

"Jesus . . . What the hell?"

"I'm sorry," I sobbed. "I can't get it to stop."

I could make out Julianne standing and walking over to me through my tears. She sat down next to me and wrapped her arms around me.

"I know, it's okay."

Finally, after a few more minutes I was able to compose myself.

"I'm so sorry. I'm not usually like this."

"I'd probably be reacting the same way if my husband had been that big of an asshole . . . right before I kicked him in the balls, that is."

"He is the biggest asshole I've ever met, but with me . . . he was sweet and loving and wonderful. I couldn't believe the things he said. I'd hoped he was just leaving to clear his head, but he never came back." I loved him so much and never expected the reaction I received.

"Men are idiots," she said with a sigh. "To answer your original question, unfortunately you will not be eligible for pay while on maternity leave as you will not have been here a year by that time."

I nodded in understanding and took a deep breath. "Then if possible, I'd like to get as much overtime in as I can."

"Have you seen a doctor yet?"

I shook my head. "I don't have one, and hadn't had the time to look for one yet. My insurance also doesn't kick in here for another week."

She stood and walked back over to her desk. "I'm going to give you the name of my doctor—she's wonderful. I want you to call and make an appointment for the day your insurance kicks in. If they can't see you because you're a new patient, let me know, and I'll get you in."

"Why are you being so nice to me?"

"Ah, I see my reputation has caught your ears," she said with a smile. "Bottom line; I like you. You're a great worker from what I've seen, with a great personality. I think you have a lot of potential, and I don't want to lose you."

When I left her office I felt better, more secure about how I was going to handle everything. Julianne said she would look into overtime but didn't think it would be a problem. Work was always piling up, and the company was in good standing.

Most of the office had trickled in by the time I returned to my desk. There was plenty of work to busy myself with, and I dug in. Anything to distract me from the pain.

Just before lunch, an email popped up. It was a company-wide press release, talking about how the company was doing, and at the bottom was a picture of Alex Cates and Gavin Grayson. He was smiling and so handsome, and I missed him so much.

My chest constricted, and a small sob left me before I could stop it.

"Hey, are you okay?" Josh asked from the cube next to me.

"Yeah, I'm fine." I nodded as I attempted to blink back the tears.

"Want to go to lunch and talk about it?"

I wiped a tear from my eye. "You want to listen to me talk about my problems?"

He shrugged his shoulders. "If my wife knew I left a woman in pain by herself, she would skin me alive."

"I'm not exactly by myself." Especially not in the literal sense. Not anymore.

"No?"

"No. There are people all around me," I pointed out, smiling as best I could.

"Very funny, Emma. Come on, I know a great place nearby."

With a sigh, I relented and logged out. Every time the elevator doors opened, I held my breath. Fear, hope, and longing raced through me. I just wanted to see him, to talk to him.

"I hope Mexican is okay," Josh said as I walked with him out of the building and down the street.

I thought about it, checked with my sensitive stomach, and decided it was worth a go. The place was packed with the usual lunch rush, and we struggled to find a table.

"So, who's the guy?" he asked after we ordered.

"It . . . He . . ." I trailed off, sighing and slumping down in my chair. "Can I have your word you won't tell anyone?"

"I know we've only been cube wall mates for a few weeks, but my lips are sealed."

Taking a deep, steadying breath, I told him all about my pregnancy and who the father was and what happened. Once finished, I was crying and was met with silence.

"Gavin Grayson. The guy who is vice president of Cates is your baby daddy?" he asked in wide-eyed disbelief.

I rolled my eyes. "I hate that term."

"But you have to admit it's appropriate in this situation."

"More like unwilling sperm donor at this point." I dipped a chip into the salsa, loading it up. It dribbled all over on its way into my mouth.

"Oh, I bet he was very willing," he said, handing me a napkin.

"Thanks," I said as I wiped up the mess. "It's still hard to believe that I'm not only pregnant, but that Gavin doesn't want us. He's the one that had all the grand plans for us."

"Maybe he was in shock?" he offered.

I heaved a sigh. "I don't think so. It's been days, and he hasn't contacted me. He won't call me back and even moved all of his stuff out when I was at work."

Josh's lips formed a thin line. "Why don't you come over for dinner tonight? Ava is making her famous pasta bake."

I stared at him as I contemplated it. Having dinner with a lovey couple and their baby, or spending the evening alone with his scent still lingering?

I nodded. "Okay, sounds like a plan."

We finished lunch and headed back to the office. Josh gave me his address, and it turned out he was only a couple of miles from where I lived. I was able to go home and change clothes before heading over.

As I walked up the flight of stairs to their apartment, I began to wonder if burdening Josh and his wife with my issues was really a good idea.

That all flew out the window when a small brunette with a cute bob cut answered the door.

"Emma!" Ava stepped forward and wrapped her arms around me. "It's so good to meet you."

It felt good to be hugged, even by a stranger. I just really needed them at that point. Ava was a very warm person. There was no stopping the tears that welled in my eyes.

"You, too."

"Ah, yeah, so Emma, this is my wife, Ava," Josh said with a shake of his head. "And that little chunky monkey is April."

I couldn't help but laugh a little. Friendly was an understatement with Ava.

"Hi, April," I said to the baby lying on her back on an activity mat. Her little feet kicked and her hands reached up as she let out delighted squeals.

"So, how are you feeling?" Ava asked. I turned to look at her, then glanced to Josh. "Oh, I'm sorry, Josh told me."

"It's fine. And things are okay. A lot of nausea going around."

She nodded. "Oh, I remember those days. Have you been to the doctor yet?"

I shook my head. "No, I have an appointment set up for next week."

"I still remember my first appointment. I got to see April when she was just this tiny nugget. Josh was totally enamored."

My smile faded at the realization that Gavin wouldn't be sitting there with me. In fact, I was going to go all alone, and when it was done, I had nobody to talk to about it.

"Emma?"

I sniffed. "Sorry."

Ava pursed her lips before turning to her husband. "Josh, can you watch April while Emma helps me in the kitchen?"

"Daddy-daughter time!" he said to April with wide-eyed excitement, which garnered a toothless smile.

As soon as we entered the kitchen, Ava pulled out a chair from a small bistro set and gestured for me to sit.

"Are you okay? Really okay?"

I shook my head. "No, I'm not."

"Josh said the father left."

I nodded, then the dam broke. "It's barely been a week, and I feel like I'm at the bottom of some pit. I'm pregnant, alone, no money, no support," I rattled off. "My parents live thousands of miles away, and how am I going to tell them what a failure their daughter is?"

She handed me a tissue to wipe the tears that fell. Ava was the first person I'd really been able to open up to about the way I was feeling.

"Look, I know we just met, but you are not a failure." She reached out and gave my hand a squeeze.

"If I'm not, then how the hell did things get so fucked up? Literally days ago I was so happy." It felt like my chest was opening up all over again, agony spilling out of every pore.

"What happened?"

I sniffed and shrugged. "I wish I had some fantastic story. That way I could understand it, maybe even explain it. It was a normal day, I wasn't feeling well when I realized I was late, took a pregnancy test, showed it to him, and then he started this massive fight, insinuating I got pregnant on purpose for his money. To trap him or something. Then I threw him out."

Ava's expression dropped. "Has he contacted you?"

I shook my head as I wiped away another tear. "I haven't seen him or heard from him since."

"What a fucking dick move."

A dark chuckle left me. "He's well known for being an asshole, but not with me. I'm so confused. He flipped out and then moved out while I was at work. I didn't plan this, I didn't trick him. This was the pull-out method failing in a spectacular demonstration of a man's inability to control himself."

"Men can be selfish bastards," she said. "But I hope for your sake that this was a miscommunication or something and that he'll come to his senses."

Desperation attempted to claw its way into my head, but I pushed it back. If he did, he was going to have to fight just as hard to get back in. "That would be nice, but I'm not counting on it. I've shifted all my focus to preparing for a baby."

The timer on the oven sounded, and she stood to turn it off. "Well, just know you're not alone, okay? I'm a mom; I'm here to help with whatever you need. It's going to be okay."

Steam filled the room as she opened up the oven and pulled out a large glass dish.

"Thanks," I said. It would be nice to have someone to talk to about everything.

"And I'd be more than happy to go with you to your doctor's appointment."

I smiled up at her, suddenly happy that I decided to come over. "I would love to not go alone."

With a smile, she turned and began pulling dishes down from the cabinets and silverware from drawers. She quickly set the table and called Josh into the dining room.

As he entered with April in his arms, she smiled up at him as he made funny faces. It was so adorable and heartwarming, leaving me more than a bit jealous, but I refused to let it show.

I moved my focus to the plate in front of me and the layer of gooey cheese. Thankfully, my stomach seemed to be fine with what I was smelling: penne pasta and tomato sauce with pieces of chicken topped with mozzarella.

"Does he work nearby?" Ava asked as she spooned some of the penne pasta onto her plate.

I glanced at Josh, who shook his head. "I didn't tell her."

Ave looked genuinely confused, so I filled her in. "He's the vice president of Cates."

Her eyes and mouth opened to perfect circles. "Oh, wow."

I nodded. "Which makes things more difficult."

"But, if you work in the same building, why don't you just go up and see him?"

"Because I'm afraid," I admitted. Somehow, she had the power to make me tell her my deepest secrets. Then again, it was an excuse for someone else to know my situation.

"Of what?" she asked.

"Of him throwing me out, of him not listening, of him firing me."

"Why would he fire you?" Josh asked before taking a bite.

"You don't know what Gavin is like," I said as I moved the pasta around on my plate. "For the weeks I dealt with him at the hotel, he was a nightmare. But when I found out why he was so awful, I began to fall in love and that's when I saw how wonderful and giving he was. But he's not a man you anger, because he will destroy you."

"Are you afraid of him throwing you out or something? Because that's what it sounds like," Ava said, her brow knitted in concern.

"He destroyed my path, and then he destroyed me. I need this job to support our baby. I can't lose it too."

"That's what child support is for," Josh said. "He makes a lot of money. You can take him to the cleaners."

"I don't want to do that." Not if I didn't have to, but with rent the way it was and daycare, I probably wasn't going to have much of a choice.

"Well, what do you want?" Ava asked.

"I want him. I want his arms around me. I want him to tell me he loves me." The tears flowed freely. "I just want him."

24th Floor

After that night, the days began to bleed together. I kept going, but every day was a struggle.

Somewhere in the back of my mind, I had always been nervous that I wouldn't be enough for Gavin in some way. I just never knew that a baby would be the issue. Maybe it was an easy way out for him. Maybe he wasn't as committed as he'd led me to believe.

Every day the depression got worse, which was only exasperated by morning sickness and a lack of energy. My pale reflection showcased the physical representation of how I felt inside. Even my lips were pale.

My heart was broken, my dreams shattered. It took everything in me to get out of bed and get dressed.

Barely two weeks had passed, but it felt like months. I hadn't heard from him. Not a single text or phone call or even a second look if he saw me at the office.

I felt like I'd done something wrong and I wanted to beg forgiveness, but I hadn't. The only thing I was guilty of was not insisting he always wear a condom.

I woke up sweaty in the middle of the night and couldn't go back to sleep. The summer heat was unbearable, and my little window air conditioner couldn't keep up. It left me staring at the ceiling with nothing but my heartache.

I missed him.

Even after what happened, I didn't hate him. Sure, I was mad at him, but I still loved Gavin. That didn't mean if he showed up at my door to take me to a nice, cool place to sleep I'd let him sleep next to me, but I'd hear him out.

As tired as I was, I still couldn't fall asleep. The fatigue was strong, but not enough to send me off to dreamland. It didn't help that I felt like I was coming down with bronchitis or something. Probably a summer cold.

Julianne granted my request for overtime so I could save up money while on maternity leave. At least I was thinking ahead of things, even if I hadn't gone to the doctor yet. My appointment was set for Thursday afternoon.

"I wish you'd be there," I said to the darkness, my fingers drawing circles over my abdomen. Tears began to slide down my temples and into my hair.

I'd had to extend my lease, which came with yet another price increase. Thankfully, the landlord hadn't rented it out yet. The budget reality was depressing, especially knowing I wouldn't have any income for at least a month after the baby came, and then there was daycare.

Sadly, staying where I was seemed to be the best option I could find. Even if I was willing to pay more rent, I could only find people looking for roommates, or too far out, or no better than what I had. Which left me right where I was—a place haunted with memories of him. Of happy times.

The temptation to sell the jewelry he gave me was strong, because I needed the money. It would all go toward his baby anyway. But every time I opened up my jewelry box and stared down at the pieces, I just couldn't do it. I couldn't wear them, either.

My parents didn't know. All they knew was that my boyfriend and I broke up. I just couldn't tell them.

I couldn't tell anyone, couldn't talk to anyone. I had *no one* in my life anymore to talk to.

That wasn't true. I did have Josh and his wife, Ava, but they had a baby and a life of their own. I didn't want to bother them too much with my problems; they had plenty of their own. Plus, they were being nice and friendly, but it was a new friendship that I didn't want to abuse, even though Ava was the one going to my doctor's appointment with me.

As weird as that was going with a virtual stranger, I was unbelievably happy to not be going alone.

After another hour of lying there, I managed to gather enough strength to get up and take a shower. The cool water felt refreshing as it hit my skin.

By the time I was dressed and ready, it was only six, leaving me two hours before start time, but I could go in as early as seven. Better than staring up at my ceiling for an hour. At least I'd get paid.

There were only a few cars in the parking lot, and I was able to get movie-star parking—right by the elevators. Luckily the little coffee shop in the lobby opened at six and they had food, so I was able to grab some granola topped with fruit and a decaf coffee.

When seven rolled around, I headed up to my desk, making sure to get a refill before I left. I was just sitting down, stuffing my purse into a drawer, when a rich, deep voice hit my ears, and I froze.

The blood pumped loudly in my veins as my heart hammered in my chest.

His voice. *Gavin.*

He was walking, his voice moving. I kept still, and stayed bent over so maybe I wouldn't be seen.

"Can I get those reports by noon?"

"Noon? You're not asking for much," Julianne said.

"Noon," he stressed.

There was a pause before Julianne let out a sigh. "How long have you been here?"

"It doesn't matter."

"Yes, it does. Did you sleep here? I swear you wore that tie yesterday. Plus, you've been a moody asshole lately."

There was a whispered, "Fuck," before he sighed. "It's personal."

The dichotomy inside me was ripping me apart. On one hand, my body sang at the feel of him so near, but on the other, I broke more knowing he wouldn't care.

All I wanted was his arms around me after I slapped him for his behavior.

"Your girlfriend?" Another pause. "What's going on? You look like hell."

"I feel like it, but it's just something I'm trying to work through."

Work through? There was nothing to work through. He'd refused to talk to me and moved out. Pretty concrete to me.

I let out a shuddered breath as tears slipped down my cheeks. As much as I wanted him, if he didn't want us, I wouldn't force him. All I wanted to know was why, so that I could tell our child when they asked where their daddy was.

Because I still had no clue what had happened.

"Thank you so much for coming with me, Ava," I said.

I couldn't go to my first appointment by myself, and Ava had volunteered. No amount of thank yous could cover how much I needed a friend to hold my hand. She met me at the doctor's office and sat with me as I filled out all the forms.

"You're more than welcome. I can't imagine going alone, so let me know and I'll be here whenever you need me."

I nodded. "Thank you."

The paperwork at the doctor's office was tedious. So much information was needed about my health as well as my family's. It was giving me a headache.

"It's your birthday today?" Ava asked as she looked down at my form.

I blinked at her, then at the current date. Sure enough, it was my birthday. That was probably why my mom had called. I'd have to remember to call her later, but I wasn't in the mood to talk to her, especially not when she was going to drill me about my boyfriend. All of that would lead to me telling her I was pregnant, and I just wasn't ready to do that. Mostly because I had no answers about why Gavin and I had broken up.

"I guess so."

"We should go out to dinner to celebrate," she said.

I shook my head. "We don't need to celebrate."

"Look at me, Emma."

I raised my head, our eyes meeting. With all that was going on, celebrating my birthday wasn't high on my priorities.

"This isn't the end of the world," she said. "I know you're hurting something awful, but you need to still be able to celebrate you."

"Emma?" a voice called out from the door, thankfully ending the conversation.

"Yes," I said as I stood, Ava right behind me.

The nurse took us back to an exam room and immediately set up to draw blood.

"Why do you have to take so much?"

"We will do a pregnancy test here as well as send out a full set of laboratory tests to check for a multitude of other things," the nurse said as she wrapped a tube around my upper arm.

My eyes went wide. "Other things?"

"Everything will be fine," Ava said as she squeezed my other hand.

It wasn't that I was scared of needles, but I didn't necessarily like them. I distracted myself my looking at Ava, but desperately wished she were Gavin.

He should've been the one beside me.

A tear slipped down my cheek, and Ava rubbed my hand as she offered me a small smile.

The nurse left, taking half my blood with her, and with a promise that the doctor would be in shortly.

"You're doing great," Ava said.

It was only a few seconds later that the door opened again.

"Emma? I'm Dr. Carmichael," a woman said as she entered. She had a soft, friendly smile that somehow put me at ease.

"Hi. This is my friend, Ava." I gestured beside me.

The doctor smiled at Ava. "Hello."

"Hi."

"Let's start with the basics, okay?"

I nodded as she went through a standard list of questions, the biggest being when my last period was.

"How are you feeling?"

I blew out a breath. "Nauseous. Tired. Nervous."

She nodded. "That's typical at this time. Your body is going through a major change." She looked over to her computer. "Looks like your date of conception was probably June eight."

When she said the date, I froze. It was one I would always remember—the day I was fired. That morning Gavin had pulled me back into the shower.

"Emma?" Ava whispered.

"It's nothing. I just . . . remember it." I remembered the cold of the tile, the hot, crackling energy that always moved between us, the way he filled me. I also remembered him pulling out, but not until after his cock pulsed once inside me.

"That would make your due date March second."

March. Nearly eight months to get everything ready.

She pulled away from the computer and stood, then handed me what looked like a thin paper sheet. "I'm going to go get a nurse to help me. While I'm gone, take off everything below the waist, put this on, and sit on the table, okay?"

"Okay."

She headed out, and Ava turned around to give me some privacy. It wasn't until I was undoing my pants that I noticed just how much the waistband was pressing against my skin when it hadn't a few weeks prior, which then led me to the realization I was going to need more clothes. It wasn't a lot, but enough that the interior button left an imprint on my skin.

Once done, we waited only a minute before she was back with a nurse pushing a screen on wheels with some other gadgets.

"Go ahead and lie back for me," she said as the nurse pulled out the stirrups.

The stirrups seemed odd, but I did as she asked. My ass felt like it was on display. Technically it was, along with everything else. It wasn't something I was comfortable with, but was probably going to have to get used to.

The doctor held up a long rod on a cord and I stared at it, confused, as she lowered it.

"Wait, that's going where? I thought they just ran it over the tummy."

She smiled at me. "This early, we do a transvaginal ultrasound. We can get a good picture this way."

The thing was huge. "At least it's wearing a condom."

Ava giggled beside me, and I caught the smile on the doctor's face along with the nurse.

I stared up at the ceiling as she pushed it in. It felt so strange to have someone sticking something inside me, then came an odd sensation. There wasn't much discomfort as it was just a lot of pressure.

"There's your baby," Dr. Carmichael said.

I whipped my head over to look at the screen. There, in the middle of a dark, black spot, was a little white peanut shape. Tears slipped from my eyes as emotion took over. A baby. Our baby, and Gavin missed it.

"Why is there no heartbeat?" I asked, and a sudden panic overwhelmed me.

"The heart has just developed and the sound waves aren't loud enough, but don't worry, give it another week or two and you'll hear it loud and clear."

I looked to Ava, who smiled. "It's amazing, isn't it?"

I nodded and looked back to the screen. There were no words to describe the feeling that took hold as I stared at my baby. *My baby*. The timing and situation weren't ideal, but that didn't matter. I fell in love instantly and completely.

"You're progressing well, but I want you to get on a prenatal right away," Dr. Carmichael said as she pulled the sensor out.

After I had my clothes back on, she loaded me up with information and a promise to pick up some vitamins. I was to return in a little over a month, and I hoped Gavin would come with me.

At least I had a picture of our little peanut, if I ever saw him again.

The days following my appointment were rough. I did as the doctor advised and got some prenatal vitamins, but I had a feeling something other than my pregnancy was to blame for my fatigue.

I had pinned the ultrasound picture to my cube wall. A reminder of why I was working so hard—my peanut.

"How's the bean doing today?" Josh asked when he came in.

Every day for weeks I'd been early, but today was late, arriving just as the clock struck eight. I barely had the strength to get out of bed.

"Another day."

His brow furrowed as he looked at me. "Are you sure?"

"Are you trying to say I don't look so good?"

He nodded. "You should go see the doctor."

I kind of hated that he was telling me what I knew but didn't want to admit. "Breathing is a bit more difficult."

"Emma, if you're sick, you need to see the doctor. Breathing issues aren't good."

I nodded in agreement. "I'll make an appointment."

There was no way I was calling then, so I decided to wait until my lunch break. The problem was that the longer I was there, the worse things seemed to get.

Every hour that passed, the heavier my body seemed to get. It wasn't that it was much worse from the morning, just more noticeable.

Until my vision blurred. No matter how hard I tried, I couldn't focus. Added to that was that the shortness of breath and my heart hammering in my chest.

Something was wrong, and it was getting worse.

"Emma, are you okay?" Josh asked.

My head was swimming as I stood. A drink. That would help.

Just as I turned to look at Josh, everything shifted. I felt myself falling, but before I even hit the ground, everything was black.

One last thing rang out in my mind. The one thing I needed.

Gavin.

Gavin

The document in my hand had stopped making sense fifteen minutes prior. In fact, I'd just been sitting there, staring at it. My mind was elsewhere, as it was every time I paused.

On *her*.

On the woman I felt more for than I ever thought possible.

"Sir?" my assistant, Amanda, called.

I blinked up at her. "Yes?"

"Are you all right?"

Was I? It was a loaded question with a complicated answer.

No, I was not all right, but I buried myself in work so that I wouldn't notice.

I cleared my throat and gathered up the stack of papers I'd been reading. "Fine."

"I'm heading out," she said with a small smile.

I glanced to the clock and noticed it was six. She should have left long ago. "Have a good night."

"You too, sir."

It wouldn't be a good night. It hadn't been in weeks.

After Amanda left, I decided to head out as well. The parking garage was mostly empty, but a few feet from the elevator I stopped in my tracks. In the first spot was Emma's Camry. I glanced back to the building.

Why was she still working? It was late. Was she up there alone? Or was she out with someone?

"Stop it," I grumbled and continued on to my car.

I wanted to turn around and get on the elevator and go to her. Because I fucked up. The utter devastation when she looked at me told me so.

I'd lost it, and I didn't know how to fix it, so I ignored the problem. I knew she didn't betray me, that she wasn't after money. I knew it, but I still lashed out, flipped out, and made a fucking mess of everything.

The Arnold Hotel was a pretty good hotel. Not as nice as the Cameo, but it did have a good-sized bar. I didn't bother going up to my room or eating. Instead, I did my nightly routine and ordered a drink.

"Bourbon, neat?" Barry, the bartender, asked as I sat down.

I gave him a nod.

He set a glass down and poured, then placed it in front of me. I downed it in seconds, the burn as it slid down my throat intense.

Barry had waited, knowing how I was after waiting on me for weeks. He filled my glass again, then stepped away, leaving me with only my thoughts.

I missed her. I missed her so fucking much my chest felt like it was on fire, and not from the alcohol.

"Hi," a soft voice came from beside me. It was familiar in an eerie sort of way.

I glanced to the side, but ignored her. I wasn't in the mood to engage in small talk.

"It's a hot night tonight," she said with a sigh, waving her hand in front of her. "Are you here on business? I am. Just got out of eight hours of lectures and training. Time to unwind."

I continued to stare straight ahead, ignoring her.

"I'm Trina." She held her hand in front of my line of sight.

My eyes narrowed as I turned toward her. "Do I look like I fucking care?" Everything stopped as I glared at her. Blonde hair, blue eyes, fake smile. Once upon a time, I had fallen for it. "What the fuck are you doing here, Katrina?"

"Oh relax, Gavin," she said with a smile. She was trying to be seductive, but it wasn't going to work on me. "I'm in Boston, staying at this lovely hotel and as I stood talking with a friend, lo and behold, my ex-husband goes strolling past."

"And you had to stop?"

"Exactly! It's been years, Gav."

"I wasn't anticipating what you had to say. I was asking why you had to stop."

She shrugged, that fucking smile grinding on me. "I thought we could have a drink for old times' sake."

"Shouldn't you be getting back to your son?"

She waved me off. "He has summers with his father."

"I see that worked out well." My tone was biting.

"Oh, well." She shrugged, so nonchalant about her behavior. "So, what have you been up to?"

"No," I said through gritted teeth.

"No?"

I pulled my wallet out and threw a couple of twenties down and gave a nod to Barry. "I don't want to fucking play catch-up with you."

"Well, that's rude."

"Have a good life," I said as I stood, having had enough of her and her shit. She was the whole fucking reason I was in my whole fucked situation.

"Gav . . . wait, Gavin."

I kept on walking, paying her no attention, but she caught up to me.

"Gavin."

"Leave me the fuck alone, Katrina. I fucking mean it. Come near me again . . ."

"What? I'll regret it?" Her voice echoed out into the lobby, garnering stares.

"Lower your goddamn voice," I hissed.

"What I regret, Gavin, is letting you walk out that door." Her tone held an edge of bitterness.

I laughed, hard and loud and filled with as much sarcasm and venom as I could muster. She had no right to be bitter. "Let me? You'd just pushed a fucking baby out. You weren't going anywhere."

"You didn't have to go home, move out, change the locks, and file for divorce. That was a little overkill."

"I'm a vindictive asshole. You knew that when we met."

"Look, Gav—"

"No, you look," I interrupted. "I don't *ever* want to see you again. If you happen to see me somewhere, look the other way."

I stepped onto the elevator and pressed my floor as I stood in the middle, daring her to try and come near me again. She glared at me, nose stuck high in the air.

In my room I paced, tossing my clothes off. My chest expanded in hard breaths. Five years since I last saw her, and it still wasn't long enough.

Her lies, her fucking men behind my back. It was all a fucking game to her, and I refused to be a participant ever again.

"Fucking gold-digging slut!" I yelled out.

Realization hit me like a truck, stopping me. They were the same thoughts I had about Emma when she told me. I was so consumed by fear that all I could think about was what Katrina had done.

That moment had been a time warp for me, and I was lost. Katrina said the baby was mine, and there Emma was telling me she was pregnant.

Fuck.

My Emma was pregnant.

With *my* baby.

The world seemed to shatter around me. Every cell in my body belonged to her, and I had completely fucked things up.

How the hell was I going to fix it?

Everywhere they told me to sign, I signed, but I wasn't mentally there. They could have taken me for all I was worth, and I couldn't care less.

Though that was nearly what was happening, only in exchange, I had keys to a house. A house I had picked out with Emma. The closing had been pushed out a few weeks by the owner, and it was fine by me.

"What the fuck am I doing?" I asked myself as I looked down at the keys in my hand. How could I live there without her?

I couldn't.

On the way back in the office, I tried to focus and not think about the huge house I was the new owner of.

"Hey, what did you get for lunch?" Julianne asked as we walked toward the elevator that let up to the lobby.

"A house."

"Oh! That's right. The one you picked out with your girlfriend."

I ignored the girlfriend comment. "What did you have?"

"I met Jonas for lunch at home."

"Home?"

She shrugged. "Jeremy is home sick, so I checked in with them."

"Does Jonas stay home with them every time?" I asked.

"No, we switch it up to be fair. I was home with Jenna two weeks ago."

We walked through the lobby, heading to the elevators that led to the upper floors. My eyes scanned the lobby, as they always did, searching for *her*. Usually there was no sight, but there she was, sitting at a table in front of the restaurant that occupied the lobby, picking at a piece of bread. It was the first time I'd seen her since she had thrown me out, and my chest fucking burned.

"How's your new employee doing?" I asked, gesturing over to where she sat. Maybe Julianne could give me some insight.

"Emma? She's fantastic," Julianne said, her expression light, a smile playing at her lips. "It's so good to have someone like her on my team. She is just soaking everything up that I throw at her." She heaved a sigh as we stopped at the elevators. "I just wish she wasn't sick."

My head spun back to her, trying to assess from where I was, my chest tightening. "She's sick?"

Julianne nodded. "She's pregnant, and it's taking such a toll on the poor girl. She takes it in stride though, tries not to let it show. I'm just afraid she's overdoing it. But I'm more afraid that there may be something wrong with her pregnancy, and she's not saying or just doesn't know."

"Why do you think that?"

Julianne stared at me, and I knew she was curious about my sudden interest in one of her employees. "I swear she gets more and more pale every day. I have two kids, and I never looked as bad as she does. She is so stressed and all alone." We stepped off the elevator and headed toward my office, though I was sure she was headed to Alexander's. "The father wants nothing to do with her or the baby, from what I hear. I can't even fathom being pregnant and heartbroken at the same time and still manage to get out of bed every morning."

I stopped in my tracks, completely gutted. I had done that to her. She was alone because I was a fucking asshole. Because I was selfish and scared and didn't think before I spoke.

"She's a tough cookie," Julianne continued, not noticing or caring about the knife she was driving into me. "Really she hoped it would make him wake up or something, but it didn't happen. It's been weeks, and he hasn't seen her or contacted her."

Weeks? I froze as I looked at her. Had it really been that long since she threw me out the door? I still remembered being stunned at her demand. It had woken me, but by then it was too late. I left to clear my head and checked into another hotel. For the entire weekend I sat there wondering just how everything had gotten so fucked up in the span of a few minutes.

I'd been on autopilot ever since then, working twelve, fourteen, sixteen-hour days. When I stopped, the pain in my chest flared and it felt like I was drowning.

"Have a good rest of your day," she said before heading down the hall.

I waved at her, but seemed to be lacking for words.

"Amanda?"

She blinked up at me from her computer. "Yes, sir?"

What did I want her to do? Call Emma up? That wouldn't look good for her.

"Nothing . . ." I stepped past her and into my office, my mind a fucking war zone.

I sat down at my desk and opened up the second drawer down and pulled out the blue satin box that I had hidden. Inside lay a three-carat diamond ring that I purchased just three days before we broke up.

Did we break up? Or were we just having a fight? From what Julianne said, it sounded like Emma thought we were over.

God, even the words seemed foreign.

Her final words came back to haunt me, and I knew that day had been the end. She wanted me gone. I didn't fight for her, but fought against her. I pushed her away. I left her. All alone.

She didn't know. How could she? I'd told her I'd been married, but had never told her what Katrina did. I just didn't give a flying fuck about my ex-wife or how her bastard child was doing.

Katrina was the gold-digging whore, not my Emma. I knew that, I did, but the situation had hit a nerve, and I reacted. It was so familiar. I had trusted that what my wife told me was truth. Our relationship hadn't been in the best shape, but when she'd told me she was pregnant, as her husband, I believed it to be mine.

Katrina was only with me for the money. A socialite trying to ride on her looks and pussy.

There I was, on the eve of proposing to Emma—not that she knew—and she dropped the bomb on me.

Pregnant.

I couldn't believe it was possible. She wasn't on the pill yet, so I made sure to wear a condom, but it didn't always happen. Those rare times, I pulled out. Not foolproof, though, I knew that.

If I were being honest with myself, it was more than the rare occasion and more the norm. Nothing felt better than being buried inside her bare, and it was a struggle every single time not to come inside her, especially when my body was crying out to slam my hips against hers and mark her insides as mine.

I knew that, and I still slapped her with the same label I'd given Katrina.

Emma had never shown me any reason to ever doubt her, and I'd lashed out at the first chance.

It wasn't that I didn't want children, but our relationship was so new. We'd only been together a few months. I knew I was being a hypocrite. The ring in my hand and the house keys in my pocket said it all.

What was my hang-up? I wanted to marry her, but wasn't ready for children with her?

I thought for the first time about the child growing inside her. I imagined her further along, her stomach protruding, round and full. Round and full with *my* child.

I shuddered, the image settling in my groin, stirring me to life. The image was a fucking aphrodisiac.

I began to wonder if it was a boy or a girl. Who would they look the most like? Would they inherit my heterochromia? I would love a child with two different colored eyes, just like me.

My mind moved further into the future. Emma laughing and playing with our infant as she bathed him or her in the master bathroom, a smile lighting up her face.

It was the vision I'd had when I purchased the ring. I wanted to spend my life with her. There was no other in the world like her, no one that affected me like her. She was the sun.

And now she was sick. Beyond regular pregnancy sick, according to Julianne.

My chest tightened, and I felt the sting of tears in my eyes. My Emma was pregnant with my baby, and something was wrong.

Suddenly, I felt sick.

Was she okay? Was the baby okay? Would they be okay? I made myself crazy with all of the questions, fears, and speculations, my hand tugging at my hair.

"Why don't you go to her?" Alexander asked from the door of my office.

My head snapped up and I stared at him, wondering when he came in and how long had he been standing there.

"I don't know what to say to her," I admitted.

"Just be honest, Gavin."

"How do you always know, Alexander?"

He let out a laugh. "Ha! It's called experience! I've been in shoes similar to yours."

He walked into my office and sat back in one of the black leather chairs opposite my desk. "Listen, Gavin, Emma is a wonderful woman, and I could see at the charity auction just how much you love her. It was quite obvious. I've heard from my daughter about her newest employee and what a 'fucking douchebag'—her words—of an ex-boyfriend she has. Is that how you want to be in her memory? An asshole sperm donor? Because that is exactly where you are headed if you continue down this path."

I shook my head. "I want . . . my family."

"Then go get your family. It may be earlier then you planned, and I'm sure that you did plan, but life doesn't always go as we see it going. You have a baby coming next year, so go get your wife now. Tell her why you reacted the way you did, make her see how much you love her. Win her back."

I jumped from my desk, grabbed the box, and ran into the hall. The elevator was too long of a wait, so I flung the door open to the stairs and flew down the four flights that separated us. I had to tell her, I had to get her back.

I burst through the door, scaring a couple of people in cubes nearby. Swiftly, I walked toward Julianne's office, only to find it empty. I slammed my hand against the frame, pushing off and moving to search for her desk.

I was causing quite a commotion as I ran up and down each aisle looking at name plates. It was my only option with Julianne unavailable, as I had no idea where her desk was.

There were a few people standing around talking, and I stopped in front of them when I saw her name.

She wasn't there.

My eyes went wide as I stared at the picture she had pinned to her wall. I pulled it off to inspect it. My mouth dropped open as a pit formed in my stomach.

"Baby Addison," it read at the top. Not Grayson. It felt like a knife was being shoved into my chest as I looked down at the tiny first picture of our baby.

I wasn't there with her. I'd missed it.

The name at the top also told me one thing—Emma really did think I didn't want them.

"Where is she?" Three people looked at me, clearly stunned. "Where is Emma?"

"Why do you care?" a voice asked from behind me. A glance down to his nameplate told me his name was Josh.

I turned toward him. "That's none of your concern. Now tell me where she is."

"No. It's none of *your* concern. You haven't even acknowledged her existence in weeks. What right do you have to come down here now? Why now of all times?"

I kept my voice low in an attempt to keep the conversation between the two of us. "I fucked up. You think I don't know that? You don't know about our situation."

"Oh, I know all about your situation," he spat back. "It's my wife going to Emma's appointments with her when it should be you."

"She's at Mass General Hospital!" a woman in the cube next to Emma's shouted as she stood.

"Wha . . . what?" My eyes were wide, and I felt the blood drain from my face.

"She collapsed. We couldn't wake her," another woman said. "The paramedics took her about twenty minutes ago."

I felt my knees buckle, and I had to lean on her desk for support.

"She's been sick."

"Not that you care," Josh spat.

I stepped forward, almost chest to chest with him. "You have no idea what I care or don't care about. Do not presume anything."

I stormed out, not waiting for a reply. There was nothing to explain to him. Only Emma.

My heart pounded in my chest, the tempo a beat of fear. With each block, it only grew in intensity. I tried not to let my mind run away with what-ifs and horrific scenarios, but after what Julianne had said, I could only think the worst.

The emergency room waiting room was filled with people, but as I scanned the faces, none of them were Emma. I went up to the reception window where a few hospital staff were sitting.

"Can I help you?"

"Yes, I'm looking for my wife," I lied. "She was brought in by ambulance."

"Name?"

"Emma Addison." I couldn't stop the tapping of my finger against the counter.

"Okay, she's in the back. Do you happen to have her insurance information?"

I shook my head. She didn't have insurance anymore; the hotel's ended when she was fired.

"We don't have it."

"Do you have a way of paying for services?" she asked.

My patience was running low. What the fuck did money matter? Nothing.

I pulled out my wallet. "Do you take Visa?"

She nodded. "Mastercard, Discover, and American Express."

I handed over my card without pause.

"I'm just putting a hold for services on."

"That's fine," I ground out.

She handed me the card back and had me sign a sheet before hitting the buzzer.

"Go through there, down the hall, and she'll be in the room on the right."

I wasted no time making my way to where she was, only to be stopped when I arrived. It was a large room with draped beds on either side.

"Shit."

Frantically I moved through the room, opening sheets and peering around others. Why were there so many patients?

Voices caught my ear, and I recognized Julianne's right away.

I pulled the curtain apart and got my first good look at Emma in weeks. She looked so weak, so frail, her body tiny and pale against the bed sheets.

It killed me to see her like that. Devastated me that something might be wrong and take her from me. I refused to let her go.

I was going to fix this mess, even if I didn't know how. Emma was mine, she always was, and she always would be.

26th Floor

My eyes fluttered open, both vision and hearing flooding in. "Wha?"

"Emma? Oh, thank God. You scared me."

My head fell to the side to find Julianne wide-eyed. Everything felt so heavy.

"What happened?" I asked. It felt like I was weighed down, barely able to move.

"Josh said you stood up and then just fell to the ground."

I'd been short of breath all morning, and I found that was still the case. "Update?"

She shrugged. "No news, but they did bring you back immediately."

A cacophony of voices filtered in and around me, only a thin piece of fabric separating us.

"How long have we been here?"

"About an hour. Just so you don't freak out later . . ." She sighed and pursed her lips. "They found that you were bleeding in the ambulance, but there's nothing to suggest anything is wrong."

Bleeding? "What do you mean, bleeding?" I lifted the sheet, which took more energy than it should have. I'd worn gray slacks

226

to work, and they were gone. In fact, my whole outfit was gone, and I was in one of the itchy cotton hospital gowns. Flipping the fabric back, there were dark rust splotches staining my skin.

"Bleeding can still happen when you're pregnant," Julianne said as I covered myself back up.

The curtain surrounding me moved back. I was expecting a nurse or doctor, but it was Gavin.

His brow was furrowed and his eyes had bags under them. He seemed to be shaking, his breath labored.

My whole body got lighter just seeing his eyes, then was crushed by the reality he'd created.

"What are you doing here?" I spat.

"Are you okay?" he asked as he stepped closer. "Is the baby okay?"

"What the fuck do you care?" The searing pain in my chest reappeared, burning like a hot iron.

"You have got to be kidding me," Julianne said from beside me. "Gavin? This is your mess?"

"Is our baby okay?" he asked, ignoring Julianne entirely.

"*Our?* So suddenly, you want us?" My tone was biting. How dare he burst in and plant himself back in my life after weeks of ignoring me.

He shook his head. "I never, for a second, didn't want you."

"Bullshit. You flipped out on me! You wouldn't return phone calls or texts. You moved out. What other conclusion was I supposed to come to?"

He opened his mouth to speak, but Julianne beat him to it.

"I'd hoped you weren't the motherfucking asshole," Julianne seethed from my side.

I'd had a feeling she suspected.

Gavin's eyes went wide. "You knew?"

"I had my suspicions, and you pretty much confirmed them when we came in at lunch."

"Would you mind giving us a few minutes?" he asked.

"No," I said. I didn't want her to go. I needed her as a buffer.

"I've got to get back to the office." She stood and took my hand. "Keep me informed, please. Take tomorrow off."

"I can't—"

"I said take tomorrow off." She set my purse next to me. "They'll probably keep you overnight anyway. Any days next week, just text me, and for HR, get a note from the doctor."

"I'll be back Monday," I insisted. I couldn't afford any time off.

"Emma, listen to me," Julianne said with a sigh. "I know you're stressed about money, but the health of you and your baby is more important. Listen to your body. Take a little time off."

"Thank you, Julianne, for everything."

She squeezed my hand, then turned to Gavin. "Better get some motherfucking knee pads." She patted his chest before disappearing.

Everything inside me tensed, which exhausted me further. I relaxed back into the bed and struggled for breath. The ceiling tiles were a much more appealing option to stare at than the man I could feel feet from me.

In my periphery, I watched as he moved to take the chair Julianne had vacated and scooted it closer. "Emma."

"Go home, Gavin."

"I want to, but that all depends on you."

"I don't get it."

He reached out and tilted my chin toward him. "You're my home, Emma. Wherever you are is where I belong."

I had to clench my jaw to keep my bottom lip from trembling. "Stop. Just stop. For weeks, you refused to talk to me, to explain yourself."

"I'm an asshole."

"Is that always going to be your excuse for everything? Oh, your dad is sorry he can't come to your recital, he's an asshole. Well, that's even if you're around," I sneered.

"You have every right to be angry," he said calmly. It made me want to slap him, but I didn't have the energy. "I failed to handle the situation, and failed you."

"I'm not a goddamn situation, Gavin. This isn't a business deal. This is love, and you latched onto the first excuse to get out of it."

"That's not true," he argued.

"You sure tried your damnedest." He took my hand in his, and I wrenched it from his grip. "Why is it when I tell you to leave me alone, you advance?"

"Because I have something you need to know. I fucked up, Emma. I'm an asshole, and I lashed out because I thought I was being duped again."

I shook my head. "Duped again? What the hell does that mean, Gavin?"

"It was like déja vu. My ex-wife said almost the same words to me once."

"Okay, what the fuck does your ex-wife have to do with anything?"

"Everything," he said before continuing. "After three years of marriage, I was done and talking with my lawyer about a divorce. One night, I came home and she announced that she was pregnant, and that put me filing for divorce on hold. She was my wife—of course I believed the child she was carrying was mine."

Believed the child she was carrying was mine. Suddenly, things started to make sense. The strange things he kept saying. It didn't make it any better, but understanding was a starting point.

"How did you find out it wasn't?" I asked with genuine interest.

"The day she gave birth." I watched as his jaw clenched and unclenched. "He had milk-chocolate skin. It was obvious then that she'd not only been cheating on me, but I knew the child wasn't mine. My knee-jerk reaction was thinking the same about you."

"Thanks for the trust," I said through clenched teeth.

He took my hand in his and wouldn't let go when I feebly tried to remove it. "I failed you, utterly. And I continued to do so for weeks, but I never stopped loving you, Emma. I'm so sorry for what I did, what I said. I've been miserable without you. Would you consider giving me a chance to make up for my mistakes?"

He killed me with his words, twisted my insides. Part of me wanted to say yes, but part of me wanted him to suffer like I had. He was trying to give me an understanding of why he had reacted the way he did. It was his turn to have an understanding of what he had done to me.

"You *crushed* me, Gavin. I'm not sure I can just sweep that under the rug and be all lovey-dovey again."

He nodded. "Let me take you home and show you how serious about this I am."

The curtain moved back and a doctor stepped in. "Hello, Emma, I'm Dr. Michaels."

I couldn't have been happier for his arrival, a reprieve from responding to Gavin.

"Hello."

"What's wrong with her?" Gavin asked, butting in.

"I'm sorry, you are?"

"The husband and father."

I glanced over to him, wide-eyed. *What did he just say?*

"Ah, right. Well, from your intake information, I want to run some tests, but the bleeding—"

"Bleeding?" Gavin interrupted again.

The doctor looked from me, then to Gavin. "Yes, Emma presented with some bleeding between the legs."

"Is everything okay? Is the baby okay?"

The doctor held his hand up. "May I speak?"

"Yes. Excuse me."

He looked back to me, clearly annoyed at Gavin. "The bleeding was nothing abnormal, but I want to do an ultrasound and check on the baby."

I nodded in agreement. "What's wrong with me?"

"I'm not sure, but we're going to find out. I'm going to have the OB on duty come check you out after we get you admitted."

"Admitted?"

He nodded. "We're going to keep you overnight."

"Overnight? Why?" Fuck. There was no way I would ever be able to pay off an overnight stay.

"For observation. You fell pretty hard, and I want to find out what's going on. I don't think you've miscarried yet, but that will be the first thing they'll check upstairs."

The blood in my veins ran cold.

"Miscarriage?" both Gavin and I asked at the same time.

Dread washed over me and panic spiked, causing tears to fill my eyes. "I could lose the baby?"

It wasn't planned, but I'd already grown very attached to the little peanut inside me.

"There is definitely a possibility," he said with a somber expression. "Someone will be over shortly to transport you."

With that, he was gone and on to the next patient.

"Everything will be okay," Gavin said from beside me.

"How do you know?" I spat.

"Because it's *our* baby."

I scoffed and shook my head. "Do you know how many women miscarry in the first trimester?"

"No, but that doesn't mean I can't be optimistic."

"I'm surprised you aren't optimistic for me to miscarry." It was a low blow, but I just needed him to hurt like I was hurting, just a little.

"Are you fucking kidding me right now?" he growled.

"That way you wouldn't have to pay child support and add me to the list of women who duped you."

"Dammit, Emma!" he yelled out. "It would devastate me if *our* baby didn't make it. Stop trying to fight me."

"At least you're fucking fighting."

"Emma?" a voice called.

We both turned to look, finding a young guy in scrubs standing at the end of the bed, a wheelchair in front of him.

"I'm Andre, here to be your wheel man upstairs," he said with a brilliant smile. Walking backwards, he was able to swing the chair right next to me before releasing the side rails, letting them drop. "Do you need help?"

I nodded and slowly moved the blanket back.

"Where are my clothes?" I asked.

Andre bent over and pulled a bag from beneath the bed. "Got them right here."

"Jesus," I heard Gavin mutter.

The gown had ridden up, and he was staring at the space between my legs. Andre stepped forward and pulled it back down as he helped me to sit up with my legs hanging off the bed before standing and, with his hands under my arms, dropping down into the chair. It took another minute for him to get me situated before handing off my belongings to Gavin and pulling the blanket off the bed and setting it over my lap, tucking it around my legs.

"Ain't nobody's business."

The gown covered all of it, but somehow, the blanket added a level of comfort and protection, even if it was psychological.

I gave him a small smile. "Thanks."

When we got to the room, Andre helped me up onto the bed, then moved to a cabinet. "Here's our lovely, hospital pageant footwear to keep your toes toasty warm and compliment your gown." I couldn't help but smile. He was making the process so much less stressful. "You can just set her clothes bag under the bed. Someone will be in shortly."

"Thank you," I said as I took them from him.

He smiled. "Feel better."

Once the orderly left, I wanted to open my legs and see just how bad it was, but I noticed Gavin looking at me.

"Turn around," I said.

"Why?"

"I said turn around, and you will respect that request or I will have them kick you out of here right now."

The blood drained from his face, and he did as I requested. "Who's the demanding one today?"

"I don't have to let you be here, you know. And I'm demanding because I have every right. You have none."

Each movement was draining and aggravated my breathing as I leaned over, spreading my legs. There was more than just the dried splotches, and suddenly I was very worried about my little peanut. I drew in a shuddering breath, which caught Gavin's attention. He turned back around, and I covered back up before he saw.

"What are you doing? Let me help," Gavin said as he sat on the end of the bed and picked up the socks. He pushed the oh-so-attractive hospital socks with their grippers onto my feet.

"Thank you."

"You're right," he said softly. "You do have every right. I was so messed up, and I'm so sorry I left you thinking I didn't want you."

"You hurt me, Gavin. Deeply. Apologizing isn't going to make it all go away." I was trying to make him understand that apologizing didn't fix it. "I still had hope you'd come back and talk to me until I came home and you'd picked up all your stuff."

"I thought a couple of days away would clear my head, but every time I started to think about it, my heart started racing and panic set in, so I stopped."

"How nice for you," I sneered. I couldn't help it. While he was busy *not* thinking about me, I was busy doing nothing but thinking of how I was going to take care of an unplanned pregnancy without him.

"I buried myself in work, and before I knew it, two weeks had passed and I didn't know how to come back. I didn't know how to make up for all that I'd assumed."

"So while I was worrying about how to support myself and a child, even thinking of selling the gifts you gave me, working overtime, you just decided to forget?"

He flinched at my words. "Selfish to the core."

"But you're not," I yelled, sitting up. "Which is why I don't understand what happened. Even with the whole ex-wife-screwed-you thing, which I get, why did you wait so long? Why did you make me suffer?"

Yelling took a lot of energy and air, which were in short supply. I was getting light-headed.

"Fear. I love you more than I ever thought was possible. I'm so in love with you that it would destroy my heart for the rest of my life if it was true."

"But it's not true! You wouldn't even talk to me . . ." The room began to spin, and I fell back down to the bed.

"Emma?"

Everything was a blur, my vision unable to focus. I managed a few, long, slow blinks, then everything went dark.

"Ah, I think she's waking up," an unfamiliar voice said.

"If I could stop doing that, it would be nice," I groaned.

"Good news, Emma. We know why now."

"Yeah?" I looked up into the soft, kind features of what I assumed was my new doctor.

"I'm Dr. Andrews, and we should have you on the road to feeling better soon."

"What is it?" Gavin asked from the other side of me.

"Well, you have iron-deficiency anemia," she said, but it didn't mean much to me. "It's common in pregnancy, but yours is a pretty bad case. We're going to give you some iron intravenously today and put you on a 120-milligram supplement every day. I still would like to run a few more tests to rule out any other issues."

"Is that why I'm so weak?"

She nodded. "Weakness, paleness, difficulty breathing, all of your symptoms are a result."

"All of those?" I had thought a lot of it was due to the baby.

She nodded. "Now, I'd like to do an ultrasound to check in on your little bundle."

"Oh, it's my friend again," I said in regard to the wand in her hand.

She let out a laugh. "I see you've met."

"Your friend?" Gavin asked.

I nodded. "I got real up close and personal with his brother a few days ago."

"I saw the picture," he said. His thumb stroked the top of my hand.

I looked at him to gauge his reaction. "You did?"

He nodded, his brow furrowed. "I'm sorry I wasn't with you, but I promise I will never miss another."

The way he said it, the conviction in his voice, made my chest clench. I believed him.

The uncomfortable pressure invaded me again, and I focused on the screen to try and block it out.

"What's that sound?" I asked. There was a soft whooshing that wasn't there days earlier.

"That's the baby's heartbeat," she said. "Good and strong."

"The heartbeat?" I asked in awe.

"It's so fast," Gavin said beside me. He took my hand in his. I glanced over and found his mouth was open, eyes wide as he stared at the screen. "Our baby." He turned to me, his brow furrowed, jaw tense.

Without warning, his lips crashed to mine, which made me squeal and tense around the rod.

His lips . . . I'd forgotten how wonderful they felt. How soft and sensual they were. A warmth spread through me that I hadn't felt since he left.

"I'm sorry. I'm so fucking sorry. I questioned your love, your loyalty because I wouldn't be able to handle that situation again. I love you so much, and I love our baby, I promise you."

I was struck by his eyes, by the pure desperation in them. They beat me down, showed me, reminded me, of the strength of our love. The fire that burned in his eyes was the fire that burned for me. It was the first major punch to taking down my wall of pain.

I loved Gavin, and he was reminding me why we were drawn together in the first place.

"Everything looks good," the doctor said, drawing our attention back to her. "The heart is healthy, and I'm not seeing anything to be concerned about. You're very lucky, Emma. I'm afraid if you'd waited much longer, you might have lost your baby."

"Really?"

She nodded. "Iron is a vital nutrient. It's the basis of our very blood. But don't worry, we're going to get your levels back up."

They set up an IV line, then brought out a bag of very dark red liquid that would, in a sense, bring me back to life.

"This is going to take a few hours, so get comfortable and we'll check back in."

With that, they headed out, leaving Gavin and I alone again.

"You should probably head out," I said.

"I'm staying."

"Why?"

He brought my hand up to his lips and kissed my palm. "Because you're my family. I love you."

I wasn't ready to let him back in, but there was one thing he definitely needed to know.

"The shower," I said.

His brow furrowed. "What?"

A sigh left me. "When you pulled me back into the shower the day I was fired. That's when."

"When what?"

I gave him a small smile. "When we made our baby."

He let out a small chuckle. "We really had quite an eventful day that day, didn't we?"

"Life altering in many ways."

They say when one door closes another one opens, and it was exactly what happened. That day changed everything in ways I could have never imagined.

27th Floor

There wasn't much sleep to be had, even as tired as I was. All the additional labs and tests came back fine, and I got the all clear to leave mid-morning. As we headed out, I was already starting to feel a little bit better. Stronger, at least.

Gavin commandeered some scrubs for me to wear and bought a pair of actual slippers from the hospital gift store.

When we got to my apartment, Gavin wouldn't even let me carry my purse or clothes as we walked. He even made me hold onto his arm.

"Fuck, it's sweltering in here," he said as we entered.

"Shit," I said as I walked over to the window air conditioner. It wasn't doing anything. Sure enough, it was dead. That could have been why it was doing such a shitty job. Good thing I had a few fans to help.

Gavin went around and started opening windows, which was good, because I wasn't sure I had the strength to open them. They always got stuck due to past over-painting.

"Well, I'm home."

He quirked his brow. "If you're looking like that expecting me to leave, you can forget it. If I have to sleep on the couch, I'm not leaving you."

"You just going to stay in your suit again?"

His lips formed a thin line. "Well, I may run and get a few things."

"Fine. Go do that. I'm going to take a nap," I said as I headed to the bedroom.

"Emma, wait," Gavin called out.

I stopped and turned. "What?"

He reached up and cupped my face, his eyes soft as he leaned forward and pressed his lips to my forehead.

"I'll be back in no more than two hours. I'll pick up the iron supplement while I'm out. If you need anything, absolutely anything, call me."

I swallowed hard and nodded. He was melting my heart each time his lips touched my skin.

"Anything," he repeated as he headed out the door and locked it.

As I stared at the door, a panic crept in. Was he really coming back? The last time he walked out, he didn't.

"Get a grip, Emma," I said to myself as I headed to the bathroom. I needed a quick shower to clean up before changing into something and falling asleep.

There was no energy left in me when I was done, and after putting on some panties and a tank, I turned on a fan and fell onto the bed. In seconds, I was out, taken down by utter exhaustion.

Twenty-four hours later, Gavin was still sitting in the heat with me. He'd kept to his promise of two hours, returning with a duffel of clothing and a couple of grocery bags. However, I ended up sleeping a lot of the day. Between the exhaustion of everything and the anemia symptoms, I was only awake for a little while every few hours.

"Here, baby," Gavin said as he moved his closed fist in front of me. I opened up my palm and he slipped the pills into my hand, then handed me a glass of water.

"Thank you." The prenatal pills were huge, at least to me. Taking pills had always been a struggle, and it was very difficult for me to swallow them. Thankfully, the iron pills weren't nearly as big.

After watching me take them, Gavin sat back down on the couch and pulled my legs onto his lap. It didn't take long for me to relax around him. We seemed to fit right back into place, but there was still the scar he left on my heart.

"What do you want for dinner? Anything sound good? Buffalo dip?"

I let out a chuckle. "Slow your roll."

"What?"

I couldn't help but laugh at the look of utter confusion on his face. "I know you're eager to please, but one question at a time."

"Does anything sound good for dinner? You barely ate any lunch."

My stomach wasn't cooperating much. Lunch had arrived and one of the dishes had to immediately go to the dumpster out back while I threw up in the bathroom.

But Buffalo dip? "I'm beginning to think Buffalo dip is my pregnancy food."

"Pregnancy food?"

I nodded. "My cousin Britney craved junior bacon cheeseburgers from Wendy's all throughout her pregnancy. It was so bad she couldn't pass one without stopping." I pulled up my phone and opened a browser window and typed in Buffalo dip recipes. "I bet it's really easy to make at home."

"Well, while you look at that, I'm going to get a burger and some buffalo dip. Anything else?"

I shook my head. "Well, maybe a side salad. Ranch dressing."

"Got it."

We'd binged the entire first season of *Stranger Things*. Gavin was totally enraptured with it, especially being an 80s' child. I enjoyed it as well, but the fatigue made me miss an episode. Gavin happily watched it over so I didn't miss anything.

I made him sleep on the couch Friday night, but I felt bad when I came out Saturday morning to find he was quite a bit longer than my couch.

The truth was, I didn't want to be hurt anymore. I didn't want to be angry with him. I just wanted his arms around me again. To feel the way I had just a few weeks ago.

As the day wore on, we'd moved from opposite ends of the couch to my legs across his lap, his hand over my stomach. He'd bunched up my tank, exposing an inch or two of my stomach, and made slow circles across my skin.

He catered to my every need, making sure I took it easy.

"I'm not an invalid," I said after I started to get up to get a drink and he stopped me.

"I know, I just . . ." He blew out a breath. "I'm just . . . afraid."

"Of what?"

"In the hospital, you were so sick. I just want to take care of you and keep our baby safe. I'm so afraid that with your anemia still being an issue, we could lose him or her."

An overwhelming need to throw my arms around him took hold, but I held it back.

I wasn't ready to show that level of affection. "Okay," I said as I sat back down and got comfy again. Really, I was at a loss for words because it was another thing that thawed me. After the number of times we'd been told how lucky we were, he wasn't taking any chances. At least not until I was better.

A few hours later a yawn left me, and my eyes grew heavy with sleep despite the naps I'd taken and the little movement.

"Bedtime?" I asked.

He nodded and removed his arms that were draped over me, and I immediately missed the warmth of his touch. My chest clenched. All I wanted was to be surrounded by him.

"You okay?" he asked, his brow furrowed as he examined me.

Was I? No, not in the least.

So much was going through my head, and my emotions were everywhere. I was scared of everything—him, me . . . us. Of what my mind decided I should do, but my heart fought against.

"Come on," I said as I stood and held out my hand. "The couch is too small for you."

He stared down at it, then looked back up to lock eyes with me. "Are you sure? I'm okay—"

"All I'm offering is sleep. Nothing else."

He nodded. "If you promise me it's okay."

"It is." With my confirmation, he slipped his hand into mine.

I turned on the fan as I slipped onto the bed and lay on my side, facing the wall. The bed dipped and Gavin brushed up against me. Unlike the last time we were together, we were both stiff like strangers trying not to touch.

"Y-you . . ." I cleared my throat, fisting the sheets ". . . can move closer. I don't want you falling off."

The bed was so small that cuddling was a necessity, but it was better than the couch. Luckily, there'd been a break in the heat, but even a sheet was still too much, especially with the added body heat.

He adjusted his position, his body inches from mine. I felt the heat pouring off him, the electricity. All things that made me want to back up into him, to feel every inch pressed against me.

"Can you get the light?"

"Sure," he said. His arm brushed across mine, his chest pressing against my back. The room wasn't quite black, light streaming in from the street lamp outside the window—I'd forgotten to close the curtains.

When he moved back, he lined his body up with mine. One arm crawled under my head while the other draped over my waist.

"Can I hold you?"

"Gavin, I—"

"Please."

That word broke something inside me. All I could do was nod. No matter how much I still hurt, I needed him surrounding me. The comfort that melted away my pain.

There was a pause, then his arms folded across me, pulling me tightly against his chest.

"I missed this," he said. His lips pressed against my temple.

A shuddering breath left me, and a few tears escaped, sliding down my cheek onto his arm. He pulled me closer, holding me like he was afraid I would leave if he let up. I wasn't sure why I hadn't told him to leave, but the reality was that I knew the answer. I loved having him there, near.

Everything he did reminded me why I had loved him so much, and how I still very much did. The pain, the trust, it just took time.

"I don't think I've ever told you what you did to me," he whispered, his voice soft.

"What did I do to you?" I stretched my neck to nuzzle his hand where it rested on my shoulder.

His touch was tender. Every time he touched me lately was that way. Soothing, healing.

"Katrina . . . my relationship with her was never like ours," he began. I froze at the mention of her again—the reason there was such a wall between us. "She was a quintessential socialite. All about money and trying to one-up her friends with the things she bought." His fingers absently brushed against my skin. "I got tired of it, tired of her. There was little affection there. When she had the baby and I realized everything was a lie, I shut down my heart, shut down my ability to love."

"Then why are you here?" That was the question I'd been asking since he'd barged into the hospital.

Gavin shifted, settling me on my back as he loomed over me. His brow was furrowed as he stared down at me. Turning my head, I focused on the wall. I couldn't look at him. There was a sob too close to the surface.

"Don't you get it?" His fingers cupped my cheek, bringing my eyes back to his. "You brought me back to life, Emma."

The dam broke, the sob pouring out of me. "You left me." *You doubted me.*

His thumb wiped away the tears that fell. "And I'm prepared to spend the rest of my life making it up to you. To restore your faith in me . . . in us. I'm never leaving again, Emma. Never."

"But . . . what if this was a sign we weren't meant to be?" I tried to settle myself, but the tears continued to choke out of me.

"Walking into the Cameo was my sign." He leaned down and nuzzled my nose. "From the first moment I saw you, I was mean, nasty to you. All in an attempt to drive you away, but you fought back. You never let me push you without giving some sort of resistance. Without putting me in my place."

He lowered his body, settling on his forearms, his hips between my traitorous thighs that spread easily for him. "Seeing you on that bed shook me to the core. Just the thought of losing you kills me. I love you. All I want is to spend the rest of my life with you."

"Please." I didn't know what I was begging for. For him to be closer? Further away? To never stop telling me he loved me?

My emotions poured from me in the form of tears. Sobs that shook my body. The weight of his words was crushing.

"Baby, please don't cry. I know I caused this. I'm so sorry."

Gavin moved us again, shifting so that he was on his back and I was draped across his body. The breeze from the fan along with Gavin's soft touch eventually lulled me. Crying turned into low sniffles, and my arm draped around his chest, pulling him closer. I wanted to burrow myself inside and never come out.

"I do love you, too," I whispered once I'd calmed down. He blew out a breath and kissed my temple again, letting me know he heard. "I'm just still hurting."

"I know. But I'm going to make sure you never doubt me again."

I stretched a bit and placed my lips on his chest, right above his heart. "I'd like that."

"Good night, my love," he whispered.

"Goodnight, Gavin."

28th Floor

By Sunday night I was starting to feel better, but Gavin suggested I take a few more days off. All of my anemia symptoms were slowly starting to dissipate. It was when that happened that I began to realize just how bad things had really been.

When the morning came, Gavin had to go back to work, leaving me for the first time since he'd gone to get clothes days earlier. "Take it easy," he said as he placed a kiss to my forehead. "Call me if you need anything."

He was still at my apartment, still sleeping curled up with me and taking care of me.

After he left, I had a few crackers for breakfast before pulling up Netflix again. There was sweat rolling down my skin, the open windows unable to provide any relief to the near boiling temperatures and heavy humidity. I directed the fan right on me, trying to cool me, but it only helped take the edge off. I'd barely made it through an episode of *Supernatural* when I drifted off.

A while later, I was startled awake by a knock on my door. My heart slammed in my chest as I blinked at the clock and peeled myself up from the couch.

"Hello?" I called through the door. It was almost noon and I wasn't expecting anyone.

"Hi, I've got a delivery for Grayson?"

My brow knitted as I opened the door where a delivery driver stood with a bag in his hand.

"Umm, let me get you a tip."

"Oh, the tip is already paid." He held out the bag.

I took it from him and thanked him as I slowly closed the door.

When I got to the kitchen, I set the bag on the counter and pulled out the containers. Right away the smell of vinegar and spice hit, and I began to salivate.

Buffalo dip.

Gavin had ordered buffalo dip for me for lunch, complete with a side salad.

Emma: Thank you

It was very sweet of him, though soon I was going to have to back off and get some healthier foods back in my system. I was just popping the lid off when my phone buzzed.

GG: You're welcome. How are you feeling?

Like I was in an oven.

Emma: Hot. Sweating like crazy. Just woke from a nap

GG: Eat, relax, and I'll check on you in a little while

Emma: Yes, Mr. Grayson

I couldn't help but smirk down at my message. It'd been instinctual, and natural to send it. So very much our relationship.

He was wearing me down, and I had to admit, it scared me.

I needed help, guidance. There were only two people I could call, and luckily, they lived together. Settling down on the couch, I pulled up my contacts list and hit the button for Ava.

"Hello?"

"Hi, Ava."

"Oh my God! Emma! Are you okay? Is everything all right? How do you feel? What did the doctor say? Josh said you were still out and I wanted to call, but he also said Gavin went after you and I didn't want to intrude."

It made me smile to listen to her rattle on. "I'm getting better."

"How's peanut?" she asked.

I smiled and looked down, my hand brushing across my abdomen. "Looking good."

"Whew! I was so worried."

"Thank you, for all of that," I said, my eyes stinging with tears. "Gavin did come, told people he was my husband to get back to me."

"Really?"

"Ava . . ." I blew out a breath. "I'm confused. An emotional mess."

"What's going on?"

"So, he stayed with me all night at the hospital and brought me home, where he continued to stay and take care of me. While we were in the hospital, he explained why he flipped out and was apologizing left and right."

"I love how it took him until you were in the hospital to finally tell you," she said, her voice dripping with sarcasm.

"Yeah. Turns out his ex-wife cheated on him and he found out in the delivery room of what turned out not to be his baby." I still couldn't imagine it, the horror. To go through an entire pregnancy thinking about seeing your baby, only to find out everything you knew was a lie.

There was a gasp on the other end of the line. "Oh, holy fuck. He thought it was the same, didn't he?" Ava caught on quickly.

"Yeah. It was a knee-jerk reaction. I get it," I said with a sigh. "Doesn't mean it hurt any less, but at least I understand what happened."

"Having an answer is huge."

"Here's the part I'm having trouble with . . . from the moment he saw me in the hospital, he has been nothing but doting to the extreme. He holds me all night, even though I know he's burning up. He gets me whatever I want and need. He even had lunch delivered for me today."

"He's trying to take care of you. He's trying to make up, to show you how much he loves you."

"He does, and I love him, but how do I move on with him?" I asked. I thought I was to the point that my heart was healed enough to give it another go.

"If you want to be with him, if you think he's paid enough and is honestly there for you, you need to give him a fair second chance. Mistakes happen in a relationship. Harsh words get said in anger, and frustrations slip out. They're not always meant, but they cut, and deeply. Words can't be taken back, but they can be forgiven. Do you love him enough to forgive him?"

Could I? Could I use all that he'd done to take care of me, all the affection, and weigh it against the pain and have it win?

There was a good chance I could.

"Thanks, Ava."

"Are you going to give him a chance?" she asked, a hopeful edge to her voice.

"Yeah, I think I am."

"Good luck, then. And give me a call whenever you need. I'm here for you and I can answer all the embarrassing pregnancy and baby questions."

I had a feeling I would have her on speed dial. "I can't thank you enough for everything you've done."

"Yes, you can," she said matter-of-factly.

"Oh, yeah?"

"Three words—double-date dinner."

A chuckle slipped out as I shook my head. "I think we can arrange that."

"Perfect. Just name a date and we'll make it work."

"Will do! Have a good day," I said.

"You, too!" she called out right before I hit the end button.

Mistakes did happen, and words were said. If I couldn't give Gavin a second chance, I would be giving up on what I knew was the greatest love of my life.

Around three there was another knock on the door. When I opened it, there was a man standing there with a large box.

"What's this?" I asked as I opened the door for yet another delivery.

"Air conditioner. Mr. Grayson requested I set one up in the bedroom and the living room," he said as he picked the box up and stepped in.

"He did, did he?"

"Yes, ma'am."

I nodded and moved to my phone.

Emma: Air conditioners?

The delivery guy set the box down and started to cut it open.

GG: It's sweltering in there

I wasn't arguing there, but it was unnecessary. **I'm used to it. Fans work fine**

GG: Until you agree to move into the house with me, I'll continue making your apartment as comfortable as possible for you

There was no winning against the man. I knew it and he knew it. Not that I was ungrateful.

Emma: If I say yes right now, will you get this guy and the air conditioners out of here?

GG: Are you saying yes?

Was I?

For four days I'd had a loving Gavin practically glued to my side. He'd taken care of me, ignored work, showed me he was there, committed.

I hit the call button at the top and bit down on my bottom lip as the phone rang. My heart hammered in my chest with what I was about to say.

"Baby?" he answered.

"I want you and I want our house and I want to forget the two weeks where you didn't love me," I said all in one long breath, my stomach in knots.

"There was never a time I didn't love you, Emma."

I chewed on my thumbnail. "I know that, but to me, in that time, you hated me."

"I'm going to make it up to you."

"You can start by getting this guy out of here," I said.

"It's really hot today. You need it," he argued.

"Fine, we'll go to your hotel then." Since he wasn't moved back in with me, he still had a room at another hotel.

There was a small pause before he spoke. "Put the guy on the phone, pack a bag, and I'll be there in an hour."

I couldn't help but giggle, and handed the phone to the delivery guy. His eyes popped wide and he nodded and agreed before putting back the Styrofoam packaging he pulled out.

"What did you say to him?" I asked Gavin once I had my phone back.

"That the air conditioners were now his," he said.

"Seriously? Couldn't you just return them?"

"It's fine. One hour."

I smiled. "See you soon."

I showed the delivery driver out, who seemed ecstatic about his gift, then moved to the bedroom to pack. If I went back to work in a few days, I would need work attire. Instead of the overnight bag, I pulled my suitcase out of the closet and began loading it with a mixture of clothing.

Making a mental list, I packed up my laptop, Amazon Fire Stick and remote, toiletries, and my pillow and blanket. I even filled up one of the paper takeout bags that had handles with drinks, snacks, and crackers.

Seeing as I didn't know how long I was going to be gone, I moved to my jewelry box and pulled out the bracelet and necklace Gavin had given me. I'd barely looked at them in weeks, remembering the sadness the last time I did.

I slid the bracelet in between my clothes, and slipped the chain around my neck. It felt so right when it settled against my skin.

The key to his heart.

Just as I was zipping up the suitcase, Gavin stepped in.

"You're taking a blanket and pillow?" he asked with a small smile.

"Yes. All part of the being comfortable theme."

He stopped when he saw the key around my neck, and his eyes snapped to mine. Two beautifully different-toned eyes that I loved so much stared at me.

"Thank you," he said.

My fingers ran across it, and I gave him a small smile. "Let's get moving. I used up a lot of energy with your one-hour demand."

"Can you handle your purse and the pillow and blanket situation?"

I rolled my eyes. "Yes."

"I'll get the rest."

The rest was a lot, especially for one trip—suitcase, laptop bag, and two brown bags filled with food and drinks. He managed it with relative ease as I locked the door.

We headed into downtown while everyone else was headed out, making the trip a breeze.

"It'll be nice to get back to work, especially so I can make sure my car is still there." It'd been days, and I wondered if they towed after a certain period of time.

"It was there when I left, so I'm sure it'll be fine."

Gavin pulled up to the valet area of the hotel and called for a cart to make things easier. The bellhop followed us up to the room.

I blew out a breath as I stood in front of the air conditioner vent.

"Feel better?" he asked.

"Okay, I relent, you were right."

"We should have come days ago," he said.

I nodded. "Yeah."

"But you weren't ready."

I reached up and cupped his cheek, loving the way he leaned into me. "No, I wasn't, but I'm ready to deal."

"Deal?" he asked with a quirked brow.

I nodded. "You promise not to leave again, and I promise not to remove your testicles with my bare hands."

He swallowed hard, his gaze bouncing between my eyes.

"I'll agree on one condition."

"There's no negotiating."

"One condition," he repeated as he dropped to the floor.

I stared at him in confusion before it sunk in. My breath hitched as I stared down at Gavin. He was down on one knee, a Tiffany blue box in his hand.

"Gavin?" My heart thundered hard in my chest, not believing what I was seeing.

He tilted the top of the box, and I stared down at the large diamond ring it held.

"Emma, you're my sun. I love you more than I ever thought possible. In a short time, you took over my every thought. I want you as my wife. Will you marry me?"

My eyes found his, the sincerity shining through. This wasn't a spur-of-the-moment question. He had a ring. He'd planned it.

My chest constricted as my heart fluttered wildly inside my chest. "Aren't things moving a little fast?" After all, I had *just* given in.

"You know I don't make rash decisions. Besides, I want to be married before our baby gets here."

He never said "the baby." It was always "our baby," and I loved that. It was one of the things that made me relent. Something so small, but it showed just how committed he was to us as a family.

"Gavin Grayson, you are a handful with dirty negotiating tactics."

He beamed at me. "But I've grown on you."

My face scrunched up, and a tear slipped down my cheek. "Yeah, you have."

"Emma, please let me make you a Grayson."

A Grayson. There was a blooming in my chest, spreading like wildfire down my arms and legs. It pulsed, sending tingles down my spine.

I wanted that. I wanted to be a family.

"Yes," I said with a shaky breath.

He pulled the ring out and slid it on my finger. It was a huge, round diamond flanked by pear-shaped side stones.

My mouth dropped open as I stared at it, but I didn't get long to look at it. Gavin stood up and took hold of my face, smashing his lips to mine.

His kiss was the match that re-ignited my soul. The fire that ravaged my body, burned away the cold, and replaced it with an all-consuming heat.

"Fuck, baby," he groaned.

I needed it, needed him inside me. Needed to feel him come in me. I was so wet for it.

I was able to get my shorts undone, letting them and my thong slip down my legs before he pulled my top up and over my head.

It was frantic, erratic as we stripped. Desperate for skin-on-skin contact.

He dipped down and picked me up, only to drop me down onto the bed a few feet later. I worked on his belt while he took off his vest and tie. As I pulled his belt through the buckle, my fingers grazed his hard length. My pussy clenched in sheer anticipation.

It had been weeks since he had been inside me, and I desperately needed to be filled with him.

"Fuck it," he spat in frustration as he loosened his tie and yanked it over his head.

Each button of his suit seemed to take forever as I stroked his length, fisting it, giving the tip a light squeeze. A shudder rolled through him, his eyes heavy and dark. He stopped unbuttoning his shirt and instead tugged it up and over his head, then pushed his pants down his legs.

No time was wasted. I had barely crawled a foot back to give him some room to get on when the head of his cock pressed inside me.

My vision blurred, and I drew in a sharp breath when he buried most of his length in one thrust. A long, low moan left me before he pulled back, then pushed his hips forward and out again.

"This is mine," he growled as he slammed in. "You are mine." Another accentuating slam. "And I'm never fucking letting you go again."

"Never."

He set up a delicious pace that wound me up more and more each time he bottomed out.

"Fuck, Gavin!"

"We have this big house with nothing in it." He flexed his hips, driving him deeper. "And I want to fill it with our family."

A moan slipped past my lips. "Yes."

His pace sped up, driving me further and further into a bliss-filled madness. The tension tightened every muscle until I cracked, my walls tightening around him.

He groaned above me, his face twisted as he slammed into me one last time, his cock twitching inside me with each jet of cum.

Our eyes locked, both of us breathing hard. It was everything I needed to remember our connection.

"I love you," I said.

His eyes softened as the back of his fingers caressed my cheek. "I will always love and be devoted to you."

Gavin changed everything in my life. I had a path, and he destroyed it. Then he rebuilt it, bigger and better than it was before. A path for us to walk together.

Life doesn't always work out like you think it will. My life was proof of fairy tales and fate.

Gavin Grayson—world destroyer and life giver.

The very unexpected love of my life.

Penthouse

Three weeks later ...

When I returned to work, Gavin did the one thing he'd threatened to do the day I was hired at Cates—he sent out a company announcement. Granted, it wasn't telling everyone we were dating, but an engagement announcement, complete with a photo taken of us from the charity event.

"What's being delivered today?" Gavin asked as he opened up a box of kitchen supplies.

The weekend after our engagement, we went furniture shopping so that we could at least move into our house. Gavin had also called for all the stuff from his New York apartment to be delivered.

"Let me check," I replied, pulling out my phone from my back pocket. I scanned for the email. "Today is the sofas for the family room, a few sofa chairs, couple of end tables, and two bed frames."

I loved our home. It may have been empty, but it was ours. Not a hotel, not a cramped apartment, but a house that we'd chosen as a couple. A place for us to live and grow our family.

It took nearly two weeks, but my iron levels finally got to a normal level and all of my symptoms were gone. The only sickness left was the morning sickness caused by our growing little peanut.

The doorbell went off, and I jumped up. "That must be them." I ran to the door and flipped the lock, then pulled it open.

But what was on the other side was not a furniture delivery, but a fifty-two-year-old man with his brown hair thinning.

"Dad?"

He beamed at me, throwing his arms open. "Emmybear!"

Instantly, I wrapped my arms around him and pulled him close. My dad. *My dad.*

"Omph!" He was laughing, but I could tell by the way his arms tightened that he missed me just as much.

It'd been years, and his hug was the world.

"Emma?"

I turned to find my mom standing behind him.

Tears filled my eyes. "Mom." I wrapped my arms around her. "What are you doing here?"

"Gavin didn't tell you?" Dad asked.

Gavin? What had my fiancé been doing behind my back?

I shook my head and sniffled. "No."

"We're moving back to Boston," Mom said as she looked me over. "He invited us to stay with you while we get situated."

"Come on in," I said, gesturing them inside.

"Oh, Emma . . ." Mom trailed off as she looked around.

"We don't have much yet, so it looks really big with all the empty rooms."

"Beats the seven-hundred-square-feet your apartment had," Gavin said with a chuckle from behind me.

"Mom, Dad, this is my fiancé, Gavin." I held my arms out like I was presenting him.

"It's a pleasure to finally meet you," Dad said, shaking his hand a little too vigorously.

"What's going on?" I asked. I was obviously missing something, because my dad knew what had happened in July. I was shocked he was being so nice.

"Turns out one of our departments was seriously lacking a key element," Gavin began. "The manager of the department and I went through the candidates from the headhunter we use, and your dad fit the bill perfectly." He smiled at me, which only caused me to narrow my eyes on him.

"Gavin, what did you do?" I asked in a whisper.

He smiled down at me and brushed my hair back. "Part of my doing everything I can to make you happy."

I stretched up and pressed my lips to his. "Thank you."

To have my parents near was like a dream, and would be especially when our baby arrived. A fact I still had yet to break to them. So much had been going on, I hadn't gotten to it.

"How about a tour?" Dad asked, his neck stretched around the doorway leading to the parlor.

"Sure," I said. We walked them through all of the bare living spaces, describing what we were going to do with them.

When we got up to the bedrooms, I stopped at what was the largest, but not the master. It appeared more like a living space with its fireplace and flanking built-ins.

"This would be a great space for you two," I said when we walked in. "We have a queen bed in another room we can bring in here, and the frame is being delivered today."

"Perfect," Mom said with a smile.

We continued on, passing a bathroom before coming upon the smallest bedroom.

"We're going to use this room for the nursery," Gavin said.

My mouth dropped open. I couldn't believe he'd just blurted it out like that. Then again, it was one way to tell them.

"Nursery?" Mom glanced down to my stomach. "Baby, you're pregnant?" my mom asked, her eyes wide.

There was no hiding it in the shirt I was wearing. My stomach had just a small bump in my abdomen. Small, but noticeable compared to the flat stomach I'd had just weeks before.

"Eleven weeks today," I said as I ran my hand across my bump. "Due to some earlier issues, we were waiting a little longer to tell you."

"Earlier issues? Emma Elaine!" Mom's eyes were wide, completely horrified. She was such a worrywart—another reason why I didn't want to tell her about my trip to the hospital.

"I have iron deficiency anemia. It caused issues early on, but I'm fine now. I take supplements and I'm fine."

My dad remained silent, still as a statue as he stared at the small room. He looked to Gavin, then to me, then back to Gavin.

"Okay. The answer is yes."

The answer?

My brow scrunched as I glanced to Gavin who held out his hand to my father.

Dad noticed my confusion. "Gavin asked for my blessing to marry you. I told him I'd have an answer when we met face to face and I saw him with my daughter."

Gavin wrapped his arm around my waist and pulled me into his side.

"Are you happy, baby?"

I smiled, my lips forming a thin line as the emotions threatened to burst out in the form of tears. "So happy."

Gavin continued to give and give. Bringing my parents back to Boston was one of the greatest gifts I could receive. Worth more than the ring on my finger, my necklace, and my bracelet combined.

He gave me my family—both the one I was born into and the one that carried his last name.

Words could never describe how much I loved the worst guest I'd ever had to deal with.

A year and a half later...

Gavin

A small cry, and my eyes were wide open. With a glance over to the monitor to check in, I saw he was standing up in his crib. Emma was a heavier sleeper than me and hadn't noticed the small peep our son made.

I slipped out of bed, letting my wife sleep.

"What's going on, Liam?" I asked as I stepped up to his crib.

"Dadada, bah-ba." His chubby fingers held onto the edge. Only recently did he start standing. Soon he'd been walking, and we'd be chasing him nonstop.

I picked him up and set him on my hip. "Okay, let's go get you a bottle."

We headed down to the kitchen, our way lit by a dozen night-lights. After retrieving a bottle and warming it, we followed the same path back up the two flights of stairs.

I sat down in the glider and held Liam in my arm, his bottle in my opposite hand. Out his window, I caught the flash of colored lights still blinking on the trees in the median. With the holidays over, my family had returned to Ohio, and our home quieted down. My hope was to spend some time in Ohio over the summer. I wanted Liam to see something besides the congested city.

Emma always said that I was the one who turned her life upside down, but the exact same could be said about her. We changed each other's lives, and for the better. Liam was proof.

She was five months pregnant when we were joined as husband and wife in front of a small gathering of friends and family. It was simple, intimate, and a show of our love for each other.

His eyes were heavy as he slowly suckled. I pulled the bottle away and repositioned him as I set the bottle down. My feet continued to lightly push on the floor as I lulled him back to sleep. As I looked down at him, I continued to be amazed that he was mine. I still hated that even for a fraction of a second I ever doubted that he was. On the day he was born, the fear was still there, in the background. I'd been there before, but left a changed, warped man.

William Alexander Grayson entered the world on March sixth, and the second he opened his eyes and looked at me, all of my fears melted away. I was hooked, so in love with him.

As he grew, his eye color began to change. He had one blue and one green eye—just like me. It wasn't the only trait he inherited from me. My boy was quite demanding at times.

I loved those moments—the middle of the night, just him and me. The days were always a mad race, but in the quiet of the night, it was just the two of us.

Alexander was setting up his retirement in two years and had officially announced me as his successor. It was an informally known progression already, but the world was now aware. We'd already started the transitioning process, but the responsibility on my shoulders was suddenly a lot heavier. I'd been with Cates for over a decade. I was there when they became a billion-dollar company, and was there as they continued to grow. The hard part was going to keep the company advancing and growing as well as keeping a balanced home life.

I wanted to spend as much time as possible with my family. I was happy and didn't want Cates to be my sole focus like it once had been.

That was my fear—being eaten up by work and losing Emma.

I strived to make certain that didn't happen.

"Baby, wake up," Emma said as she roused me.

I drew in a breath as my eyes went wide. I'd fallen back to sleep on the rocker, Liam in my arms. Emma lifted Liam from me and set him in his crib before taking my hand.

"Come on, Mr. Grayson. Shower time."

The morning wood in my pants twitched, excited about the idea. "I like that idea very much, Mrs. Grayson."

She looked back to me, a sly, naughty smile playing on her lips.

Forty-five minutes later, I headed down to the kitchen to help with Liam so that Emma could finish up. My mother-in-law stood at the counter by the coffeepot while Emma sat at the table with Liam in his high chair.

"Morning, Kathy," I said as I entered the kitchen.

"Good morning. Coffee?" she asked as she held out a mug.

I nodded as took it from her. "Thank you." I headed over to Emma and draped my jacket over a chair.

While Emma's parents living with us was supposed to be temporary, we were going on almost two years with them still with us. Our home was big enough, and we were grateful to have the help with Liam, but at the same time there was something to be said about the lost privacy.

Fucking my wife on every surface of our home was taking longer than it should have.

Emma was feeding Liam while she ate a yogurt, and I took over so that she could finish eating and getting ready. She popped up once done and gave me a quick kiss before heading upstairs.

She came back down fifteen minutes later as I wiped banana from Liam's mouth. "Ready?"

I nodded, giving one last swipe to his mouth before picking him up. "Let's go."

"Bye, Mom!" Emma called, waving at Kathy. "Have a good day."

"You, too. Bye, Gavin. Bye, Liam."

I waved Liam's arm at his grandmother before following Emma out. Tom, Emma's father, had already headed out.

We loaded into the car, Liam in his seat, and headed to the office. I loved our drives, even though they were short, because it was a few minutes of the day when it was just us.

"Isn't it a little cold for a skirt?" I asked as I set my hand on her leg. Normally she wore pants in the winter.

"Yes, but I was so hot when we got out of the shower."

"It was a hot shower."

"Mm-hmm."

I loved it when she wore skirts because I knew what she was wearing under them. Nothing turned me on as much as her thigh-highs. I pushed her skirt higher, sliding my hand over her silk stockings until I reached the soft skin of her upper thigh.

"Where is that hand going, sir?" she asked.

I gave her a lopsided smile. "Wherever it wants to."

"This morning wasn't enough?"

"I can never get enough of you."

She bit her lip and tried not to smile. "Better not let my husband hear you say that."

A chuckle slipped out, and I squeezed her thigh. "I'll keep that in mind when I've got you laid out on my desk later today."

"I don't know if my boss would like me to be missing from my desk."

"Baby, I'm your boss's boss. She'll have to deal." I swung into my parking spot and threw the car into park. "If you want to keep your job, you'll be in my office at noon."

She gasped beside me, eyes wide. "But, Mr. Grayson, you can't do that."

Fuck, I loved our little role play. "Oh, I can, Emma. My office. Noon."

She gave a little nod and looked down. "Yes, sir."

I took hold of her chin and pulled her closer. "Such a good girl." My mouth was on her, lips parted, tongues mingling. A taste to hold me over until I saw her again.

It was difficult pulling away from her, but I managed with a slight adjustment of my dick as I exited. I unclipped Liam's carrier while Emma grabbed his diaper bag.

We walked in together and dropped Liam off on the tenth floor before stepping back onto the elevator.

"Have a good day, baby. Love you," Emma said when we reached the seventeenth floor.

"I love you," I said. My lips pressed to hers before she stepped away, her hand still in mine. Our eyes were locked all the way until the doors closed. Fuck, did I love my wife.

It was Emma's idea to create a company daycare. I was resistant at first, but when she laid out some of the benefits, including less missed work, happy workers, and happy wife, I couldn't refuse. Especially when Liam arrived and Emma went back to work, it was extremely convenient to have him close by. In the first month, tardiness was down by fifty percent at our Boston office. Seeing the benefits, I approved the program at our other locations around the country.

We did charge a fee per child, but it was a fraction of the cost of daycare and strictly to help with getting quality staff. Not a single person complained, and nearly everyone with young children signed them up. We were also about to launch a version for older kids for when summer break came along

"You're making some great changes, Gavin," Alexander said as we sat in his office discussing the financial reports an hour later.

"Thank you, Alexander."

"The daycare is flourishing."

I nodded. "I have to admit, if it wasn't for Emma pointing out the need, I might not have thought of it."

He smiled at that. "Morale is up, attendance is up, and employees seem happier, which is a good thing."

"Very. Production has been up as well."

"You know, from the moment I met her I knew that girl was special, but it's amazing what she's done to you."

"Done to me?" I asked, a brow quirked.

"You're no longer thinking about this as just a job. This is the livelihood of your family, and everyone who works for you is part of that family."

He was right. Cates's success was financial security for many families, not just my own. The weight was tremendous, but it was all about the balance, and I was determined not to lose sight of either of my goals—a thriving company and family.

An hour later, there was a familiar knock on my door, breaking me away from the email I was writing. A smirk grew on my face—it was a knock I'd know anywhere.

"Come in."

"You wanted to see me, Mr. Grayson?"

Fuck. I *loved* my wife.

My assistant must have been away from her desk, otherwise she wouldn't have started our naughty boss play.

"Yes, Emma, come in."

She started walking, but as she approached, her smile dropped and she bent over, eyes closed as she blew out a breath.

I was immediately out of my chair and rushing over to her. "Are you okay?" I asked as I ran my hands up her arms, directing her to a chair.

Her brow was furrowed as she nodded. "Yeah. I just think I'm coming down with something."

"Make a doctor's appointment."

She nodded. "I might. Mom's off today, and she can get Liam and me."

"Don't worry about Liam. I'll pick him up at five."

She smiled up at me. "Thank you." Her expression dropped, and she froze.

"What?"

"Well, I was just thinking . . . I've felt like this once before."

"What was it then?" I asked.

"A baby."

I froze as I stared down at her. "Do you think . . .?" I trailed off as I pressed my hand against her abdomen. With our first child, she was alone when she took the test, but I wasn't going to let that happen again. "Let's go." I took her hand and headed toward the door.

"Go where?"

"There's a drugstore a block away." I stopped and turned back to her. "No, wait. You stay here, I'll go. Just wait here."

"Gavin, I have work to do."

"Please, baby."

She nodded and sat down. I placed a kiss to her forehead before racing out and down to the nearest drugstore.

Round trip, it was only fifteen minutes before I was back in my office.

"You're hogging my employee," Julianne said as I entered.

"Technically, she's my employee as well."

Julianne quirked a brow. "Just because she's your wife doesn't mean she gets special privileges."

Emma snickered, her lips turning up.

I lifted the bag up that held the tests. "Give me another fifteen minutes, and she's all yours."

Julianne's eyes narrowed. "Is that a pregnancy test?"

I took hold of Emma's hand. "Fifteen minutes."

"Fine," Julianne huffed.

I dragged Emma into the women's restroom, receiving a startled gasp from a woman washing her hands before she scurried away.

"You're abusing your power," Emma said as she stepped into the stall of the women's bathroom, tests in hand.

"Trust me, Julianne has used being Alexander's daughter in the past."

After Emma had healed from Liam, I wasted no time fucking my wife anytime I could. Being my wife, I also no longer saw any reason to pull out. I made sure she was never left wanting, and it made me hard knowing each time I came inside her could get her pregnant again.

I was actually surprised it took this long. Liam's first birthday was coming up. The sound of the toilet flushing echoed around the tile walls and she stepped out, setting the tests on the counter.

She stared down at them, her lip caught between her teeth. It took almost no time before markings appeared. I looked down at the box for the results, then down to the tests.

A smile stretched across my face as I stared down at the two little lines. "Pregnant." I looked to Emma to find her face was pale as she stared down. "Baby?"

She blinked and shook her head. "Sorry. I was having a bit of a flashback."

I tipped her chin up and locked my eyes with hers. "We're going to have another baby, and I am so fucking excited," I said, knowing she needed to hear it. I needed to make up for the last time we found out we had a baby on the way. "I love you. I love you so much, and I am so happy we are adding to our family."

"Really?" Her brow was furrowed.

I pulled her to my chest and wrapped my arms around her as I kissed the top of her head. Her fingers clenched around my jacket.

"Over the moon excited." And I was. "Though your parents may never be able to move out."

She laughed at that. "Don't say that." She sighed and leaned into me. "I guess it wouldn't be so bad. It's a big house."

"I hope it's a girl," I said. "As beautiful and strong as her mother."

"I'd love a little girl."

"Then we can have a boy. Do an alternating pattern."

She pulled back and stared at me. "I am so going on birth control when this baby is born," she said.

"Why?" I asked.

Her eyes were wide as she looked at me. "Baby, you may love me being pregnant—"

"I do," I interrupted her.

She rolled her eyes. "I don't want to just be a baby maker. Two kids is plenty."

"I always saw us with three or four."

She shook her head and smiled. "Let me have a breather of a couple of years, then we'll talk about it. There's plenty of time for more later."

I ran my hand over her stomach and our baby inside. "You're right. I just . . . I fucking love that you're pregnant."

A smile grew on her face. "Because you claimed me?"

I nodded. "I fucking did."

It was months later when baby girl Grayson came into the world. We named her Amelia.

Life always came with ups and downs, but we handled everything together. Emma and our babies were my world. I loved them with my whole heart, my scars long healed, because Emma had shown me what true love could be.

About the Author

K.I. Lynn is the *USA Today* Bestselling Author from The Bend Anthology and the Amazon Bestselling Series, Breach. She spent her life in the arts, everything from music to painting and ceramics, then to writing. Characters have always run around in her head, acting out their stories, but it wasn't until later in life she would put them to pen. It would turn out to be the one thing she was really passionate about.

Since she began posting stories online, she's garnered acclaim for her diverse stories and hard hitting writing style. Two stories and characters are never the same, her brain moving through different ideas faster than she can write them down as it also plots its quest for world domination...or cheese. Whichever is easier to obtain... Usually it's cheese.

Amazon - http://bit.ly/KILynnBooks
http://www.kilynnauthor.com/
Facebook - http://bit.ly/1qbp5tx
Twitter - https://twitter.com/KI_Lynn_
Instagram - https://www.instagram.com/k.i.lynn

More Books from K.I. Lynn

COCKSURE
A life altering lie, ten years, and one wild night later, the game has changed.

Niko
My life is great. I love my job, have awesome friends, and a great family.

Women love me, even if they know it's just for a night.

I always thought love at first sight was bullshit. Then she came storming into my life. She tore through my every rule, rocked my world, and knocked me on my ass.

There's only one problem...she lied.

Turns out my best friend's little sister isn't so little anymore.

Everly
I stole a night with my fantasy. Lied to him.

After ten years of not seeing each other, Niko doesn't even recognize me.

So I take what I want from him, what I need from him. Without worry. Without consequence.

What I didn't count on was the lingering need for him.

Once the truth is out, the game changes. There are consequences.

I should have known nothing in my life is ever simple.

My brother is going to kill his best friend and I have nine months to figure out what I want.

BECOMING MRS. LOCKWOOD

Every girl has dreams of meeting Prince Charming, or at least I know I did.

A fairy tale-like meeting of love at first site.

Real life and fairy tales are very different.

I'm just a small town Indiana girl that had a chance encounter with one of Hollywood's golden boys. You may think you know where this story goes—not even close.

Life is different. Marriage is hard. It's even worse when you're strangers.

SIX-

I had a one-night stand. It wasn't my first, but it would be my last.

A gun to the head.

A trained killer.

A deadly conspiracy.

Kidnapped and on the run, my life and death is in the hands of a sadist captor who happens to be my one-night stand. Armed with countless weapons, money, and new identities, the man I call Six drags me around the world.

The manhunt is on and Six is the next target. Can we find out who is killing off the Cleaners before they find us?

Two down, seven to go.

When it's all over he'll finish the job that dropped him into my life, and end it.

Stockholm Syndrome meets bucket list, and the question of what would you do to live before you died. The questions aren't always answered in black and white. Gray becomes the norm as my morals are tested.

Death is a tragedy, and I'll do anything to stay alive.

Are you ready for the last ride of your life? Six has a gun to your head—what would you do?

This isn't a love story.

It's a death story.

BREACH BOOK 1

Existence is more than just a word, it's a state of being. More importantly, it's my state of being. Day by day I go through the motions of living—eat, breathe, work, sleep.

That is until I finally get some help at work in the form of Nathan Thorne. He's sexy, cocky, arrogant, an asshole, and total bullshit.

I see through the façade to the turbulent man beneath, but I'm not the only one who can see through masks.

One late night the tension between us explodes, starting a lust filled craving for each other. All it takes is that night and his dirty talking mouth, and I'm his.

Now sex is in the mix. Violent and dirty and passionate and everything I need to fill the void inside me but one thing is missing—he can never love me.

It's not enough for me to leave, even though I know I should.

More than my heart is on the line, and I don't know if I'll survive our breach.

NEED BOOK 1

I was Kira's from the first moment I saw her. Maybe it was love at first sight, but I was only ten.

She became my best friend.

My crush.

The girl I can't live without.

But I have to.

She was almost mine, but my father took away my chance.

Now she lives across the hall from me. Instead of the title of girlfriend, she's now my stepsister.

But that doesn't stop how I feel, how I want her. Thankfully, I'm off to college two hundred miles away, but even that doesn't help.

She's under my skin, all around me, and I watch her morph from a sexy teenager to an irresistible woman.

I can't take it anymore, I need her.

Is it possible to ever be happy without the one person you *need*?

"I'm Brayden, baby. The man you've been dreaming about your whole life. And I'm about to fucking show you why."

Part 1 of a 3 part series.